Advance Praise

In *The Trion Syndrome*, Tom Glenn packs an emotional
punch. Finding inspiration in—and using as a plot point—the
Trion myth as well as the work of Thomas Mann, Tom Glenn
takes readers to the coldest depths of desolation and back
to the warmth of human kindness. Glenn's tale of betrayal
and forgiveness serves as a lesson in self-awareness and self-
acceptance.

> — Eric D. Goodman, author of *Tracks: A Novel in Stories*

Tom Glenn's *Trion* is a serious work of fiction. It is a story
about damaged people and how the darkness that enters the
spirit can erode a life until it is nothing more than basic living
without light or hope. *Trion* presents the reader with a "who
am I?" challenge. What about my past is creating my present?
I do not believe any reader can experience the lives of the two
primary characters and not ask himself or herself whether the
darkness presented in the story is also present in ourselves. These
characters have wounds that have not scabbed over, even though
they occurred long ago. These wounds are so unspeakable,
to their minds, that they cannot be spoken of, even to save
themselves. I found this book hard to put down and I was eager
to get back to the story despite the darkness in the tale. This is a
book I will remember for a long time. Tom Glenn has written a
masterful work of fiction.

> — Larry Matthews, author of *Take a Rifle from a Dead Man*
> and the Dave Haggard thrillers.

It's 1996. Professor David Bell thought he left the Vietnam War behind him, but PTSD hovers in the middle distance. A recurring dream—shadowy, accusing—always climaxes with the swift, efficient slaughter of a child and evokes the Greek myth of Trion, son of Ares the war god. Trion takes such pride in his savageness in combat that he actually disembowels his own son. Even the gods are appalled and curse him by making him incapable of getting or giving love. Bell fears that's his own fate.

His life intensifies with divorce and the loss of his job, and he vanishes to avoid the alimony and child support he can't pay. Soon it's just himself and that dream, in a small New England town in deep winter. In effect he's following the ancient Greek Odysseus to the land of the dead and that child. And like an archeologist, Bell must dig down to a prehistoric city razed by war and search the grave he comes upon for an ancient treasure.

Bell is a complex character, a welter of contradictions. He wants to do what's right and simultaneously cut and run. Or attack and hurt. Read this harrowing, ultimately affirming book, filled with people you'll want to slap and then hug. It's that good.

— Grady Smith, author of *Blood Chit*

The Trion Sydnrome is a gripping story that explores the horrors of war, childhood trauma, and family dysfunction in a mythic story-within-a-story. Told in alternating viewpoints by its protagonists, Washington, D.C. university professor Dave Bell and his wife Mary, the novel chronicles the couple's increasingly venomous struggle for primacy in their tattered marriage. When Dave discovers an unknown manuscript by Thomas Mann—the story of Trion, a "man who could not love"—he sets off a power clash in the seemingly genteel halls of Lincoln Christian University's German literature department. Banished from the institution he loves, Bell abandons his family and flees to a remote town in Maine. Here, in his despair, he is ministered to by the town's denizens, a band of wise eccentrics. Soon, a young stranger arrives in the town, one who, in his innocence, may possess the key to Dave's redemption. Beautiful language, finely drawn characters, and hurtling pacing—the novel's final pages read like a thriller—make this novel an absorbing and rewarding read.

— Ellen Kwatnoski, author of *Still Life With Aftershocks*

The Trion Syndrome

For Gary
– may its read
prove helpful.

Tom Glenn
21 June 2018

The Trion Syndrome

Tom Glenn

Apprentice House
Loyola University Maryland
Baltimore, Maryland

First Edition

Printed in the United States of America

Paperback ISBN: 978-1-62720-071-4
E-book ISBN: 978-1-62720-072-1

Design by Emily Earenfight, Apprentice House

Published by Apprentice House

Apprentice House
Loyola University Maryland
4501 N. Charles Street
Baltimore, MD 21210
410.617.5265 • 410.617.2198 (fax)
www.ApprenticeHouse.com
info@ApprenticeHouse.com

To all combatants who suffered damage to their souls
while serving their country

Contents

Foreword

The Trion Syndrome is at once a domestic novel of marital infidelity, angsty teenagers, and job strife, and a disturbing psychological study of long-held and barely repressed trauma.

Like his protagonist, Tom Glenn is a scholar of Thomas Mann and of the German language. This is not my world. But I see much here that I know and fear. Glenn's protagonist is, again like Glenn, returned from Vietnam. Dave Bell is returned but not yet home. The dreams come every night: the darkness, the bridge, the moment after which nothing will ever be the same. Bell has made a life in the world with a wife and kids, a good job, and some small portion of success in his field, but his war isn't over. He is a high functioning yet highly damaged human being.

Something in Vietnam changed Bell—and I shan't give that away here. He returns to America and immerses himself in his studies, travels to Germany to complete his academic research, then returns home again to begin a life, a family, and an academic career. When it collapses—the pieces shattering one by one until Bell's instinct to flight finally vanquishes his resolve to fight—the collapse is sudden and complete.

Glenn has written in a somewhat experimental style, employing multiple points of view: sometimes first person, sometimes third person. This, it must be said, seems a bit jarring at first, but in time the reader understands there is a message in the medium and in the story. As well, the parallels in characterizations between Bell and his object of study, the Trion of the title, urge the reader to download, order, or visit the library for some Thomas Mann.

Throughout *The Trion Syndrome*, Glenn leads readers through Bell's labyrinthine journey of self-discovery. We see and feel Bell's anguish and his longing for love, and we accompany him on the journey—I'm sure the Germans have a thirteen-syllable word for this. I should ask Professor Bell.

On this voyage, Bell discovers and we might, too, that the things we have done are a part of us as much as an arm or an eye. As Faulkner famously wrote in *Requiem for a Nun*, "The past isn't dead; it's not even past." Each of us lives with our own past, we carry it around with us like belly-fat, we hear it whispering to us—a wordless keen from some cold black space inside us that wakes us in the long dark night and ages us in dog-years.

But as much as each of us must live with our own past, we all must also live the pasts of others—both collective and individual. We send men and women off to war. We strip them of the trappings of the civil society and urge them to kill with God and country behind them. Then we bring them home without so much as a pat on the back to try to re-enter the society that they left behind. We spend months, even years, training them to kill, and scant days—if that—returning them to "the world."

Quite often there comes with all of this a sense of betrayal, and a result psychiatrists call a moral injury. Words like morality and ethics and moral order are often used among philosophers and ethicists in their studies and academic papers. But words like integrity, trust and honor have tangible meaning among warriors. When a soldier's sense of integrity or honor is betrayed, there remains a wound to the soul—a moral injury.

In the Civil War, doctors described the symptoms or what we think of today as Post-Traumatic Stress Disorder—then called Soldier's Heart—as nostalgia: an inability to focus on the present due to remembrances of things past. In World War I, soldiers with blood and bone wounds were authorized a wound stripe on their uniform and a pension; soldiers with Shell Shock, the term of art in use then, were not. In World War II we called it Battle Fatigue but understood it no better. Today, blood and bone wounds warrant a Purple Heart medal, PTSD doesn't. It's important to remember that not all wounds are visible, that a moral injury is a combat wound but that, because it deals with the mind, we know precious little about how it happens or how to properly treat it.

The Trion Syndrome takes on most of this. For those who are returned from war or wars, it is worth the read because it may help us discover a way of thinking that could be a way home. For others, it might be a window through which one might view a world only hinted at, and not discussed openly or honestly.

— *Ron Capps is the author of* Seriously Not All Right: Five Wars in Ten Years, *a memoir published by Schaffner Press. He is a combat veteran of Afghanistan.*

The Trion Myth

Ares, the god of war, beheld a maiden washing herself in a stream. Overcome with lust, he plunged into the water and ravished her. The girl bore a male child, Trion, who throughout his days would be afraid of water. Bent on revenge, the girl carried the infant Trion to the city of Thrace to confront Ares. To her surprise, the god doted on the boy and taught him the secrets of war.

Larger and stronger than other boys, Trion grew to become a fierce warrior, renowned for savagery in battle. Indifferent to pain, given to brute force, and addicted to dominance, he earned the enmity of Hera because of his cruelty to the vanquished. He fell afoul of all the gods when, as the leader of Spartan forces, he disemboweled his own infant son to demonstrate his ferocity. Aphrodite cursed him—he could never know love. At the peak of his success, Hecate sent the Eucharides, three female monsters, to destroy him. Trion fled to Delphi and consulted the oracle but refused to heed her warning to change his ways and make penitential sacrifices. The Eucharides trapped him at the mouth of the Strymon River, where it meets the Aegean Sea. There they drowned him.

December, 1996

Where the Eucharides Wait

He studied his hands in the moonlight. He couldn't see the blood, but it was there. "Baby killer," they'd yelled. "Butcher."

He sloughed off the blankets. The cot wobbled under him. Cold. The shed wasn't insulated. He shivered in his sweat clothes, felt for his mukluks, slipped them over his socks. Through the window, he could see the Mackinaugh River, white in the moonlight between two shores of pale blue. To the north, before it disappeared around the bend past the highway bridge and railroad trestle, snow dusted its frozen surface. Farther south, toward Winter Bay, the ice darkened, turned gray, then black as the salt water and tides melted it. How cold did it have to be for the ocean to freeze? A man wouldn't last long in that water.

Fresh snow lay on the hillside all the way down to the river. That was to be expected, Old Nate said. Maine got the most snow in December. Except for January, of course. And February. Dave moved closer to the window and looked at his watch. Four-twenty.

He tilted back his head and closed his eyes. All he wanted was to stop the pain. He *had* killed their child. Then he'd left Inge. Her sobs rang in his ears. Sometimes remembering hurt so much that he couldn't think. He was heavy, heavier than Helen. When his body hit the water, it would sink. The destruction of Dave Bell, the man he'd come to hate as much as Chip did. The man who shamed his children. God could forgive him what he'd done. He couldn't forgive him what he was. Killer of children. The Eucharides awaited him at the water's edge.

He found his boots. By the door, he put on his parka, gloves, and stocking cap. Outside, the cold sliced through his gut like the knife he'd used. *Good. Let it.*

He stumbled down the hill toward the river, snow creaking under his feet. He saw Chip before him, saying, "No way." Jeannie studying her ring, refusing to look at him. Ashamed of him. Inge's weeping scarred his ears. Long Dinh. The frozen scream.

The river stretched away from him, now gray in the moonlight. His boots crunched on the stones and dirt. He stepped out on the ice. Slippery. As it had been each time before. No cracking. After a dozen steps, he looked over his shoulder. Already the shore was far behind him. Half way up the hill, the shed was a smudge among the leafless, snow-lined trees. He turned south toward the bay. No smell. Too cold. The ice darkened before him. Maybe they'd never identify his body. He carried no ID. Wrong. His PhD ring. His name was in it. Dread roiled in his chest. He quelled it.

"You go all the way through the ice into the deep water," Nate had said, "and it's all over. Current. No way you can find the hole again. No man can last long in water that cold." Dave would sink like Helen's car. Shocked by the cold, struggling not to breathe, water sucked into his lungs. A minute and twenty seconds, then silence. He understood how Helen did it.

He heard the crack before he lost his footing. He went down fast. Freezing water in his ears and nose and eyes. Taste of briny ice. The nerves in his belly screamed. His heart beat against his breast bone as if to break free.

His throat locked like a vise. He tried to open it, suck in water. His boots struck bottom. His legs, on their own, catapulted him up. His head bashed the ice. Faint light behind him. He twisted toward it, thrashed, reached. The hole. His hands grasped the jagged edge. His face broke through the surface. His throat opened and gasped.

Current tugged him toward the ocean. He grappled at the raw edge. It broke in his hands. He reached over it and spread his arms. "Lie spread eagle," Nate had said, "so your weight isn't all in one spot." He inched onto the ice. It broke. He submerged, struggled to the surface, pushed his arms over the ice, and shimmied. The ice cracked. He laid his cheek against the frozen river, spread his arms and legs, and listened. The cracking stopped. Wind hissed past his exposed ear. He tried to raise his head. His cheek had bonded. He tore it loose. Red flesh and bristles of gray beard clung to the ice. No cracking. He brought his arms to his body, tucked his elbows under him, and used them like crutches to edge forward. Still no cracking.

He slithered north toward the bridges, toward the white, away from the black. His leg muscles kinked. Wet hair stiffened into ice. After ten feet, he risked getting on his hands and knees, crawled another thirty feet, and knelt upright. So far so good. He staggered to his feet. His clothes were rigid. He turned toward the shore.

Up the hill, slipping, falling. His gloves were frozen when he fumbled with the door latch. He lurched to the utility closet, turned on the water in the tiny makeshift shower stall, and stripped. His clothes clattered to the floor. At last the water turned hot. As he crouched under the shower head, ice fell from his hair and crackled on the plastic floor. Slowly, the quaking stopped, and the numb turned to pain.

Coffee. Dressed in dry sweats and wrapped in a blanket, he shuffled to the cast iron stove, blew on the coals until the wood chips caught, and added kindling. When his spit sizzled on the stove's top, he carried the coffee pot to the sink in the utility closet, filled it, and dumped fresh coffee into the basket.

Hunched cross-legged next to the stove, he forced down hot coffee and surveyed his body. Everything worked. The side of his face burned. He must not have been in the water long—two or three minutes. Every time he remembered, he started shivering again.

What had stopped him? Shallow water. He'd hit bottom. Panic. Involuntary reflex. He was too much of a coward to control his body long enough to die. Maybe next time he'd do what Mann's Trion did—load his body with weights to drag him to the bottom and hold him there.

He looked at his watch. Stopped at four thirty-eight. The alarm clock told him it was nearly five-thirty. Christmas morning. Merry fucking Christmas. Shaking his watch didn't make it run. One more chore, buying a replacement without explaining to Ed in the Thrifty Mart why he needed a new watch. He needed clocks and watches. Gave his life the patina of routine. But when he was alone in the dark shed, when there was no routine, shame came out of hiding.

PART ONE

March, 1996:
Takoma Park

Chapter 1

Retreat to Cuxhaven

Dave took his parka from the hall tree and opened the front door. The sky was gray. If it snowed, he wouldn't be able to run Monday. He drew his coat closer around him and sat on the porch steps.

The dream again. It always left him feeling uneasy about Chip and Jeannie. He didn't want them to know. You have to live up to how your children see you even if they're wrong. He'd hunkered on the bedroom floor in the dark and felt for blood, his hands wet, shaking. He'd smelled them. No blood. Mary's breathing was deep and even. How could she sleep through the scream?

It had been more than twenty-five years. He could sit through Fourth of July fireworks. He could take the children camping without getting the shakes at night. But he'd never forget attacking Jeannie after she dropped a bottle of milk while his back was turned. And the dream never left him.

It was always the same. He and the other two are in a hootch or in the jungle or in a ville. Jerry Devereaux, big and black and dripping with sweat. Dave, crouching, ready to spring, unable to make a sound. And the woman. Dave can never see her face. Jerry won't fire his M-16. Dave lunges with his knife. The scream.

He focused on the dormant, leafless tangle that would turn into wild roses after the thaw. Before spring, he'd have to prune them. The cherry should be old enough to bloom this year. The crocuses would be up soon. Have to be sure the kids didn't trample them.

The front door opened and closed. He stiffened, waited for Mary's voice. Finally he turned.

Jeannie stood on the porch. She wore her car coat over pajamas, her uncombed dark hair caught in the collar. Her doe-eyes were large, green, and bright in the half light. Mary's eyes. Her skin was pale with sleep. Dave allowed himself to gaze at her, but only for a moment—so that she wouldn't say, "Oh, *Daddy!*" She sat on the step, shivered, and leaned against him.

He put his arm around her. "Chip up yet?"

She nodded. "Wants to get to the gym early so he can have the Z home by lunchtime."

"I promised we'd change the oil this afternoon before I go to campus."

"Mom wants to ground him."

"He didn't have any marijuana."

"Scary. Mom tried and tried to call you." She shrugged. "Anyway." She was quiet, then, "Can I have a Thai princess ring for my birthday?"

"They're too gaudy for your age." At least Mary thought so.

She frumped. "Then how about taking me out to dinner? Some place in D.C."

"How about Mustafa's? Your mother and I used to go there." Long ago. When things were different. Odd thing was, when he'd taken Helen there last week, the maitre d' remembered him. Maybe he shouldn't take Jeannie there. Never mind. The maitre d' didn't know who Helen was. "We'll sit by the fire. No, wait, we couldn't, either. The tables near the fireplace are for two."

"I hoped it'd be just the two of us. Chip's such a jerk."

"Okay. When?"

"My birthday."

March 7. He'd be in the middle of PhD comps, but only four candidates. He could swing it. "If you promise to smile."

"Don't like people to see my braces. The bands keep coming unglued, and that means that I'll have to wear them forever."

Dave squeezed her. "I'll call Doctor Morgan Monday. Maybe there's some other tack we could take—different kind of adhesive or something."

His children would never go through what he went through, but the goddamned dream . . . Maybe he was like his bastard of a father. Claimed he never got over World War II. His excuse for the bad checks and the chiseling and the shame. The son-of-a-bitch disappeared when Dave was six. Dave had promised himself that if he ever had children, he'd take care of them.

But he'd lie to them, wouldn't he? Covering about Helen. If the kids ever found out . . . No one knew except Harry, Helen's brother, who'd walked in on them last week. God, it had to end.

"We could fix pancakes," Jeannie said.

He grinned. "How about salt pork and black beans?"

"I *hate* salt pork and black beans."

"That's what my mother used to fix. Even for breakfast."

"Oh, *Daddy!*"

Dave chuckled. "Okay. Pancakes. You mix and I'll grill."

• • •

Dave lay on the dolly and struggled with the crankcase bolt. "Damn." He turned the dolly and grasped the right front tire with his feet. "Why the hell did I put it in so tight?"

"You didn't," he heard Chip say. Chip bent over to look under the car. His red hair grazed the cement floor. "You always told me to tighten it up as far as I could."

Dave banged the bolt with the wrench on both sides.

"Let me try," Chip said.

Dave rolled from beneath the car. Chip lowered himself onto the dolly and scooted under.

"I got it," Chip said. "Give me the drip pan."

Dave watched Chip slip the pan under the crankcase and open the bolt all the way. It fell into the pan with a clunk followed by gurgles of black oil. Chip rolled from under the car.

Dave tossed him a rag. "Wipe your hands." He helped Chip to his feet. "Always carry a grease rag in your hip pocket when you're working on cars."

"You told me."

"Then why don't you do it?"

"Forgot." He handed the rag to Dave.

"Put it in your pocket. How'd you get the bolt loose?"

Chip shrugged. "Kept pushing."

Dave squinted. He had to look up to see Chip's eyes. Mary's eyes, like Jeannie. Red hair and green eyes. Chip looked like an ad for Christmas. Except for the smear of oil on his cheek.

Dave pulled the rag from his own hip pocket and wiped Chip's face. "How much you weigh?"

"Little over two-thirty."

"Jesus, you outweigh me."

"Not by much."

"How much weight are you bench pressing?"

"Hundred-forty. You?"

"Almost up to five sets," Dave said, "twelve reps, hundred and ten. Can you do that?"

"I'm going for higher weights and lower reps."

"When did you first do five sets of one-ten?"

Chip shrugged one shoulder. "September."

Dave slugged him lightly on the bicep. "That's great, son, but—" He smiled. "Don't let anything, you know, extra-curricular, get in the way of schoolwork."

Chip's jaw tightened. "I'm not on drugs."

"Okay, okay. Let's get the oil in."

Chip didn't move. "They locked us up in this dark cage with all these creepy guys. I was scared shitless. When Mom showed up, she was, like, *mad.* She said she had half a mind to leave me there to teach me a lesson. She tried to call you in New York, but they said you weren't registered at the hotel. When we got home, I called the conference number. They said you weren't signed up. All day Sunday, Mom was in her cold fury mode."

Dave's jaw clamped. The lying to his children had to stop. The thing with Helen had to end.

"Dad, I didn't use any weed that night." Chip's face was grave. "It's the truth. I couldn't lie to you if I tried."

"Let's get the oil and the filter in."

"Fuck it."

"Chip, the oil."

Chip lowered himself to the dolly and rolled under the car. As Dave reached for the fresh oil, he tripped over Chip's foot.

"Ouch!" Chip yelled. "*Goddamit.* Plug's in."

Chip rolled from under the car, touched his cheek, and looked at the blood on his fingers.

Dave knelt beside him. Cut below the cheekbone. "Let me clean that and get something on it."

"Fuck it."

"*Now,* Chip," Dave said through his teeth.

He led Chip to the bathroom, sat him on the commode, and washed the cut with soap and water. "Quit jumping around."

"Stings."

Dave doused the wound with peroxide. Chip hissed. Dave applied Bactine and a band-aid.

"Can I use the Z tomorrow?" Chip said. "Paper says the reflecting pool at the Lincoln Memorial will be solid enough to skate on. I asked Cindy."

"Will Mom's car be here?"

"Nissan 300Z's a lot cooler than a Honda wagon."

"Why not Metro?"

"Aw, Dad."

"Okay, okay." Dave smiled. "Let's get the oil in."

Back in the garage, they put in the new oil filter. Dave opened the plastic bottles and passed them to Chip.

"Done." Chip straightened and banged his head on the raised hood. "Damn."

Dave grinned. "You'll learn not to do that."

Chip started to close the hood.

"Hold it," Dave said. "Always check with the dipstick."

"I just put the oil in."

"Check it. Happened to me once when I was working in a gas station while I was in grad school. Forgot to put the plug in. Customer burned up the engine."

Chip showed him the dipstick. "See?" He closed the hood. "Mom's, like, still mad at you. Where were you?"

The lie. "They had my name wrong. Had to stay in a hotel uptown."

Chip put his hands in his pockets. "It's a whole lot easier to deal with her. She gets mad. You get, like, crushed."

Dave wilted.

"Dad, I didn't use any pot that night."

"You got stoned other times?"

"Twice."

Dave closed his eyes.

"But not that night," Chip said. "We were whooping it up in the park with beer. Then the police came."

"If there's ever a second offense . . ."

Chip looked at him without blinking. "There won't be."

"Did you ever buy any marijuana?"

"No. The guys know where to get it. A creep called 'The Gator.'"

"Did you ever use anything besides pot?"

Chip looked away. "Sniffed some glue. Tried angel dust once."

Bad news all the way. What could Dave do? Since he had to lie about Helen, maybe he could try the truth. "Once upon a time, a long, long time ago, I got stoned sometimes. In Vietnam. And in Germany. Even used cocaine once. But I found out I can get high on better things than pot. Like the buzz I get when I run. Like the spike I got when I discovered Thomas Mann's *Trion* novella. Like the feeling I get when I hit a new level in lifting. I can't do those things if I'm flying on drugs."

Chip's face was blank.

"Chip, a man is a man when he's strong, nurturing, and wise."

A faint grin lighted Chip's face. "Where have I heard that before?"

"And you can blame fate for your problems, but only you can solve them."

Chip rolled his eyes heavenward.

"Okay," Dave said. "Then stay away from drugs. And don't get any girl pregnant."

Chip blushed.

"You and Cindy?" Dave said.

"She's not pregnant."

"Even if she's not, women expect a long term relationship when there's sex." Take, for example, Helen. "Think before you fuck."

Dave wished he'd had someone to advise him.

• • •

Dave dialed Helen's number. If Harry answered, he'd hang up. Helen answered.

"Harry at home?"

"He's at the library on campus. Says you assigned extra reading. He's been working his tail off."

"Doesn't look that way to me."

"He might have mono. He's gone and gotten himself a part-time job."

"Maybe if you didn't take such good care of him, he'd grow up faster."

"He's my brother, Dave, the last of the Serenis."

"Look, this isn't . . . Can you meet me at the office?"

"Harry's got the car."

"Take the Metro."

Silence, then, "You're scaring me."

"Five okay?"

Long pause. "Okay."

• • •

One more. Dave strained with everything in him. His muscles screamed. His breath was gone. The barbell rose above him. He'd done it. His biceps quaked as Bob helped him lower the bar into the bracket.

Bob beamed. "Nice goin', Bell!"

Dave pulled his gym towel from the bench. "Let's see what you can do, Scarff."

Bob added two ten-pound weights. "Think you'll ever catch up with me?"

"I've got ten years on you."

"And a wife and two kids."

"You don't know what you're missing."

Bob lay on the bench and grasped the barbell. "Do, too. I've been that route, remember? Now I get to have my cake and eat it, too." He winked at Dave.

They finished their routines, stretched, and eased into the sauna.

"Got to make this quick," Dave said. "Have to stop by the office."

"Same here. Meeting a client at six. Business session, then a long leisurely dinner at her place."

"What a racket! Help them divorce and bed them down in one fell swoop."

"All in a day's work. Speaking of which, that secretary in your department office is one nice package."

"Helen Sereni?"

"Anybody fucking her?"

Dave stifled the impulse to slam his fist into Bob's grin.

Dressed, Dave crammed his workout clothes into his bag and walked toward the campus police station. He showed his ID, signed the log, and got the officer on duty to admit him to Scully Hall. Inside the glass doors of the German Literature front office, he hesitated. Leave the doors unlocked? Someone might notice. Helen had her own key.

He walked past Helen's desk and turned down the hall to

his office door and unlocked it, drew the blinds, and switched on a lamp. Too edgy to wait, he opened his single-drawer safe beside the desk. He'd bought that safe out of his own pocket to protect Mann's *Trion* manuscript, then discovered that the original measured over twelve by twelve inches. With its pages in acetate sheaths bound within a black leather cover and stored in a clear plastic case, the manuscript was too large for the safe. He'd had to buy a chart-size carrying case to lug the original and the copies from Los Angeles. He'd gotten the largest strong box the college had, locked the manuscript in it, and stored it in his office cabinet. Talk about irony. The manuscript was the one thing he wanted to protect. Instead, his in-basket, still stacked high with papers, lay in the bottom of the safe drawer where Helen had left it when she closed up Friday.

On top was a phone slip from George Eckland, student reporter at the *Lincoln Log*. What did that bastard want? "Journalist's honor," he'd said. His article on the *Trion* find hadn't done any real harm except that now everyone, even Robin McAndrew, who covered education for *The Washington Post*, knew they were using *Trion* for the comps. McAndrew had been after Dave for an interview, but Dave wanted to break the news of his discovery of an unknown Thomas Mann novella in his own way—probably with a news conference. He'd invite McAndrew, but not Eckland. Snotty twit. He'd never forgiven Dave for the D in German Literature in Translation. Too intelligent to study. The opposite of Helen's brother.

Next was a slip from somebody named Hans Lehmann at Christ House. The hospital for the homeless? Doctor Johann Lehmann had been one of Dave's professors in Nürnberg in 1975, but he never called himself "Hans." A third slip from Horst Vinzing at Für Ein Fremdes Land. Dave's book order was in. The fourth was from Robin McAndrew. "Talk about *Trion* find after alumni lunch on 15 March?' was written in Helen's hand.

Dave wasn't attending the luncheon. That would piss off Jerry and Jake Colson, the college president, but Dave hated politicking. He was a scholar, nothing more. "Dave, this is ostensibly a Christian college, originally founded as a seminary," Jake had said. "One of the values enshrined in our charter is brotherhood. You act unbrotherly and the backers get antsy. We need them."

Dave didn't. Give no quarter and take none. His motto since he was six.

He replaced the in-basket and locked the safe. Then he opened the mahogany cabinet with his key, unlocked the strongbox, and took out the original of *Trion* and all copies along with his article and translation. He'd go over the passage about soul damage at home. Carla had questioned his translation of *verstehen* as "knowing" rather than "understanding." Once he'd assured himself that "knowing" was closer to Mann's intent, he'd make copies of the German text and the final version of the comp questions. Then, when the comps were finished, proving that Lincoln College shared its research with its students, he'd schedule a news conference and look for a publisher. *The German Literature Review*, top in the business, couldn't turn him down.

His fingers, on their own, withdrew the *Trion* manuscript. As his hands turned the acetate-bound pages, his eyes traveled along the fourteen-point typescript. This story, more than any other of Mann's, touched Dave's soul. Trion Kretzschmar's struggle between his desire for dominance and his craving for love, his horror when he finds that he cannot love, the climax when he sends his son to his death, his sickening suicide by drowning—all of it lived inside Dave's skin. "Evil has no understanding of love," the old exorcist tells Trion, but was Trion really evil? He just settled for less than he could have. He chose domination over love. Or maybe his evil was camouflaged by its banality, as Arendt had said of Eichmann. Maybe he sold his soul for dominance. Mann's ambiguity, Trion's "questionable" motives.

So many similarities with Mann's *Doktor Faustus*. The name Kretzschmar—the same name he used in *Faustus*—the issue of the evil being unable to love, the equivocation, dependence on a myth as the basis for the story. Best guess was that Mann put aside *Trion* and rewrote, ending up with *Faustus*.

The scene of Trion's drowning still made the hair bristle on the back of Dave's neck. Mann left nothing to the imagination. The water forcing its way into Trion's lungs as his weighted body plummets to the bottom of the river, his feeble struggle, all reflex, as the water suffocates him. Dave shuddered. He'd never overcome his hydrophobia. He'd gotten through Army Ranger water training by an act of self-control, his will over his terror, a capacity to overcome panic that had later earned him a Silver Star during the ambush when Jerry nearly got killed.

He'd forgotten where his fear of water came from until it surfaced in his dreams. He'd been barely more than an infant. They were in a river, near a bridge. His father, up to his chest in water, his eyes under their dark arching brows bluer and brighter than the sky, had held Dave out at arm's length and turned him around so that Dave was facing the bridge. Dave had struggled. His father laughed and dropped him. Dave plunged deep into the river, sucking in water, and fought his way to the surface. Through the froth, he could see his father smiling, barely out of reach. Panicked, unable to cry out or breathe, he'd beaten the water and gone under. His father finally pulled him out and carried him to the shore where he slapped him until his weeping and coughing ceased.

Helen slipped in, closed the dead bolt behind her, and tossed her coat and purse on his desk. Dave closed the manuscript and slid a copy into his briefcase. As he stood, she wrapped her arms around his neck.

He patted her back.

She raised her head. "What's the matter?"

He let go of her. "Tense, I guess."

"I know how to take care of that." She reached for his belt.

"We need to talk." He walked to the window. Through the slats he saw the dark blur of Scully Field two floors below.

"What's wrong?" Helen asked.

"How did Harry react to finding us in bed?"

"He took it okay."

"He acted strange in class," Dave said. "Still didn't have his paper on Günter Grass ready to hand in."

"He's been sick."

"He's cramming for the comps?"

She looked away. "You think he'll do all right?"

"I wonder if he's in over his head. I advised him not to take the comps this go-round."

She slumped. "May I sit down?"

"What a question."

"You're acting distant."

She sat in the chair by his desk. "Since the *Log* article came out, he's been reading Thomas Mann."

"What texts?"

"Different things." She massaged her hands as though washing them. "What's the use? I knew it was coming. Then the way you touched me. You know, don't you? It was wrong. I've prayed for forgiveness. What can I do? I'll tell Harry not to take the comps."

He took a deep breath. "We have to stop."

Silence.

"After Harry found us," he said, "I realized that I couldn't go on. The children—the lying and hiding and cheating."

She gawked at him, her head cocked.

"I'm sorry," he said. "Sorrier than I've ever been about anything. I should have thought before I—" He sat on the edge of the desk and put his hand on her arm.

She pulled free. "Please, no." She took tissues from her purse, struggled to her feet, and stumbled away from him.

"Helen, it was wrong. Wrong for me."

"Harry said you were using me." She laughed. "'Sewer trash. That's what they think we are. Does Dave hold his nose when he makes love to you?'"

"Stop it."

"You love me, Dave?"

He held his breath, afraid of what he might say.

"Did it ever occur to you," she said, "that I love you?"

"Maybe in a different place, a different time—"

"You love your wife?"

He swallowed hard. "Yes."

She slapped him.

The rage left her face, and her body shook rhythmically as she tried to swallow the spasms of weeping. He put his arms around her, but she faltered out of his grasp.

"Helen—"

"Leave me alone." She wiped her face with her hands, picked up her coat, and opened the dead bolt. As if reconsidering, she leaned her head against the jamb, then opened the door, went out, and closed it behind her.

He fell onto the chair. He wanted to weep. He couldn't.

Chapter 2

Counterfeit

The first one up, I'm at the kitchen table with my warmed-over coffee. I wish I had a fire. The big fireplace is in Dave's "study." Used to be our living room. Now he's got his desk and computer and printer and files in there. Always keeps the door closed. And builds himself a fire. These days, except when he's courting the children, he's absent, even when he's home, even when he's sleeping next to me.

I could put on Dave's parka and brave the cold to look for logs small enough to fit in the fireplace in the family room. Better to turn up the thermostat—no, then Dave'll complain. I'll put on flannels under my robe when I go upstairs. Or get dressed.

We used to have fires in the family room. When the kids were little, Dave and Chip foraged for wood at building sites and hunted for fallen trees. I'd hear them outside as they split logs. Dave was always coaching Chip. "A man is a man when he's strong nurturing and wise," he'd say. And another time, "Life doesn't make us unhappy. We make ourselves unhappy by trying to be what other people want, by wanting things we can't have." If Dave knows all that, why doesn't he act on it? He's changed. That was before Dave started having firewood delivered, before he got into running and weight lifting, before he spent all his time working behind closed doors.

In the old days, Sunday mornings were for togetherness. The

first one up made coffee and brought it to the bedroom in the carafe with the mugs we'd gotten on our honeymoon in Munich. We read the paper together in bed. We talked about the world, work, the kids. He cracked up at my characterization of Clinton as the only person I'd ever come across who charmed me so much that I actually enjoyed his lies. We showered together and made love before the kids woke up. Dave wanted to make love to me then. Before he saw what I really am. More than a year since he's touched me. Even before that, he locked me out of his life.

I sag. Living's got to be more than something to be endured. I get to my feet, dump last night's coffee, and start a new pot. I have to get the step-stool to reach the mugs from the top cabinet. Spoons. Napkins. Cream pitcher and sugar bowl. Out into the snow to retrieve *The Washington Post*.

While the coffee finishes, I go into the half bath and close the door. I straighten my hair, pull it away from my face, and hold it with combs. Rouge, lip gloss. I zip my blue silk robe to the neck. Dave always said it makes me look like one of those tall, blonde Giotto madonnas.

I dash to the kitchen, coffee into the carafe, up the stairs. I set the tray on my bedside table. "Wake up, lazy."

Dave opens his eyes. He wasn't asleep. Those eyes, blue like the sky above the last of the sunset, lashes black like shadows.

"What brought this on?" he says.

"We haven't done it in so long." I hand him a mug and sit on bed. "I brought the paper."

He slides until he's leaning against the headboard. He's all shoulders and chest and hair. "You really want to do this?"

I clamp my mouth, turn, and put my feet on the floor. "Of course not. Lost my head there for a minute."

He catches my arm. "Sorry. I'm not really awake."

"You want me to stay?"

His eyes are somber. His lips smile at me.

"Then, afterwards," I say, "let's have a fire. My tush gets cold when the leaves fall and stays that way until the jonquils bloom."

He looks bruised. He used to laugh at my jokes.

"Our problem," I rattle on, " is that we have too much in our lives. Kids. Work. By the way, Shirley Devereaux called. Wants to know if we can get together with her and Jerry and Robin McAndrew and his wife for dinner before the comps."

Dave groans.

"What's the problem?" I say.

"Jerry's politicking again. He wanted me to do a spiel on *Trion* at the alumni lunch. I said no, so he asked Robin to speak. Let's stall. I have an awful lot going on."

"You always have a lot going on. I hoped that when you got older you'd stop trying to conquer the world. Master of the universe, top dog, king rat."

"Sarcasm brings out your natural bitchiness."

"And you risk being arrested for impersonating an asshole."

I'm too good at snapping off one-liners. I didn't come up here to claw at him.

He shuts his eyes. "What's going on with you?"

"Boring administrative stuff. Not up to your level."

Dave swallows. "Try me."

"Carla Brecht and I had lunch Thursday. Wish you'd come."

"Carla and I don't get on. She's a little short on the milk of human kindness."

"You're not known for your outgoing charm, either."

Dave grunts. "Look who's talking. What's going on in the office?"

"Usual panic. Getting all the computer records straight on course assignments. Would you believe Lincoln College has more students assigned to classes than it has registered for the spring semester? They're holding *me* responsible." My laugh sounds shrill.

He smiles.

"And we're famous for our math department," I say.

His face takes on life. "We're *really* going to be famous when the story gets out about *Trion*, beyond that slag Eckland published in the *Log*. I know you think it's silly, but an undiscovered Thomas Mann novella turning up in the nineteen nineties?"

I study my mug.

"Doesn't interest you at all, does it?" he says.

"Did the first four times. Minor story by a German writer most Americans have never heard of."

He grinds his teeth.

"God," I say. "I'm sick to death of German."

"Watch it. My mother was German."

I nod. "And a lush and your father was a son-of-a-bitch who wrote bad checks and deserted you. Get over it."

"Mary, what do you say we call a truce?"

I put out my hand. "Deal."

We shake.

I hold onto his hand. "We can get into counseling sessions in April. They have openings."

He pulls away.

"Then how about you go alone?" I say. "Tell them about your dreams. Even if you won't tell me."

"I've gotten where I am by depending on myself, no one else."

I clench. "Would it shrink your manhood to ask for help?"

"Stop it!" He slugs down coffee.

"Why did you tell Chip he could take the Z?"

"That's the deal. He maintains it and pays for gas. He gets to use it when I don't need it."

"You going to let him off?"

"He didn't use any pot that night."

I snort. "You curry the kids' favor, like you're afraid they won't love you if you're not everything they want you to be."

"Come off it."

"You force me to be the bad guy."

"What would you do?"

"Ground him for a month. Take away his allowance. Pull him off the wrestling team. No more gym—"

Dave puts down his mug. "Why don't you just castrate him and be done with it?"

"He got himself arrested. I get a call at three in the morning from the park police."

Dave shakes his head slowly. "Sounds like you want to punish him for what he put you through. You should see your face. Medea incarnate. Watch out for your vindictiveness, Mary. Someday it'll bite you in the ass."

"The truce," I say.

"Sorry." He isn't.

I rock the carafe. "Empty. Ready for a shower?"

I know how to excite him. He's always said my body is his ideal, makes him tingle with desire. We dry each other and hurry to bed. He kisses my breasts. His lips and tongue leave my skin wet with saliva. His stubble rasps across my nipples. I shut down. Something in me congeals. I try to act aroused, but I'm cold. How long will he take? He's poised to enter me, lifts his body with his arms. I sneak a look at the clock.

He recoils as if I'd slugged him, shifts his weight off my body, rolls away.

"What's the matter?" I ask.

"Get me turned on and kick me in the balls."

I put my arms around him. "Come on. You know I'm willing."

"Get your hands off me."

"I haven't told you in a long time," I say. "I love you."

He sits up. "Don't lie to me, Mary. Not about that. Zing me about impersonating an asshole or being king rat. Call me a charmless. Mock the way I treat the children. But don't tell me you love me."

He swings his feet to the floor. I catch his arm.

He yanks free. "No thanks. If I'm going to masturbate, I'd rather do it alone."

He throws on his sweats and stomps out.

I fall back on the bed and stare at the ceiling, gray in the half light. I'm an impostor. I lack the basic sexual instinct men sense in a woman. I must give off subliminal signals. I used to be able to satisfy Dave, and it wasn't really pretense, even though I had no physical sensation. I did find fulfillment in his passion, holding him in me through his wildly thrashing orgasms, feeling his sweat on my breasts and arms and face, muffling his cries in my hair, smelling his semen, like the odor of milkweed. Then, somehow, I couldn't fake anymore. Maybe it was my anger at his wrapping himself in his work. Maybe it was the onset of menopause. Maybe it was my growing sense that I wasn't a real woman at all. He thinks I don't love him.

The first time I saw him, he was across the patio at a party in Berkeley. He'd walked into the light from the doorway where

I stood. His eyes were blue and hungry, his body massive. He scared me. This man was strong enough to kill me with his bare hands. No, strong enough to protect me from any raw-boned yokel who might try to hurt me again. He smiled. I said something arch to cover. His smile melted, and his eyes looked through mine to the woman inside.

He was always a loner, always tried brute strength first and only used his brain when all else failed. Always fought first, asked questions afterwards. Always had a short fuse. But he never once hurt me. He was always there to protect me and take care of me. Not any more.

I've watched other women watch him. He gets their signals. I can see it in his eyes. He might answer their call—no, he's too decent. He wouldn't do that to *me*. He used to love me. He still loves me. That's why he's hurt. What have I done to him?

The front door opens and closes. Dave going out to the porch to sulk. He couldn't have left for the gym. He isn't dressed. I hate the gym the same way I hate his office, especially in the last year since he stopped making love to me.

I roll on my stomach. If only I could get past that terrifying moment when my insides freeze. We'll be doing fine, enjoying each other. He gets amorous, I'm pleased he wants me. Then something locks up. When I feel that place slam shut, my desire to please him takes over. I learned over the years when to coo or draw my breath in quickly. I know when a moan excites him, when digging my nails into his arms will make him come.

At least I used to know. I've lost my touch. He sees me for the impostor I am.

When I'm around other women, I never let on. I know when to laugh or raise an eyebrow. They never see that I'm counterfeit goods. Why couldn't I have been a full-blooded woman with normal erotic feelings?

I wish I could talk to other women. Maybe there are others like me. Maybe it's not me, maybe it's Dave. I've never made love with another man. I don't want to, but what other way is there to find out? Would another man have Dave's magic? When he holds me, I want to surrender. Everything about him makes me love him. Then he starts pawing, and I shut down. Nothing is so lonely as being the object of lust.

I drag from the bed and poke in the closet. If I don't get downstairs before the kids fix breakfast, I'll have to nag and maybe yell to get them to clean up. Dave will be off in his study healing his wounded ego or out in the garage working on that damned Z with Chip. Jeannie will feel left out, and it'll be up to me to make it right. Profoundly unfair. Does he think he's the only one hurt?

• • •

I tell Emma I'm going to lunch, and head out of the office for the elevator. Carla said she might be a few minutes late—meeting with Jerry at eleven-thirty. I'll wait in the German Department's outer office. Dave will be in class until twelve-thirty.

The elevator doors hiss open at the first floor. I walk the length of the marble hall to the atrium. Snow powders the decagonal skylight above me and clings to the glass walls. The pencil beam spotlights have been turned on against the dark of the day. As I turn toward the glass doors, three heavy, graying men mount the concrete steps from the street and push in, huffing from the cold. Alumni. Here for some function or other in the second floor banquet room. They rumble past, then I step through the doors and down the stairs to the sidewalk.

Snow is still falling in irregular swirls, but the sidewalk is clear except for a coating thick enough to show footprints. I turn toward Scully Hall.

Dave will never forgive me. I mocked his manhood. I shudder. He's unmasked me for what I am. Passionless. Last Spring, he shocked me. "Do you know how long it's been since we made love?" he'd asked. "Three months. You didn't notice, did you?" I hadn't.

Across the street at the end of the block, I see Scully Hall, nothing but glass and steel. I am as I am, deficient. He is as he is, normal. I can do nothing.

I head into Scully Hall, ride the elevator to the second floor, and go through the glass doors into the German Department front office.

"Hi, Helen."

"Doctor Brecht's still meeting with Doctor Devereaux, Mrs. Bell," Helen says.

I settle in a chair and pick up the *German Literature Review*. Why is achievement so damned important to Dave? I know. Something he said one time about an archaic German word, *Ungeminnt*—incapable of loving, unlovable. He repeated the word. I watched his lips, rounded, then spread as if in a grimace of pain, his eyes like ice picks. If he couldn't love or be loved, he'd earn respect and admiration.

That's part of his craziness that makes me love him. Of course he can love, but something in him denies it. If only I could show him.

Helen answers the phone. I hate her. Flowing sleek black hair, high cheekbones, eyes turned up at the outer edges giving her face an elfin cast. Short with a narrow waist, classical breasts, a slim rear to die for. Helen has the confidence beautiful women always have. And yet—I let my eyes rest on her, ready to dart to the journal the instant she glances toward me—Helen radiates need.

My need's locked inside where no one can get to it. Helen's presence in the same world is an indictment of me.

Why did God do this? Wire in need and deny the tools for fulfillment?

Carla and Jerry Devereaux, minus their suit jackets, emerge from the door labeled "Chairman." Carla, carrying an overstuffed manila folder, waves and disappears down the hall. Jerry smiles his way to me.

"Dave's teaching until twelve-thirty," Jerry says, all charm.

"Carla and I are having lunch."

"You and Dave pick a date for dinner with the McAndrews?"

"Ask Dave. He's the one with the busy calendar. Is Carla invited?"

Jerry's smile falters. "We want to charm McAndrew, not subject him to frostbite."

Carla marches in, her battle-ship gray overcoat buttoned to her chin, her chignon freshly knotted. "It's snowing. Let's eat on campus."

We trudge through the snow back to Thurston Hall, take the elevator to the fourth floor alumni dining room, dark in velvet and satin, and take a table close to the roaring fire. For the first time in hours, my bones thaw.

Carla gives her napkin a sharp snap and spreads it in her lap. "Your husband is annoyed with me."

And furious with me. Are Carla and I twins? "Dave is easily annoyed."

Twins. The thought makes me squirm. Twin to the Iron Maiden, as the grad students call her.

"I sent him my translation of the first chapter of his *Leverkühn Tragedy*," Carla says. "He mentioned that Smithson will be bringing out a second printing of the English edition of *Leverkühn* next year, and that Brenz-Verlag had approached him about a German translation. I offered to collaborate."

Brenz-Verlag? Ah, yes, in Wiesbaden, the publisher of Dave's German-language *Thomas Mann: Künstler und Philosoph*. Carla's most recent book on Schiller, published in East Germany before the reunification, is out of print. Publish or perish, right?

"Dave's a card-carrying lone wolf, Carla."

She stops moving. "Wolf? You know that and do nothing?"

I laugh. "*Lone* wolf."

"Ach, yes, I see. The department, indeed the entire college, is aware of Dave's uncooperative spirit. Doctor Colson invited him to speak at the alumni luncheon on his discovery of *Trion*. Dave told Jerry he won't be attending."

Just like him. Give no quarter and take none. Especially never depend on another human being. Another craziness that makes my heart hurt for him. When we were first married, he was distant, cautious. Slowly, he opened up. Then, when our love-making shriveled, he shut me out.

"We always talk about Dave," I say. "What's going on in the department?"

Over shrimp salad and rolls, Carla chats about the new copy machine, her inability to master the computer system, the forthcoming comps, and Helen.

"Helen's brother is our problem child," Carla says over her wine glass. "I asked Jerry and Dave not to let Harry take the comps. He's not ready."

"Can you disallow him? Dave says by the end of the semester he'll have completed his course work—"

"Something's wrong with that boy. Emaciated. Jumpy. Dresses like an Ivy League student of twenty years ago, chinos and those shirts with the alligator. Dave should never have championed him for graduate school. Jerry and I were opposed to his admission. It's been a four-year struggle."

"Dave's tried to help him. Even tutored him on Günter Grass—"

Carla stiffens. "Profoundly unfair to the other students."

I study the fire, willing its heat into me. "Dave knows what it's like to flounder."

"And since last fall, when *Helen* started working in the office—" The words float in the air. Something in her tone.

"Helen?" I say.

Carla pushes her plate away, touches her lips with her napkin. "Enough department gossip. How's my Jeannie doing with her braces?"

"All right."

Helen?

• • •

The Z's in the driveway. The snow. Dave can't run. I leave my umbrella on the porch next to his and hang my wet coat on the hall tree. From the kitchen comes the sound of laughter, Dave and the kids must be cooking. When I stop at the kitchen door, his smile sours.

During the meal, Dave keeps a running trialogue with Chip and Jeannie about skating, proper tire pressure, and tasteful jewelry for teenaged girls. When dinner's over, he mumbles something about the office and leaves the house. I badger the kids into doing the dishes and cleaning the kitchen. Dave always makes such a mess. Then comes the routine scene over homework before television.

Exhausted, I collapse into the easy chair in the family room. No fire, of course. No wood. I think of calling upstairs to Chip. No, better to let him study. I wrap myself in the throw from the sofa and switch on the tail end of *The News Hour*. The phone rings.

"May I speak please with Doctor Bell?" asks a German-accented male voice.

"He's not here. May I take a message?"

Silence, then, "When it would be best time to call him?"

Never. He doesn't live here anymore. "Is this business? You might want to try his office—"

"I have left message three times."

"How can he reach you?"

"I am at Christ House." He gives me the number.

"May I tell him what you wish to speak with him about?"

"You are Mrs. Bell, yes?"

"Yes."

A pause. "It is family business."

"I didn't know he had any living relatives."

Long silence, then, "I am related to his mother."

"I'll leave the message for him. I didn't get your name."

"Hans Lehmann."

Chapter 3

The Streets of Baghdad

Mustafa's was halfway down the block on N Street, Northwest. The maitre d' greeted them just inside the door. "Ah, Doctor Bell. You bring another beautiful young lady to visit us tonight."

"My daughter, Jeannie." Dave handed him their coats.

"By the fire?"

"Please."

Dave filled his lungs with the aroma of spiced meat, sesame oil, and burning wood. As they passed between stone braces that disappeared into the void above them, he saw that they were heading into the open expanse in front of the fireplace to the same table he and Helen had shared.

"Who's the other 'beautiful young lady'?" Jeannie asked.

Dave turned his face to the fire. "A visiting professor."

"Young and beautiful?"

"The maitre d' is a pro."

"It wasn't Mom?"

"Your mother hasn't been here in a long time."

Over curried lamb and stuffed grape leaves, Jeannie told Dave that their school spring trip was to Charlottesville. "Ever been there?"

"Beginning of last month."

Jeannie squinted at him. "That's when you were in New York."

He felt his face redden. "You're right. Must have been last fall."

When their dinner dishes were cleared, Dave reached into his jacket pocket. "Happy birthday."

With a grin, she took the gift and shook it. "Is it—?" She tore it open and lifted out a black velvet box. Slowly, she opened the top and gasped. "Princess ring!" She slipped it on. "Oh, *Daddy!*" She held her hand out toward the fire, palm down, and tilted it. The flattened cone-shaped setting of multicolored stones caught the light.

"Sorry you don't like it," Dave said with a smile. "Guess I'll have to exchange it for gym socks. Mom says that's what you need."

She flew from her chair and threw her arms around his neck. "Thank you."

"Your mom thinks princess rings are kind of tacky. She doesn't know I got you one."

"*She* gave me gym socks. She's weird."

"Kids always think parents are weird."

"Did you?"

Dave looked at the fire. "No, you know the story. My dad gone. My mother drunk. Being on welfare. Always had to do for myself. Learned not to trust anybody."

"Don't you trust me? And Chip?"

He smiled. "Sure."

"Mom?"

"Her, too." Another lie.

• • •

Dave stretched, poured himself more coffee, and carried it to the study window. Less than a week until the alumni lunch.

Jerry had been pestering him. Gave the wrong impression, Jerry said. Reinforced Dave's image as a loner, sneering at the college's Christian origins. Dave had held fast. Never mind. The crocuses had come and gone, and the jonquils were in bud. Soon he'd have to put down lawn fertilizer, prune the hemlock, and plant the flower beds. He'd taken a decisive step in giving up Helen. Now he'd turn inward, toward his family. He'd court Mary all over again. He'd take the kids camping in West Virginia, bird watching at Assateague Island, hiking at Cunningham Falls. He shuddered. He'd come *that* close . . . Thank God no one had found out. Harry'd been right about one thing. Dave *had* used Helen, like he'd used Inge long ago, before Mary.

He squatted before the hearth and poked the embers. Back at the desk, he put on his glasses and picked up the third comp paper. He'd like to pass all four PhD candidates.

The phone rang. Carla Brecht.

"Have you read paper number three?" Carla said in German.

"Just starting."

"It is a fraudulent paper, David."

"Carla—"

"It's too good. The translation is astute. I suspect he or she probably had studied the German text of *Trion* before Thursday."

"Some of our candidates are very accomplished."

"David, I'll come straight to the point. It looks as though you helped candidate number three."

"Are you suggesting—"

"I'm going to call Jerry."

Dave hung up, took off his glasses, and rubbed his eyes. So like Carla. He picked up paper number three.

It began badly. Banal statements about the greatness of Thomas Mann, but the second paragraph noted that the manuscript's typeface suggested the nineteen-twenties. The third paragraph dwelt at length on Mann's discussion of the protagonist's questionable motives at the end of the novella. The fourth mentioned the use of the name Kretzschmar, the gloomy texture, the Gothic writing, and even the focus on the soul. "*Trion* might have been a preliminary sketch for *Doktor Faustus*," the paper said, "which may be why Mann never published this story."

The rest of the paper analyzed the story's exploration of the idea of soul damage. It offered translations to support its arguments. It translated *verstehen* as "knowing."

The candidate had obviously had access to Dave's work—both his unpublished article and his translation—but nowhere had Dave mentioned in writing the typeface as a way to date the story. He and Jerry and Carla had talked about it. And he'd mentioned it to Helen.

Helen . . . Had she stolen copies of everything for Harry? Vengeance? How could she have gotten into the strongbox? It didn't make sense. She'd even arranged for another secretary, Rose from the English Department, to type the exam papers and code them. No one, including Helen, could identify the authors. Yet no one else knew where he kept the copies of the *Trion* original. He pulled his briefcase across the desk and took out the sealed envelope with the identifying key. He tore it open. Number three. Aroldo M. Sereni. Harry.

The phone rang. Jerry Devereaux. "Carla called me. I think she's on to something."

"Jerry, who has access to the department offices and the locked furniture? And strongboxes that belong to the college?"

"Campus police have keys to everything, I think, and I have copies of the keys to everything in the department in my desk."

"Who has access to your desk?"

"Me. And Helen."

"I checked the list, Jerry. Paper number three is Harry Sereni's."

"Jesus. You'd think he'd be smart enough to realize that we'd recognize the crib."

"There are some dead giveaways," Dave said, "Like 'knowing' for *verstehen*."

"Look, let's not do anything rash. We'll get together in the morning and hash this through. I want to go over the paper again and be sure there's no other explanation." He hung up.

Dave picked up the paper again. He recognized Harry's writing style—his use of "in order to" and the past progressive and his tendency to string present participle clauses at the end of sentences. Harry had thrown in a few clinkers to make it look less obvious, but there were too many coincidences. Besides, Harry wasn't that smart. Dave drew a deep breath and called Helen's number.

"I've been going over the comps papers," he told her. "Harry's is especially good."

"Thought you weren't going to look at the key until after all the faculty deliberations."

"I wasn't. Until I read Harry's paper."

Helen said nothing.

"Did Harry have a copy of the German text, my translation, and my article? Did you give him a copy of the comp questions?"

Silence.

"You could have opened Jerry's desk," Dave said, "got the key to the cabinet and strongbox, and made copies. You knew the computer password for the comp file."

"I tried to tell you," she said in a shaking voice, "the day you said you didn't want to see me any more. I thought you already knew."

"You stole the copies before we broke up?"

"I've got to see you and explain."

"Chip has my car. Mary's gone in hers."

"I'll come to your place."

"You can't come here—"

She'd hung up. He dialed her number. No answer.

The doorbell rang less than thirty minutes later. He admitted her without speaking. She wore her dark coat and a beret. Her face was drawn and gray. He led her to his study. She sat on the edge of the recliner without taking off her coat.

Dave looked at her steadily. "Mary and Jeannie will be home in an hour. Let's get to the point. You made copies of the text, my translation, and my article and gave them to Harry."

She lowered her eyes and nodded.

"You told him everything I told you about *Trion*," Dave said.

"After Harry walked in on us, he said he'd known about us almost from the beginning. He was waiting to cash in. He said we'd found the golden goose. He told me I should pretend I was pregnant and ask you to pay for an abortion, or if I really wanted to get you by the balls, I should get pregnant. He knew he couldn't pass the comps on his own. He wanted to force you to help him. If you refused, he was going to tell people in the department about us, call your children."

Dave closed his eyes.

Her shoulders drooped. "I knew he'd do what he threatened. I didn't want you to be hurt. So the next morning, I went to the office early and made copies of everything. I warned him to be careful so no one would suspect."

Dave dropped into his desk chair.

Helen took a deep breath. "He was home when you called this afternoon. He said that if you don't pass him, he'll call your wife."

Dave stifled a gasp. "And this is the man you sacrificed everything to help?"

"He's my brother." She took a folded paper from her purse. "You remember this?"

He took it. A burn copy of a computer note.

OAK 3.91 MESSAGE TEXT FOLDER: BELL

PASSW: KISS

DATE: 12 FEB 96

FROM: DBELL

TO: HSERENI

SUBJECT: NEXT WEEKEND

HELEN, I TALKED TO HARRY. WE'RE GETTING TOGETHER FOR SOME COACHING. REMEMBER OUR DEAL. I'LL TAKE CARE OF HARRY IF YOU'LL TAKE CARE OF ME. <SMILE> DAVE.

"Harry has the original." Helen said.

"How did he get it?"

"He asked for it. I gave it to him."

Dave wanted to vomit. "Blood is thicker than semen, isn't it, Helen?"

She turned her head sharply as though he had struck her.

"Does he really think," Dave said, "I'm so craven I'd help him to save myself? No way. Tell him that."

"Dave," she said, her voice in tatters, "don't let it end like this."

"Me? The slob who used you and couldn't wait to wash off the smell of you?"

"I love you."

"Come off it." He folded his arms. "It's too late to help Harry. Carla spotted the similarities. She called me and Jerry."

Helen's lips parted.

Dave got to his feet and walked to the window. The lawn still awaited his attention. The jonquils were still in bud.

He said in a low voice without turning toward her. "Tell that stupid bastard to withdraw his exam paper. You understand that your job is in jeopardy?" He looked over his shoulder at her.

Her face was stricken. "No, I didn't think—"

"It pays to think before you—" He looked at the jonquils. "Helen, you and Harry set me up, didn't you?" He spit. "What got into me? Thinking with my gonads."

Her coat rustled and she gasped. Dave turned. Mary and Jeannie, shopping bags in hand, stood inside the door. Mary's eyes were taut, her face pale. She looked at Helen, then Dave, then Helen.

Half running, Helen pushed past her. Footsteps, then the front door opened and closed.

Mary's eyes settled on Dave. "How long have you been sleeping with her?"

She walked into the room and put her parcels in the recliner. Jeannie stayed by the door, her face blank.

"You bastard," Mary said. "It couldn't be a little hooker down on Fourteenth Street. It had to be the bunny at the office."

"Will you give me a chance to explain?"

"What were you planning to do when the kids found out?"

Dave stammered.

"You'd risk your soul for good sex, wouldn't you?" she said.

She picked up her parcels and headed for the door, then wheeled. "The weekend Chip got in trouble . . . You never went to New York! You were with her, weren't you?" She took Jeannie by the hand and left the room.

Dave's heart was pounding so hard he could see the pulse in his eyes. He fell into his chair, spread his hands on the desk surface, and glared at the wet hand prints.

Harry's exam papers. Had to get Jerry and Carla's copies. He'd call them. Tell them that Harry planned to withdraw. He dialed Carla.

"Carla," he said, trying to get the shakes out of his voice, "the author of paper number three wishes to withdraw."

"Who is it, David?"

Dave considered. Carla would find out anyway. "Harry Sereni."

"Sereni? Helen's brother? David, the truth. Did you help Harry?"

Dave clenched his teeth. "I did not help Harry."

Silence.

"Carla, give me paper number three tomorrow. I'll get Jerry's copy, too. I'll return them all to Harry and allow him to withdraw."

"You want all copies? Where is Harry's original?"

"In my safe on campus."

"You realize that you are asking me to collude with you in consigning all copies of the fraud into your hands."

"What are you implying?"

"I want to talk to Jerry."

She hung up.

Dave bit his lip. Pointless to call Jerry now. He had to think. He got up and walked to the fire. He had to act. He had to

. . . He went to the desk and sat. He thought the whole thing through again.

The phone rang.

"Doctor Bell, this is Harry Sereni. Helen talked to me. I'm terribly upset."

"Under the circumstances, Harry, the only thing you can do is withdraw."

"That's why I called, Doctor Bell. I want you to know, sir, that I had no intention of doing anything dishonorable. I thought the materials you sent me were to help me in my preparation. Since the help came from you, I didn't realize I was doing anything wrong."

"Harry, you think anyone would believe I'd help you in an unethical way?"

"I didn't know it was unethical. I thought it was because you are my advisor . . . and because of your special relationship with Helen."

"Harry, Helen said you were going to blackmail me."

"I have to warn you that I'll do whatever I must to defend my honor and protect Helen. We both acted in good faith. And if I'm asked, I'll be forced to say that the help I got came from you."

Dave hung up.

• • •

The following morning, Dave skipped his workout and went straight to the office. Rose from the English department was sorting the weekend faxes and mail at Helen's desk. He took his mail. "I won't be taking any calls."

A small man with a blond beard, an earring, and round rimless John Denver glasses sat next to Helen's desk. George

Eckland. "Doctor Bell, can you spare me a minute?"

Dave locked his teeth. "Come on in."

George followed Dave to his office. A note, in Jerry's hand, was taped to the door: "Dave—emergency meeting in my office. Waiting for you." Dave ripped it from the door and waved George in. "Why have you been calling me?"

"No need to be hostile." George eased into the chair next to Dave's desk. "I wanted to do a follow-up on the *Trion* discovery story."

"You won't get any help from me. You can't be trusted."

"Sorry about that. *Trion* is an important find."

"What about your pledge of 'Journalist's Honor?'" Dave said.

"My first duty is to my readers."

"Even if the information was confidential, provided off the record?"

George squared his shoulders. "You wanted to orchestrate the announcement of the discovery to get the maximum publicity, right?"

"What the hell is your problem?"

"I could have graduated *cum laude.*"

"You thought you were so smart you didn't have to study."

"German literature is an elective, not required for a journalism major."

"I see," Dave said. "Not worth your time."

"I'm here for another reason. An anonymous tip. Caller claimed there was cheating on the German PhD comps and that you're involved."

Dave's scalp crawled. "Get out."

"I'm going to find out anyway, Doctor Bell."

Dave stood and started toward George. "Out."

George scrambled from the chair and got to the door. When he saw that Dave wasn't following him, he composed himself and gave Dave a fatuous grin. "Have a great day."

Jerry and Carla were at the conference table. They were a mismatched pair. Jerry, a smiling black fullback; Carla, gray, sour, and brittle.

"Here he is," Jerry said. "Dave, I took the liberty of postponing your eight o'clock until tomorrow morning at ten."

Dave sat.

Jerry paced. "Damage control. Comp paper number three bears all the signs of cheating, information from Dave's unpublished article, phrases from his translation. The only person with access was Helen Sereni, and candidate number three is Harry Sereni."

"Yesterday afternoon," Dave said, "Harry told me Helen gave him copies of everything. He said he didn't think there was anything irregular about using my work to prepare for the exam. I'm his advisor, and he thought I'd sent them to him." Dave grunted. "Bullshit."

"No need for that kind of language, David," Carla said.

"Jerry," Dave said, "call Helen and ask her."

"I called Helen before the meeting," Jerry said. "Harry told me she was at the doctor's. He repeated what he told Dave." Jerry cleared his throat. "He added one important piece of information. He says that since October Helen and Dave had been . . . keeping company."

Carla took off her glasses.

Dave winced. "Helen and I were seeing each other, but the rest of Harry's story is fabrication. Helen came to see me. She admitted she had taken the papers from the strongbox and made copies for Harry, without my knowledge."

Carla put on her glasses and studied her pencil. "You are asking us to believe, David, that despite your . . . *relationship* with Miss Sereni, you gave Harry no help?"

Dave turned his body full toward her. "What are you accusing me of?"

"Dave," Jerry said, "this is no time for surliness. If you ever needed your friends' support, you need it now."

Dave flashed. "*Friends?* Support me or not, as you see fit. I've never asked for help from either of you. I'm not asking now."

"This whole issue," Jerry said, "is complex. Whatever else happens, I counsel you to avoid discussing this matter with anyone." His eyes moved from Carla to Dave. "Meanwhile, let me have Harry's test paper—the original and all the typed copies. I'll ask Harry to withdraw. That's all for now. Dave, I'd like to talk to you privately."

Carla stalked from the room.

"Does Mary know about Helen?" Jerry asked.

"She overheard my conversation with Helen yesterday."

"What's she going to do?"

"Nothing—as far as I know."

"Jesus." Jerry looked down. "I'm with you on this, buddy. Let me know if I can help. Meanwhile, there's no need to turn on me and Carla." Jerry played with his papers. "I wouldn't be alive if it weren't for you. The ambush . . . you saved my ass. Then you took me under your wing—"

"Jerry, this is no time—"

"I wasn't nothin' but a knowless nigger from Loosianer. I never would have found out I had a flare for languages. I learned my first German from you. If it hadn't been for you pushing me . . ." Jerry put down his papers. "We both did pretty well—for a couple of guys who started out with nothin' but street smarts."

His grin faded. "Except for Long Dinh."

Dave said, "I don't even remember it."

"Used to be we'd get together for a beer once in a while—"

"Can we talk about it some other time?"

"You've gotten downright eccentric—wanting to use the Mann manuscript for PhD comps, locking everything up in a safe you bought yourself like you're protecting the Romanov jewels, buying a 300Z. And now, for the last year, this health kick. You work out every morning?"

"Fuck it." Dave left without looking at Jerry.

In the outer office, Rose stopped him. "Doctor Bell, phone messages." She handed him yellow slips. "Mr. McAndrew. And a Mr. Hans Lehmann has called twice."

Dave pocketed the slips and went into his office.

• • •

By the time Dave parked the Z down the block from the Für ein Fremdes Land bookshop, street lights along Carroll Avenue were flickering on through freezing rain. He eased from the car, sat in the downpour by the pink-and-blue gazebo, and gazed across at Horst's shop. The dim light from the display windows was warm, comforting. Lights were on upstairs, too, in Horst's apartment.

Chip and Jeannie. And Mary.

He studied the puddles on the brick pavement. He pictured Mary's sculpted face. He didn't want to love her anymore, but he did anyway. What could he do to make her forgive him? All right. He'd go to counseling with her. Alone, too. Anything she wanted.

He wiped the rain from his face and edged across the sidewalk and onto the street. The pavement was slick. The "help wanted" sign was still taped to the inside of the shop window. "Live-in assistant manager. Desire graduate student." Horst's English. A jangle announced his entry, sounding for all the world like the shattering of glass. He turned, surprised, and saw a set of brass bells hanging from the door. There were eight of them, ranging from five or six inches in diameter at the top to an inch at the bottom, joined by leather thongs that vibrated while he watched.

"Temple bells," an accented contralto voice said. "From Ayutthaya. My gift to Horst."

A woman in a beige suit stood in the dim light at the end of the cashier's counter. Her honey-colored hair was swept back from her face to the top of her head, held with combs, and she wore small dangling earrings. Her makeup was careful enough to alert him that she was probably not in the first bloom of youth. She gave him a radiant smile. "I am Arianna d'Amori. Visiting from Maine."

"Dave Bell."

She took his hand in hers. "Horst is detained. Care to rest at table?"

"I hope I didn't interrupt—"

She waved her hand back and forth, palm down. "Not to derange yourself. Horst will be along directly."

Horst came down the steps and unlatched the chain with the sign that read No ADMITTANCE. His glasses caught the light, hiding his eyes, but his smile was genuine. "*Ach, Herr Doktor Bell!*" In the half light, Dave could make out Horst's tiny frame, bald head with fluffs of white hair above each ear. "Your order is in. *La Divina Commedia*, and I have a special book of poetry for you by Rumi. But you are soaked. You have met Arianna?"

"I must be on my way." She slipped into a midnight blue

rain coat, arranged the hood, and slid on blue kid gloves. "You will come to visit me in Maine." She picked up a large briefcase. "I will look forward to it." She gave him another smile and was gone.

Dave watched after her and caught the scent of lime in her wake. "Is she Italian?"

"From Venice originally. She's in town on business."

"Your lady friend?"

Horst smiled and shook his head. "A friend. A fine woman. Generous. Good-hearted. Some time you must ask how she came by her name." He scanned Dave's face. "You are not well, David?"

"Not my best."

"I see." Horst guided him toward the rear of the shop. "Tea will improve your constitution."

Dave breathed in the scent of old books, dust, and tea. As he passed the shelf on German literature, he spotted three copies of *Leverkühn*—his book analyzing Mann's *Doktor Faustus*—and one of his *Thomas Mann: Künstler und Philosoph*. He sat at the tiny table.

"A new Darjeeling." Horst came through the arched doorway from the office. "Found it at a little place in Kensington." He put down a tray with cups, napkins, a tea pot, and a plate of almond cakes, and sat across from Dave. "I saw Eckland's item in the *Log*. When will I be able to see the Mann manuscript?"

"Summer."

"You found it in Los Angeles?"

"His daughter's estate allowed Lincoln to take it for study. They retained the rights to royalties but gave us permission to publish it, do a translation, and share our findings."

"Trion?" Horst said.

"The Greek myth. Dramatized by Sophocles and Euripides. Mann was fascinated with Trion, a sort of a Greek prototype of masculinity pushed to the edge."

Horst nodded slowly. "The Spartans revered him, yes? Impervious to pain?"

"In himself and others. He murdered his own son, disemboweled him. In the Euripides version, he didn't know it was his son—kind of like a reverse of the Oedipus story. The Eucharides drowned him."

Horst cocked his head. "Eucharides? The grateful ones?"

"Greek irony. Like calling the Furies the Eumenides, the kindly ones."

"Yes, of course. Mann would have loved all that."

"He set his novella in the nineteen-twenties," Dave said. "Called his protagonist Trion Kretzschmar, a German army officer who never knew love as a child. Mann uses the archaic term *Ungeminnt* to show that Kretzschmar can neither love nor be loved. Mann sums it up, 'Evil has no understanding of love.' Kretzschmar is *Unverzeihlich*, unforgivable because of what he is. What's heart-breaking is that Kretzschmar, unlike a true psychopath, understands his dilemma and craves love. Then, in the pivotal scene, Kretzschmar chooses power over the possibility of love. He sends his bastard son to his death— disembowelment—in battle. The battle is won, Kretzschmar is credited with a great military victory. He looks in the mirror and sees that he has no reflection, steps into the sunshine and looks down. No shadow. He has lost his soul. At the height of his success, he flees to Cuxhaven, where the Elbe meets the North Sea, and pleads with an ancient exorcist for help. The old man tells him that only by loving can he save himself. But

Kretzschmar doesn't understand love. He loads his body with all the weapons of his trade and throws himself into the Elbe. The weight of his weaponry drags him to the bottom and he drowns."

Horst smiled. "Genuine Mann."

"It's sort of an 'Every*man*' story—maleness unchecked, Dionysian extremes without the Apollonian counterforce, the Yang without the Yin. In some ways, it's a cautionary tale. Mann is warning against strength without love, dominance without mercy, loss of the soul."

Horst gave him an appraising look. "Why does Trion's fate fascinate you?"

Dave's heart jumped.

"Your eyes," Horst said. "So like your father's. They tell me much."

"You used to read his eyes, too?"

Horst nodded. "When your father, the young Corporal Bell, described the Fräulein he wanted to take to the states, his eyes told me everything. I counseled him to marry her at once, before her family learned she was pregnant."

"I don't know anyone else who knew him," Dave said. "I wonder if the son-of-a-bitch is still alive."

"No. He was a troubled man pursuing his own ruin, even when I knew him. Unlike his son." Horst reached across the table and put his hand on Dave's. "Forgive him his weakness. Free yourself of that burden. You are not like him. We are who we choose to be. You chose aloneness, and kindness, even to an old man."

"*You* made all this." Dave spread his arms.

"I could never have gotten to the states without your help." Horst brightened. "It was on that trip that I met Arianna. She, too, is a bookseller. But we were speaking of you. I see those same eyes, your father's eyes, again telling me of trouble."

Dave told him. The whole sordid story. "All day I've been remembering the first time I saw Mary. She was standing in a lighted doorway at a party in Berkeley. She looked like a dancer except that she was too tall. Greenest eyes I'd ever seen. 'You play football, don't you?' she said. 'For adulation or for the sports scholarship?' I didn't answer." Dave swallowed the lump in his throat. "You think I can win her back?"

"The tea will be ready." Horst smiled. "The mystics tell a tale about a man searching for a key by night on the streets of Baghdad. A young boy comes upon him and asks him where he lost the key. The man points and says, 'Over there.' 'Then why do you search here?' the boy asks. The man answers, 'Because the light is better here.'"

"Good story," Dave said.

"Search for her love in the right place."

"Where?"

"She is your wife, not mine."

Dave tasted the tea.

"Tell me the dream again," Horst said.

Dave studied his hands. "It changes. Sometimes we're in a hootch and the VC are at the door. Sometimes we're in the jungle. Jerry is always there with his M-16. And the woman. I can never see who she is. The VC close in. All I have is a knife. I try to tell Jerry to fire, but he freezes. Then I lunge. I hear a scream and wake up looking for the blood."

"What happened in Vietnam?"

"It's what happened afterwards. For years, I didn't sleep well. Loud noises made me want to dive for cover. When I was startled, I went into the attack mode, even hit Jeannie one time.

Some odors gave me the shivers. I'll never forget the mob that greeted Jerry and me and the others in San Francisco. They spat on us, screamed 'baby killers' and 'butchers' at us."

"David, what happened *in Vietnam?*"

"I don't remember."

"You were there with Jerry and a woman."

"No, there was no woman. That's only in the dream."

"So you do remember. Tell me."

"I don't—" But in his mind Dave saw the snaking vines, felt the heavy air on his skin, smelled the rot. His mouth went dry. "We were near Long Dinh. In a sort of a hut. Someone was trying to get in. Jerry pointed his M-16 as the door opened." Dave was panting. He could see the blur framed in pale light. "And there, in the doorway—" He could see it, the figure in black, raising its arms. "Jerry froze. I tried to tell him to fire, but I couldn't speak. All I had was a knife." Dave's throat locked. He was shaking. The person in the doorway. The lunge. The scream. Then the blood.

"Your tea will be cold," Horst said.

Dave lifted his cup. His hand was trembling.

"Who is the woman in your dream?"

"I don't know," Dave said.

"Is she Mary?"

"No. She's . . . I don't know."

"Describe her."

"Blond hair."

"Mary is blond."

"It's not Mary," Dave said. "The woman in the dream hates me."

"Why?"

"I don't know."

"Tell me why she hates you."

"The person in the doorway."

"What did you do?"

"I . . . I only had a knife—"

"You stabbed the person at the door?"

The memory closed down as though the light had gone out.

Horst patted his arm.

Dave drew his handkerchief across his forehead and cheeks.

"Perhaps, my friend," Horst said, "you need to search for the key not in the light but in the dark."

"Is there only one key?"

Horst smiled.

Chapter 4

Blood and Fire

My call to George Eckland is brief and sharp. "Cheating on the PhD comps in the German Department," I whisper. "Check on Doctor Bell and his relationship with the sister of one of the candidates."

"Who is this?" Eckland says.

"Call me anonymous. Check it out, George."

My finger glides over the disconnect button. I take a deep, shaky breath, wipe the sweat from my palms, and lean back in my desk chair. It rolls an inch. I grasp the edge of the desk. As soon as I stop quaking, I open the door to the outer office so Emma won't think anything's strange.

Before lunch, I call Carla. She avoids the subject of Harry, makes it clear that she doesn't feel free to discuss anything with me.

"But this news has shocked me, Mary," she says. "Count on me as a friend."

I have a hell of time getting home in the freezing rain—the station wagon slithers all over the street, especially on the hills up to the house. The Z isn't in the driveway. Inside, no one around, but I see Jeannie's car coat on the hall tree. I hang my coat, go upstairs, and stop at her door.

"Where's Chip?"

"Gym. Went on the Metro."

She's lying on her bed twisting her hair, a book and binder open in front of her. She's wearing the princess ring.

My stomach turns. "You wore that thing to school? I told you it makes you cheap."

She rolls on her side, her back to me. I go to our room long enough to change out of my suit, head downstairs to start dinner. Will Dave be here? Chip?

While I'm chopping cabbage for slaw, the phone rings. I hear Jeannie scamper into our room to answer it.

"Mom," she yells from the top of the stairway.

I dry my hands and pick up the kitchen extension.

"Mrs. Bell? This is Harry Sereni. Your husband is my advisor—"

"He's not home yet—"

"I was hoping he wouldn't be," he says. "I thought you and I should talk."

Cold spreads in my chest.

"From what my sister told me," he says, "I gather you know Doctor Bell and she have been seeing each other?"

I don't answer.

"Mrs. Bell, your husband forced himself on Helen— threatened to fail me if she didn't let him have his way with her, as they say. Out of love for me, she did what he asked but did nothing to protect herself."

I should hang up on him.

"They had unprotected sex."

I swallow but can't speak.

"Are you still there, Mrs. Bell?"

I manage to make a sound.

"If she bears his child, Mrs. Bell, we'll have to make some kind of arrangement—unless, of course, he decides to stay with her. I believe he's leaning in that direction—"

I slam down the receiver. *If she bears his child.* None of this is true. Harry is making it up.

Forced himself on her? Dave? I wring my hands. She's going to bear his child?

"Mom?" Jeannie from upstairs. "How soon's dinner?"

Maybe Helen and Harry were in this together from the beginning. Dupe Dave into divorcing me and marrying her.

"Mom?"

He must care nothing for his children.

"Mom!"

"Half an hour," I yell. "Why?"

"I want to start typing my paper at Dad's computer. How soon's he going to be home?"

"Go ahead."

I hear Chip hanging his coat in the hall. His face is still flushed from his workout, shower, and the walk from the Metro.

"What's happening?" he says.

I return to my chopping. "Start your homework."

While I'm doing dishes, Dave comes in and goes straight upstairs. I clean the stove and follow him up. He's already in bed. I perch on the edge.

"What are you going to tell the children?" I ask.

"That I slept with Helen Sereni. I didn't help Harry cheat."

"Are they going to ask you to resign?"

He puts his arm over his face. "Of course not."

"Are you going to leave me?"

"No."

"Is she pregnant?"

"No!" he says "Why do you ask?"

"You still seeing her?"

"I broke it off last month."

I bite my lip. "Is she sexy?"

"Not as sexy as you."

"I thought I was your leading candidate for the international Mrs. Frigid competition."

"You're the sexiest woman I ever met."

"If you really think I'm that sexy," I say, "why were you fooling around with her?"

"When I make love to you, I feel like I'm forcing myself on you. I want you to want me."

"She wants you?"

"Yes."

"She's good in bed?"

"Why do you ask?" he says. "It's over."

"Is she better than me?"

He trains his eyes on the ceiling.

"As erotic as you?" I say. "God. You two must have melted the bed springs."

He sits up. "Stop it. Whatever else you or I may think about Helen, she knows how to love a man. You, *you*—Satan put you on earth to drive me insane."

"Now you link goodness and sex? You're nothing but one big penis."

"Never read Dante, did you? You know how he depicts evil? Frozen in ice from the waist down. Tell me what it feels like."

I swing at him. He catches my wrist. I swipe with my other hand. He catches that one, too. His hand is big enough to hold both my wrists while he raises his free hand and holds it trembling over me. Our eyes lock.

"Go ahead," I say through my teeth. "Beat me up. Make it perfect."

With a single motion he shoves me away. "I'll sleep on the sofa."

• • •

"Morning, Emma," I say with a bright smile. "Unbearable
weather. Still have icicles on my eyelashes. We have coffee yet?"
I wheel toward the coffee machine, but something stops me. I
turn to Emma. She's avoiding me like I'm the body at a funeral.
The gossip mill must have reached her.

"I left the mail on your desk." She busies herself with a heap
of papers.

She's awakened the butterflies in my belly. With a
nonchalance I didn't know I could muster, I pour myself
coffee and head into my office. As I put my cup on my desk,
I do a double-take. Dave's picture, dead center on my desk
blotter, smiles up at me. It covers almost half the front page of
today's *Lincoln Log*. The headline reads, "Sᴇx Sᴄᴀɴᴅᴀʟ Rᴏᴄᴋs
Lɪɴᴄᴏʟɴ." The subtitle says, "Professor Accused of Cheating."
The byline is George Eckland, Student Reporter. The date is
Tuesday, March 12, 1996. I ease into my chair.

> In the worst scandal to strike Lincoln College in its fifty-year
> history, a German professor was accused yesterday of cheating for
> sex. Doctor David Schliemann Bell, associate professor of German,
> is alleged to have secretly provided copies of Thomas Mann's
> unpublished novella, *Trion*, and related materials to Aroldo (Harry)
> Sereni, a German graduate student, to assist Sereni in his PhD
> comprehensive examinations. Sources report that Bell's motivation
> was his intimate relations with Elena (Helen) Sereni, secretary in
> the German Department and sister to Aroldo Sereni. Bell attracted
> international attention recently because of his discovery of the
> Mann novella. He is married to the former Mary Bergstrom of
> Saint Paul, MN, and the father to two children, David Bell, Jr.
> (Chip), 17; and Jean Bell, 15. Mrs. Bell is Chief of Administration
> of Lincoln College . . .

He named the children, even gave Chip's nickname. I can't
read any more. I did this. Shame flushes through me. Shame for

Dave. Shame for myself. *What have I done to my children?* I had no idea . . .

I dial George Eckland's number.

"Eckland."

"I need to see you immediately," My voice is jittering.

"Who's speaking, please?"

"I'm on my way over."

I sweep across the snowy sidewalks and icy crosswalks to the other side of campus. At the Student Union Building I show my ID to the security guard, making no secret of my impatience. On the second floor, I barge into the *Lincoln Log* office without knocking. A large room crowded with desks and computers and printers and stacks of paper. The windows are filthy, the floor littered with paper wads and candy wrappers. All faces turn toward me.

I'm panting. "George Eckland . . ."

A blond wisp of a man in wire-rim glasses stands.

"Is there some place we can talk?"

He waves me toward a door. Inside is a windowless room the size of a closet. He sits at a desk. I squeeze into the chair opposite.

"You've seen today's *Log*." He's smiling, as though he expects to be congratulated.

"I want you to retract the story."

His smile vanishes. "Who are you?"

"Mary Bell."

His eyebrows go up.

"That story is a garbled lie," I say.

His smile, smug and triumphant, returns. "My sources wouldn't agree with you."

"You were tipped off," I say. "Anonymously."

His face turns serious. "How do you know that?"

"I was the tipper."

He registers genuine surprise.

"I shouldn't have done it." The jitter is in my voice again. "Your story will hurt people. My children . . . I want your promise that you'll recall all copies immediately, retract the story, and print nothing more on this incident."

He shakes his head. "I can't do that. It's my obligation as a journalist to report the truth as I see it. Nothing else matters. Besides, you weren't the only source."

I clutch. "Who else?"

"I'm not at liberty to reveal that. Anyway, it's too late. Robin McAndrew of *The Washington Post* called this morning to congratulate me. They're thinking of running an item." He leans forward. "You all right?"

"Tell McAndrew the story was a mistake."

He tilts his head and offers me a comforting smile.

I feel tears coming.

He rises, the smile still on his lips. "Wish I could help you."

Why did I tip George? I close the door to my office and weep. *Dave* had the affair. To betray me with that woman. I remember Helen at the desk while I waited for Carla. A beautiful sensuous woman who knows how to love a man. I wish she were dead.

I flip open the directory, find the number of Bob Scarff.

"Can I see you today?"

"Has something happened?"

"Have you seen today's *Lincoln Log*? Read it before I get there. Save us some time."

• • •

Dave's lying on the bed. I sit on it and look at him. My rage boils.

"What are you going to do?" I say.

He puts his forearm over his eyes. The phone rings downstairs. "I suggest you not answer it."

"You wanted a whore," I spit, "I was a madonna."

"You used to want me to make love to you."

"You never interested me in bed."

"What were you doing? Faking?"

"I was fool enough to try to please you."

Dave bolts upright. "You used to—"

"Never."

"I don't believe you."

"*You* believe what you want to believe."

He reels from the bed. The phone is ringing downstairs. "Jesus," he says. "For twenty years?"

"Go to Helen," I say.

"That's over."

"Pity. Because I want you out. As soon as you can move."

Dave catches his breath.

"Lawyer says I should have clear sailing," I tell him.

"You're going to divorce me?" he says. "Because of Helen? Mary, for God's sake. Chip and Jeannie—"

"Start your new family without any ties." My smile dies. "Maybe she can support you. Because when I get through, you won't have a pot to piss in or a window to throw it out of."

Dave gives me a look like none I've ever seen, as though resigned to his own execution. He gets to his feet and heads out. I hear him on the stairs, the door to the study closes.

Chip and Jeannie come home from school quiet and edgy and avoid my eyes. They've seen the *Log*. After dark, I fix them something to eat and go to Sligo Creek Park. I walk and walk and walk. I don't even feel the cold. I burn with hatred for him, despise myself.

At nine o'clock, I'm home.

Dave heads me off at the stairs. "Chip and Jeannie deserve to know what's happening."

"I'll tell them to meet us in the family room."

Dave goes to the family room, and I call the children. Dave is seated on the hearth. I take the chair next to him. Jeannie eases into the room as if trying not to be noticed. Chip, pale and tight-lipped, stomps in and sits next to Jeannie on the sofa.

"You've seen today's *Lincoln Log*?" Dave says.

Jeannie nods. Chip goes on looking at Dave.

"I want to set the record straight." Dave's short of breath. "The story about me and Helen Sereni is true. We did have an affair." He can't meet Chip's gaze. "It ended last month. The accusation that I helped Harry cheat is a lie."

Chip is still watching him. Jeannie goes on studying her ring. My heart aches for them.

"Your mother," Dave says, "told me this afternoon that she's filed for divorce."

Chip's mouth opens. Jeannie raises her head.

"We haven't talked details," Dave says, "but I guess I'll be moving out. You need to think about what you want to do. I want you both to come with me—"

"No," Chip says.

"You're free to decide for yourselves," Dave says.

Jeannie covers her face with her hands. Her body vibrates. Chip puts his arms around her. She breaks from his embrace, comes to me.

I hold her. "Hush, honey."

Dave puts his hands on Jeannie's arms. "Hey, love—"

Jeannie pulls away from him and buries her face between my breasts.

Dave slowly stands upright. "I see. You have to make your choices and live with the consequences." He gives us a bitter smile.

• • •

I awaken alone. Dave's last day in the house. I told him to go. He can come back later and get the rest of his things. I can't bear to look at him. I'll wait until I hear him leave before I go downstairs. No point in trying to go to sleep again, even though it was after three before I finally drifted off.

The taste of vengeance in my mouth, like blood and fire, has turned to ashes. I brush my teeth, floss, gargle. My moment of glory came when I told him I'd been pretending, all those years. His face had twisted. I'd hurt him. Deeply. Good.

Then his eyes teared. I had to squelch the impulse to take him in my arms. What's the matter with me, wanting to hold him and tell him I loved him and it would be okay?

It won't ever be okay.

At least neither of my parents is alive to say "I told you so." They tried to get me to come home to Minnesota, forget my plans for graduate school, marry a local God-fearing, tobacco-chewing, raw-boned yokel. Norwegian Gothic. They chose the boy from the adjoining farm, because he'd serially raped me when I was fourteen. They told me it was my fault, never spoke to his parents about it, never said a word about it to anyone. After the botched abortion they insisted on, they refused to take me to the emergency room when I hemorrhaged. I was contaminated. Shame. I've never told anyone, not even Dave.

Dave was my passport to freedom, but they were right. He's
no good. Let him and Helen try to make a life together. By
the time I get through with him . . . I'll even get a shot at his
pension.

I tear my nightgown off and turn on the shower. I sit naked
on the edge of the tub. The cold, white enamel chills me. I want
to hide my body from men's leering eyes, from the pain of that
boy's penis tearing me open. Killing shame. I'm damaged goods,
incapable of loving a man. But I do love Dave and the bastard
betrayed me. I step into the shower. I'll ruin him. I already have.
I tip my face into the hot jets of water and feel my smile return.
His career's in the toilet.

"You did the right thing," Bob Scarff told me. "Strengthens
our case."

"I didn't think Eckland would turn it into a sex-on-campus
extravaganza," I said.

Bob laughed. "Men aren't born monogamous." He gave me
a suggestive smile. "Women, either."

A couple of times Dave and I had dinner with Bob and his
date of the moment, always a woman whose divorce he was
handling. Handsome, with that crooked smile under the lock
of brown hair falling over his forehead. Boyish, innocent. More
than once, even when he was with a date, he looked into my
eyes a little longer than needed. And the time he helped me with
my coat . . . Dave warned me about him. "Lady killer. Reputedly
the biggest skirt chaser in the seven counties."

Jesus, this whole business is fixating me on sex. I work
shampoo into my hair. Dave says Bob's a lousy father. Has
two children he sees at Christmas and once or twice during
the summer. Not that it matters. By reputation, Bob's the best
divorce lawyer in town. He's sure of himself and comforting. He

told me to let him handle everything. All I have to do is follow his guidance, like closing out the bank accounts and canceling the credit cards before Dave had a chance to do it.

Chapter 5

Unauthorized Transactions

Dave put his hands on Jeannie's arms. "Hey, love—"

Jeannie pulled away.

"I see," Dave said."You have to make your choices and live with the consequences."

He walked through the patio door, down the steps, into the darkness. He stood on the brickwork he had laid and looked toward the rhododendron, the yews, the flowering cherry he had planted.

The wind bit his flesh. Sleet lashed him. His wife and his children had turned on him. He was on his own now. Always had been. His family was a delusion. He'd given up Helen because he didn't want to lose Jeannie and Chip. Just as he'd given up Inge twenty years ago to come home and marry the only woman he'd ever loved. Mary was right. He'd risked his soul for good sex and lost.

Dave follows the woman across a rope bridge over a chasm. They move forward slowly, silently, putting one foot in front of the other on the single strand. Jerry is already on the far side, concealed in the undergrowth, covering them. When they are almost across, the woman stops and turns. "Killer!" she whispers. Dave can't see her face. "Killer!" The bridge sways. From nowhere, the VC are in front of them, between them and Jerry's hiding place. One is hacking at the bridge with his machete. The bridge drops half an inch and shudders. Dave can feel each chop on the rope beneath him. The bridge drops again, nearly a foot. Jerry emerges and raises the M-16. Dave tries to order him to fire, but he can't make a sound. Dave forces his way past the woman and struggles to reach the end. The bridge trembles and lurches. Jerry still doesn't fire. Dave unsheathes his knife and lunges . . .

The scream threw Dave from the sofa. In the dark he couldn't see his hands. He clasped them. Moist.

He staggered to the wall and threw the switch. The ceiling fixture flooded the room with bleak light. The clock on the VCR told him it was not yet five. Still panting, he headed upstairs to the bathroom.

In the dark, he pulled on his sweats, stuffed his feet in his sneakers, and carried his gym bag, suit, shirt, tie, and street shoes to the car. He arrived at the campus in plenty of time to work out. Too early for Bob Scarff. Dave went on without him. His body was slow and uncooperative, his mind distracted. He wasn't able to make his numbers, but he went through his entire routine. As if it mattered.

In the office, he'd hung up his coat when the intercom sounded. Jerry.

"Jake Colson has appointed an investigative committee. Unusual, but a college president can do it. We're meeting tomorrow morning in Halsey 313. Carla and I are both on it. The chair is Sharon Wise from Chemistry. Be there at nine, all right?"

"Isn't this kind of sudden?"

"Seems the alumni and trustees are going bonkers over the item in the *Log*."

Dave huffed. "They must have too much time on their hands."

"You forget. Lincoln was originally Lincoln Christian

college. Some of our most generous supporters cherish their
memories of the old days when Lincoln was a seminary. Now
McAndrew has run a piece in the *Post*. Looks like he's talked
to Eckland and maybe even to Eckland's anonymous tipster.
Colson wants action, fast."

"Who else is going to be there?"

"Wise and the three of us. And Harry and Helen."

"So. You and Carla will get to hear the truth from Helen.
I'm relieved."

"Meanwhile, Carla and I will be taking over your classes
until all this is resolved."

"And office hours?" Dave said.

"Don't see anyone."

Dave nodded to himself. He saw how it was going to go.
"Need the time to move to a motel."

"Oh, Dave—"

"Yeah. She's filed."

"God!"

"When Mary sticks it to you, she doesn't fool around."

Dave hung up. Too much happening. Couldn't keep his
grip. Had to think. Find a place to stay. Get a lawyer. See about
money. Try for a reconciliation? He remembered Mary's face
when she told him to move out, Chip and Jeannie when he
said he wanted them to come with him. No, his sin was mortal.
They'd never forgive him. He couldn't even forgive himself.

For what? Sleeping with Helen? That wasn't it. It was . . .
what he was. He was *Unverzeihlich*, unforgivable. Because . . . he
didn't know why.

By nine o'clock he'd phoned the Shady Vistas Motel on
Route 1 south of Laurel and reserved a room. Long way from
campus but cheap.

Next he telephoned Bob Scarff.

"Never thought I'd be calling on you for professional help, Bob."

"Mary talked to me yesterday. Retained me to handle her case."

"You're representing *her?*"

"Sorry, guy. Have a pencil?" He gave Dave the names and numbers of three lawyers.

Bob representing Mary. If Bob so much as leered at her . . . He stopped himself. Mary knew Bob. She was on her own. He picked up the phone and dialed the first lawyer on the list, a Thomas Vickers, and got an appointment for the following Monday.

After lunch, too tense to work, Dave left the office, went home, and packed everything he could carry. He'd have to keep his stuff in the car. When he had a place to live, he'd go back and get the rest of his possessions from the house. Maybe. Did he even care enough to go to the house and claim his things? He drove north on Route 1. There, amid used car lots, fast food restaurants, and discount outlets, he found the Shady Vistas Motel. Not a tree in sight and the only view was the gravel parking lot and the three-story windowless brick building beyond.

When he entered the office, crowded with vending machines, racks of paperback books, and magazine displays, he caught the acrid scent of pizza. Hesitant, self-pitying dialogue of a TV soap opera drifted through the door behind the counter.

"Be right with you," a voice said.

A bloated, middle-aged woman with hair that looked like a Dolly Parton wig came through the door still chewing.

"I have a reservation," Dave said. "Name's Bell."

"How long will you be staying?"

"I'll pay for one night."

"Fill this out."

While Dave wrote, she set her Coke on the counter and ran his MasterCard through the electronic reader. It hummed, growled, and went silent. She scowled at the machine. "Declined."

"Pardon?"

"The system won't accept the charge. It says for you to contact your financial institution."

Dave blinked. "Would you try it again?"

She zipped the card through the machine. More hums and growls. "Declined."

"Try my American Express."

She sliced the card through the reader and waited. A moment later, the machine responded.

"'Declined. Please contact your financial institution.'"

Dave coughed once. Mary must have closed the accounts. "Guess I'll pay cash."

The room was spare. It smelled of Lysol, bleach, and urine. The walls were dark synthetic panels peeling at the light switches. Dave turned on the heating unit and hung up his suits. Nothing to do now but wait until tomorrow.

After nightfall, he found a convenience store, bought cereal, milk, and instant coffee, and went to the ATM to get cash. The screen flashed "UNAUTHORIZED TRANSACTION, PLEASE CONTACT YOUR INSTITUTION." He tried their checking account. Same result. He opened his wallet. Less than a hundred dollars. He drove to the motel.

The next morning, Dave found Halsey 313. The room was long, narrow, and windowless, lit from above by recessed fluorescent lights that drained the color from everything. The floor was deeply carpeted. The seminar table, large enough for ten, reminded him of a corporate board room in a bad movie. Polished wooden chairs with padded seats lined the table.

Harry and Helen sat on one side. Harry held his topcoat in his lap. His dark suit and tie made him look like a priest. Helen wore her beret and her long coat over a black turtleneck. When Harry saw Dave, his face darkened. Helen, her flesh pinched and colorless, looked at her folded hands. Dave sat opposite them.

A stately gray-haired woman in rimless glasses came in carrying a briefcase. She took Dave's hand. "I'm Sharon Wise."

She moved to Harry and Helen. Helen raised her head. She had a bruise under her chin. She pulled the turtleneck higher.

Doctor Wise sat at the head of the table and took a file from her briefcase. Jerry and Carla came in and sat on either side of her.

"We're investigating," Doctor Wise began, "possible misuse of information in a comprehensive examination last Thursday and Friday in the German Department. Let's keep it informal. Doctor Devereaux?"

Jerry repeated the facts of the case, ending with Dave's admission of the affair with Helen.

"Thank you." Doctor Wise surveyed Dave. "Doctor Bell, have you anything to add?" Dave shook his head. "Doctor Brecht?" Carla mouthed "no." "Mr. Sereni?"

"Yes," Harry said. "I am threatened with expulsion. I must speak."

All except Helen watched him.

"As some of you know—" He glanced at Dave, Jerry, and Carla. "—I'm not exactly a stunning success as a graduate student. Helen and I grew up orphans in The Bronx. With

Helen's help, I made it through college. Four years ago, Doctor Bell admitted me as a probational graduate student. I made it up to the comps level, then everything fell apart."

Harry's eyes moved from face to face. "Last fall, Helen got a job as a secretary in the German Department, so I could qualify for the family tuition program. From the start, Doctor Bell showed a lot of interest in Helen. Then in October—" He took a deep breath. "In October, Doctor Bell told my sister that if she'd sleep with him, he'd see to it that I got my PhD. If she didn't, he'd flunk me and get her fired."

Dave's jaw slackened. Doctor Wise leaned toward Harry. No one else moved.

Harry took Helen's hand. "Helen has always put my good before her own. She's been looking after me since I was four. She saw to it that we stayed together after our parents died as we were shunted from one relative to another. She was determined I'd get my PhD, no matter what it cost. She . . . She did as Doctor Bell wished."

Dave felt as though he'd been kicked in the groin.

"I didn't know about any of this," Harry said. "Then, last month, Doctor Bell, who was my advisor, offered to share the Mann story he had discovered. He invited me to his office, showed me the manuscript, and allowed me to study his translation and an early draft of an article he was writing. He even made copies of *Trion*, his translation, and his article and gave them to Helen for me. I was flattered by Doctor Bell's interest and what I thought was his kindness. When he asked me not to tell anyone, I agreed. I didn't know *Trion* was going to be used for comps. Then when it came out in the *Log*, I realized I had an advantage, but it never occurred to me that I was the only candidate who'd seen *Trion*."

"Harry— " Dave began.

Doctor Wise shushed him. "Let him finish."

Harry turned his head to the side and looked down. "I didn't realize that Doctor Bell expected me to be sneaky about what I wrote in my comp paper. I didn't understand until he called Helen and told her that Doctor Brecht had figured out that I'd seen the *Trion* papers. As soon as I realized I'd had an unfair advantage, I called Doctor Bell and asked to withdraw from the comps. That's when Helen told me that Doctor Bell had forced her to have sex with him."

Harry drew a folded set of papers from his breast pocket and tossed it on the table. "Here is a copy of the official complaint we filed with the college this morning against Doctor Bell." He bit his lip. "Then, in the middle of all this, they think I have mono. Lab reports will be available in a day or two."

Silence. Carla took off her glasses.

"I don't know where to begin," Dave said in half a voice. "Miss Sereni and I did have an affair. It ended last month. Miss Sereni was under no compulsion. I've come to suspect that she seduced me. Then she and her brother could blackmail me into helping him pass the comps. No question I was a fool, but I never threatened Harry or Helen. I never showed him any of the *Trion* papers. I gave him no copies, nor did I help him in any way improper for a faculty advisor."

He wiped his hands with his handkerchief. "Helen told me that she'd taken the *Trion* papers from my office without my knowledge. She made copies for Harry. She says she did it because Harry was going to blackmail me into helping him. She knew I'd never give in. Helen can verify what I've told you."

"Miss Ser—" Doctor Wise said.

"Please," Harry said. "My sister has been ill for the last

week."

"Helen," Doctor Wise said gently, "did Doctor Bell threaten to flunk Harry and fire you if you didn't sleep with him?" Helen nodded. "Last October?" Helen nodded again. "Did you steal papers from Doctor Bell's office?"

"No," Helen said in a barely audible voice. "He gave them to me for Harry."

"Doctor Bell sent the *Trion* papers to Harry through you?" Helen nodded.

"Was Harry going to blackmail Doctor Bell?"

"No."

"Helen," Dave said in a soft voice, "how did you hurt your neck?"

She raised her head.

"Why are you doing this to me?" Dave said

Harry leapt to his feet. "Haven't you tortured her enough?" He lunged at Dave across the table.

Jerry grabbed Harry's arm.

Red in the face and trembling, Harry pulled back.

Doctor Wise was on her feet. "Mr. Sereni!"

Harry sat and glared at Dave.

"Mr. Sereni," Doctor Wise said, "you and Miss Sereni have made serious charges. Have you any proof?"

Harry reached again into his breast pocket. "He sent this to my sister the week before he took her away for the weekend."

Harry handed a folded paper to Doctor Wise. She opened it, read it, and handed it to Carla. She read it and passed it to Jerry.

"May I see?" Dave said. Jerry handed him the paper. A printout of a LAN message. It read:

OAK 3.91 MESSAGE TEXT   FOLDER: BELL   PASSW: KISS

DATE: 12 FEB 96

From: Dbell

To: Hsereni

subject: Next Weekend

Helen, I talked to Harry. We're getting together for some coaching. Remember our deal. I'll take care of Harry if you'll take care of me. <smile> Dave.

"Doctor Bell, did you send this note to Miss Sereni?" Doctor Wise said.

All faces turned toward him.

"Yes, but . . . it's not—"

Harry helped Helen to her feet. At the door, he stopped. "Doctor Bell exploited my sister and me. Our future is at stake. We demand justice. We'll go to the courts if we have to." He eased Helen out and closed the door behind them.

Dave turned to the others.

"I hope," Dave said, "that it is obvious to you that Harry has fabricated his charges against me."

Carla raised an eyebrow. "David, I have heard nothing to contradict Harry's charges."

Doctor Wise took off her glasses. "Doctor Brecht has a point. It sounds as though the Serenis will sue if this committee decides against them."

"Forgive my bluntness, David," Carla said, "but Miss Sereni is a very attractive young woman. One is forced to ask why she should have been interested in a man nearly twice her age."

"I don't know why," Dave said. "Women find me attractive."

All three looked at him in silence.

Jerry cleared his throat. "I'm not sure that it's proper to be discussing all this with Dave."

"Of course," Dave said. "But the note I sent Helen was completely innocent. She was worried about Harry. His work had gone to hell. I told her that if she'd worry less, I'd spend some time with him. That was the deal I mentioned in the note. I did coach him—on Günter Grass."

He couldn't read their faces.

"Ten minute break," Doctor Wise said.

Dave went to the men's room. A movement to his right. Jerry was at the next urinal.

"You might want to consider, Dave. If you made a move before the committee reports to Colson, you might be able to do some damage control."

"A move?"

"Tender your resignation."

Dave turned his head toward Jerry.

"You've forgotten Lincoln's religious roots," Jerry said. "We tell the world we are the leading non-profit college with a distinctly Christian heritage. The alumni are scandalized. The trustees are pressuring Colson for a quick resolution. Sharon's worried that Harry and Helen might resort to litigation. Whole thing's gotten out of hand."

"Resign because I slept with Helen?"

"To head off the sexual harassment charge."

"But the charge is preposterous."

"Carla and Sharon don't think so."

"Oh, come on."

Jerry stepped away from the urinal. "Put yourself in Colson's shoes." He washed his hands. "You're in serious trouble." Jerry blotted his face with a paper towel. "Don't look so freaked. It'll all work itself out." He tossed the towel in the trash holder and left.

Chapter 6

The Cold at the Top of the Stairs

By Wednesday, everybody's avoiding me like I'm tainted. Adulterated. I want to scream it's not me, it's *Dave*. Instead, I go out of my way to be gracious.

At home, no Z. Chip's snacking in the family room. I put my hand on his shoulder, feel him tense. "How're you doing?"

His eyes are fixed on his popcorn. "Fine."

My heart sinks. Won't show his feelings. Just like his father.

I head upstairs to change. As soon as I go into our bedroom, I see something's not right. The box Dave keeps his cuff links in is gone from the chest of drawers. I pull open the top drawer and lift the lid of my jewelry box. Rings, my diamond bracelet, the sapphire earrings—all where they should be. But the clock radio is missing from the night stand. I open the closet. Dave's suits and shoes are gone. The clothes basket he keeps on the shelf for his sweats, the boxes of dress shirts from the laundry, the belts on hooks on his side—all gone. In the bathroom, I open the medicine chest over the double sink on his side. Empty.

Fine. I'm glad I'm rid of the son-of-a-bitch. He could have left a note or something. He could have called me at work . . . No. It's better this way. The way I treated him, I wouldn't have expected him to . . .

I'll call him. I'll tell him to come home. I stumble to the telephone and lift the receiver. When I put my finger to the key pad, I stop. I don't know where he is.

• • •

My vagina is torn open. I feel his sweat, hear his harsh panting in my ear. The acrid stench of chewing tobacco suffocates me. I can't scream, people will know. I hear sobs, so far away they might not be real. I open my eyes. I was dreaming. I hold my breath and listen. The sobs again. I look for the clock radio. It's gone. I flip on the lamp and blink at my watch. Three-twenty-one. The keening, now a high-pitched moaning, is faint. I have to strain to hear it. I slip from the bed and follow the sound.

I ease down on Jeannie's bed and stroke her hair. "Bad dream?"

She rolls away from me. I switch on the lamp.

"Jeannie?" I reach for her.

She makes a sound.

"What?"

"Leave me alone," she says.

I stay beside her for a long time. She doesn't move. My chest hurts. I turn out the light and go to bed.

• • •

In the office Thursday morning. Emma's still acting like the floor is made of thin ice. Mid-morning I get hold of myself and telephone the German Department to find out where Dave's staying, even if it's with Helen.

"German Department," a voice says. It's not Helen.

"This is Mary Bell. May I speak to Doctor Bell?"

"He's in a, um, meeting, Mrs. Bell. I can take a message."

"Let me speak to Doctor Brecht."

"She's in the same meeting," the voice says.

"All right. Doctor Devereaux."

"Doctor Colson called a meeting of the investigative

committee, Mrs. Bell. They're all there."

I call Bob. He says he can see me for a few minutes between appointments. I tell Emma I'll be back shortly.

"Did Eckland print what we lawyers call demonstrable falsehoods?" Bob asks me.

"That's not the point. It's the damage. George is a vicious bastard—"

Bob laughs. "He's only a kid trying for a big story. Look, the article helps our case. Now we can show he subjected you and the children to public humiliation."

"So," I say, "there's nothing I can do legally to get them to retract the story." Sick rage flushes through my veins. "I'll find a way to make George suffer for this, if it's the last thing I do."

Bob puts his arm around me. His smile is lop-sided, his teeth perfectly formed, white and shining. "Don't take it so hard."

He's looking through my eyes to the me on the inside. I pull away.

"Our case is solid." He moves to his desk and looks at his calendar on the computer screen. "Next—"

"It's hard for me to get time off from work," I say.

"How about evenings? Maybe you could drop by my place for dinner. Tomorrow night? About seven?"

"What can I bring?"

"Yourself." There's that look again.

I get to my feet. I'm still shaky. "I don't know how I'll get through this."

Instantly, he's at my side. "Put yourself in my hands." He smiles. "They're very capable hands."

I ease away from him. "Thank you, Bob. I have to depend on you." I laugh. "What choice do I have?"

"That's the spirit." He escorts me to the door.

I go to the office and finish the day. Work is piling up. I try to concentrate on the backlog in getting grade reports entered into academic files. I see Bob's glowing eyes. He *is* making a move on me.

Friday morning. Only have to get through today, then I can hide from the world for two days.

Emma pokes her head in the door. Something's wrong.

"I thought you should, um—" She tiptoes into the room and slides the *Log* onto my desk.

"BELL ACCUSED OF SEXUAL HARASSMENT," the headline reads.

Dave's smiling photograph is set beneath it on one side. On the other, the text of George Eckland's article reports that Aroldo (Harry) Sereni yesterday accused Doctor David Schliemann Bell of forcing his sister, Elena (Helen), secretary in the German Department, to sleep with him to keep her job and to save Harry from academic failure. Doctor Jacob Colson, the college president, had convened an investigative committee at which the Serenis made the charge.

The accusation is patently absurd. Anyone who knows Dave

. . .

The intercom buzzes.

"Mr. Robert Scarff for you on line one," Emma's voice tells me. I press the button.

"Have you seen today's *Log*?" I ask.

"That's why I called." He sounds jubilant. "I'll send that kid a box of cigars. He made our case a breeze and enriched you."

"The charges are ridiculous."

"Who cares? These things drag on forever. By the time it gets hashed through, we'll be home free. Have you considered sole custody?"

"Bob, Eckland has to be stopped. He's destroying my family."

"Get hold of yourself, Mary. The kid's doing us a world of good."

"I've got to find a way—"

"Mary, listen to me. Don't get in Eckland's way. Promise me you won't do something silly."

"I can't stand by—"

"Let me handle it, okay? Trust me."

I'm shaking. I take a deep breath. Tears come. I order them away.

I don't want to see anybody. I eat at my desk and riffle through grade reports, add-on lists, and drop notices. I have to get them to data processing this afternoon, so I'll hand-carry them, then I'll check the printouts. I sort the papers by date and put them into a manila folder. I head past Emma, eating a sandwich at her desk, into the hall. En route to the computer shop, I head around the corner by the banquet room.

The banquet room door wheezes open and Dave stumbles out. A kid who looks like Chip is pushing him. He staggers toward me, wrenches the kid's hands off him, and almost runs into me. I stop short and drop the folder. Papers scatter. Dave's flushed. Sweat glistens on his forehead. Blood is dripping from the corner of his mouth. He falls to his knees, scoops at the fluttering sheets.

"Leave them," I say.

He loosens his grip. Papers skitter to the floor.

Two security guards jog up and pull Dave to his feet.

"Understand there's been a disturbance," the larger one says. "Doctor Bell, would you come with us, please?"

One on each side, they hook their arms in his.

Dave yanks himself free.

"You'll have to leave the building, Doctor Bell."

The smaller one takes Dave by the arm and urges him toward the elevator. The door opens and two women step into the hall. They frown at Dave. The guards escort him in. They turn before the doors close. Dave, still breathing hard, is staring at the floor. The guards don't look at me.

My God, what's he done now? I can't think about it. My head is pounding, but I have to finish the day. The divorce is going to take up all my vacation time, and I hate to say I'm sick. I telephone Carla. She doesn't know anything about a disturbance at the banquet hall, says she can't talk about the investigation. Finally, Emma and I close the office. Chip's not home. Jeannie says he's at the gym. She's still wearing that princess ring. She doesn't look at me when she speaks. I touch her hand. She jerks away as if I had shocked her.

"Jeannie, what is it?"

"You did something, didn't you?" She's glaring at me. "Otherwise, he wouldn't have . . . are you seeing someone?"

"*No!* How dare you—"

"The way you treat him—"

I can't breathe. "I have always loved him."

"But you don't anymore. Otherwise, he'd be here."

"Marriages are not all sweetness and light."

"Will you let him come home?"

"He wants to be with *her*."

When I reach for her, she lurches away from me.

I'm late to Bob's. I've covered the stress in my face with makeup. At least his place is easy to find—the highest building in Bethesda. The clerk in the lobby has to telephone him and get permission for me to take the elevator to his penthouse. The doors open on a room with glass walls, gossamer drapes, dimmed lights, a fire roaring in a stand-alone fireplace in the middle of the room. Bob, in cargo pants and an open-collar shirt that shows off his chest hair, steps into the center of the carpet with a tray, a cocktail shaker, and two frosted martini glasses. He sets the tray on a nesting table in front of the love seat by the fire.

He takes my hands. "Come sit by the fire." He leads me across the room. "This'll warm you up." He pours me a drink, disappears with my coat, and returns with a plate of hot pastry shells filled with braised crabmeat. He eases down next to me on the love seat.

I bring him up-to-date—Dave's move, Jeannie's hysterics, Chip's moodiness, my running into Dave outside the banquet hall. "Everybody acts like I'm the villain."

"Everybody blames the woman, even the Bible. Never mind. The law doesn't see it that way." His smile melts. "The assumption is that when a man strays, his woman gave him cause. Did you give Dave cause?"

"Jesus, not you, too."

He puts his hand on my shoulder. "We need to be prepared for whatever Dave might bring up in court. Was there ever anybody else? Money problems? Anything with the kids?"

"Nothing. He did spoil the children. I got after him about that. Made me the policeman."

"Then I'm forced to ask—forgive me, Mary—how were things in bed?"

I guess I should have seen this coming. I have to tell him the intimate details of our sex life. He'll condemn me, too.

"We hadn't made love for more than a year. Dave thought I

didn't love him. Said I was cold and unresponsive."

"Were you?"

His teeth glint in the soft light. It dawns on me that this place is really a love trap. In his eyes, I see the same lust I saw in the yokel in Minnesota and in Dave. I turn to the haunted skyline beyond the penthouse balconies. *Biggest skirt chaser in the seven counties.*

"I'm not very sensuous by nature," I say.

"When a woman fails to respond, the man's a lousy lover. Was Dave?"

I stumble. "I have no idea."

He grasps my elbow, moves closer. "Stop beating yourself up. You're a beautiful woman who got stuck with a man who didn't know his way around a woman's body." He refills my drink. "I didn't mean to get into all of this first thing, but I could see you needed to vent. Feeling better?"

I don't answer.

"Hope you like grilled tuna." He gets to his feet. "Bought some this afternoon from a little place that has it flown in from the coast. Marinated it in olive oil and lemon juice, the way they do in the Greek islands. I have the grill heating."

He slips away. I gaze at the view, all dark shapes and rutilant dots with pale stars flickering above. I taste the martini and admire his drink mixing—just the right dryness, bracing, yet relaxing. I feel the tautness in my legs ease. I can see him through the glass door to his balcony. Smoke lit by flames from below make him a silhouette.

We eat at a bistro table on another balcony, this one glass-enclosed. We have candles, crystal, and Châteauneuf-du-Pape. Afterwards, we warm our cognac in snifters by the fire. I'm not used to the alcohol in my veins. Makes me feel warm and safe.

I close my eyes and rest the back of my head against his arm stretched across the love seat.

"Mary," he says sincerely, "Dave's a fool." His face softens into a smile. "I'm not."

His hand goes around my shoulder. He kisses me, gently, sweetly. His body is reassuring, his touch soft. I feel the scratch of his beard against my cheek. I shouldn't be doing this. God, I'm scared. But it's so good to be held . . .

• • •

Saturday morning, the roses arrive. Clear glass vase, fern, baby's breath. The card reads, "With heartfelt thanks for a lovely evening. B."

Thank God Chip's at the gym. He used my car and took Jeannie to the ice rink. I'm still in my blue robe, zipped to the throat. I'm queasy from last night. And I feel a dull ache behind my eyes. I flutter them to clear the fog and lift my coffee mug with a shaking hand. I'm not used to being made love to. I think I'm actually a little sore down there. The hurt reminds me of the yokel. Lots going on I'm not used to. I'm not used to being alone. I'm not used to getting roses.

The phone rings.

Bob's voice is low and husky. "Wish you could have stayed the night. How are you this morning?"

"A little under the weather."

He sounds distressed. "Let me come over—"

"*No!.*" I didn't mean to sound abrupt. "No," I say more softly. "I'm all right. I'm not used to—"

"How about lunch?"

"Bob, I can't. I have to . . . to wash my hair."

Why did I say that?

"Dinner?"

"Not this weekend."

"I'll call you at the beginning of the week." He sighs a little too audibly. "I'll miss you until then."

Off the phone, I slink to the kitchen table. I'm cold. Bob's touch was gentle. His bed was warm. I'd forgotten the pleasure of being wanted. I was content in his arms. Until I froze up. I hope I didn't hurt his feelings. Guess not. He wouldn't have called.

God, I barely know this man. What was I thinking? I shouldn't have . . . Why not? Dave did it. What's fair for the goose . . . I feel a glimmer of victory. Maybe Dave doesn't want me, but other men do.

But I clutched with Bob, same as with Dave. It *is* me, isn't it? Maybe I need time to loosen up. Maybe . . . No, it's me.

I take the roses, vase and all, out the kitchen door and dump them in the garbage. I make sure they're covered with banana peels, last night's empty pizza box, and greasy plastic wrappers. The children will never see them.

The front door bangs. Chip's telling Jeannie to hang up her coat. His voice is kind. Odd what misfortune will do to people. She goes upstairs. He comes into the kitchen, shoots a quick look at me, goes to the refrigerator.

"Come sit for a minute."

I can see he doesn't want to. He pours himself a glass of milk and snatches the leftover pizza. He takes a chair opposite me and chews.

"You'll be able to see your father. You haven't lost him."

He shakes his head sharply.

"Have the kids at school . . ."

He stiffens. "The bastard cheated on you. You dumped him.

'Nuff said."

He puts his glass and plate in the dish washer and heads upstairs.

It's so quiet I think I'm going to howl, just to hear something other than my own heartbeat. After dinner, the three of us watch television, just like a normal family. I tell Chip he can use my car if he wants to go out. He mumbles. I ask Jeannie what her plans are for Sunday. None.

"Let's rent a movie tomorrow," I say. "We'll have Chinese food delivered."

Nothing. Defeated, I creak to my feet and head up to bed.

Dave and I should have been planning our retirement, setting aside a little more, maybe. We could have finally got the addition on the house so Dave could have his study and I could have a real living room again. I suppress a shudder as I remember that the mortgage payment is due.

I hadn't thought about money. If Dave's career is ruined, he won't have any money for child support or alimony. The kids and I will be essentially living on my salary. I'll have to talk to Chip about college. Even with the scholarship, George Washington's going to be out of the question. How will I pay for Jeannie's college? Why didn't I think of all that before I tipped Eckland?

Watch out for your vindictiveness, Mary. Someday it'll bite you in the ass.

Is Dave always right? I want to cover my ears. Instead, I force myself to stand straight. I shed my clothes, leave them on the floor, put on socks and the one pair of sweats I own. The sheets are cold. I roll toward his side of the bed out of habit. He used to sleep on his back. I'd snuggle up next to him and put my leg and arm across his body. His arm would go around me, and

I'd be warm again.

In the dark I hear Jeannie, later Chip come upstairs and settle in. Tomorrow I'm going to rent a movie and order Chinese food. If they don't participate, then they can stay out of my way. I'll—

A soft clump from downstairs. My eyes snap open. Did Chip remember to lock up the house and turn on the outside lights? I hold my breath and listen. There it is again. My heart thuds so hard I can feel it in the roots of my hair. What will I do if someone's broken in? I'd always wake Dave and tell him to go down and check. He'd mutter and throw on a robe. He'd be back a minute later. He'd be asleep before I could even get resettled. I'd cuddle up against him to get warm, and—

I hear it again. From now on I'm going to double check the locks before I go to bed. I'll get one of those alarm systems put in. I'll— Again. Closer this time. Sharper. Is someone coming up the stairs?

The yokel tears my panties off, covers my mouth with his hand. He forces himself in—

"Chip," I call as loud as I can, trying not to scream. "*Chip.*"

The hall light goes on. He comes to my door in his boxer shorts, his eyes smudged, his hair tangled. "What?"

"I heard something. Go check downstairs. *There.* You hear it?"

He gives me a look somewhere between disgust and pity and disappears. I hear him on the stairs. The sound again. What if he gets into a fight with the robber? Footsteps coming up the stairs. I block the scream in my throat.

Chip's face in the doorway. "Pine tree at the corner of the house. Wind's blowing it against the siding. Tomorrow Dad and I—" He stops, fumbles. "I'll trim it." He moves from the doorway, and the hall light goes out.

Still trembling, I wobble from the bed and grope for the extra blanket on the shelf in the closet. I crawl in bed, try to get warm. I'll never be warm again.

Chapter 7

Despiséd and Rejected

Friday morning, Dave went for a prolonged workout.
No need to get to the office early. He showered, shaved, and
dressed at the gym. It was nearly ten by the time he pushed
through the glass doors into the office. Rose, the substitute
secretary, gave him a wary look. His mail tray was full. At least
that hadn't changed. Phone slips. One from Robin McAndrew
at the *Post*, two from Hans Lehmann and four from George
Eckland. Beneath them was the *Lincoln Log*. "BELL ACCUSED OF
SEXUAL HARASSMENT." Dave's own face smiled up at him, this
time a large color photograph. George Eckland's article, in cool
journalistic neutrality, recounted Harry's tale minus any mention
of mononucleosis.

Just past eleven-thirty, the intercom buzzed.

"Dave, this is Jerry. Can you come to my office? The
committee has reported to Jake Colson."

"And?"

"I'd rather not discuss matters of this import on the
telephone."

For Christ's sake. What a time to be pompous. Dave resisted
the impulse to snap. "Be right there."

Jerry sat at his desk staring out the window. "Close the door
and pull up a chair."

Dave did. "Well?"

Jerry swivelled from the window and gave Dave a grave look.

"The committee sided with Harry."

Dave fell back in the chair as though Jerry had struck him. "Get serious."

A shadow of indignation brushed across Jerry's face.

"What did they tell Jake?" Dave said.

"That the evidence shows you forced Helen to have sex."

"Harry's cockamamie story?"

"And Helen's."

"But Jake knows me," Dave said. "He knows I wouldn't pull shit like that."

"Colson asked for your resignation."

Dave's heart thudded. "It's Harry's word against mine."

"And the LAN note. Helen's word, too, Dave. You keep forgetting that."

"Helen was under duress."

"Carla and Sharon didn't think so."

"They're biased," Dave said.

"Why? Because they're women?"

"Because they're maiden ladies—ready to believe all men are brutes."

Jerry's wet upper lip curled into a tense smile. "I'll pretend I didn't hear that."

"Did you talk to Jake yourself?"

Jerry picked up a pen and squinted down its length as if sighting a rifle. "He said he'd been worried about you—not a team player, tending to use intimidation to get what you want."

"*What?* Come on. Jake knows me better than that."

"You play awfully hard sometimes."

Dave looked at his trembling hands. "I want to talk to Jake. Maybe get a lawyer."

"Colson won't see you until he has your resignation in

hand."

"He said *that?*"

"Not in so many words."

"Doesn't sound like Jake."

"Anyway, I seriously doubt he'll listen. Everybody's screaming to have this settled. Robin McAndrew called Colson. The *Post* will run a story tomorrow."

"My God." Dave sagged, then straightened himself. "Look, I'm as anxious as anyone to have this settled, but fair is fair."

Jerry raised his eyes from the pen. "You might have been able to salvage something by resigning before he got the report."

"After the article in today's *Log?*" Dave's throat was dry.

"About your resignation—"

"How soon?"

"As soon as possible," Jerry said. "Dave, I tried like a son-of-a-bitch. They wouldn't listen."

Dave found his way to his feet. "Yeah . . . thanks."

He left in a daze. Carla was coming toward him.

"Did he tell you?" Carla said in German. "I'd like to say I'm sorry, David, but I'm not. You violated every principle of decency. Forgive me for saying so, but the result is unjust only to the degree that it is not severe enough."

Dave sparked. "You dare judge me?"

"We were unanimous."

Dave fought off an impulse to draw blood. He started into his office, then stopped. "Unanimous?"

"No one, not even Jerry, could condone what you did."

Dave's skin prickled. Was Jerry a complete coward? Couldn't be true. Carla was biased. He and Jerry had been through too much together.

He stumbled into his office, slumped into his chair, and put his head in his hands. He had to . . . He had to . . .

The intercom rang. Rose.

"Doctor Devereaux asked me to draft a pro forma resignation for you. I'll bring it in and let you review it. If it's all right, you can sign it and I'll handle the distribution."

He was imagining all this, right?

"Doctor Bell?"

"Not yet, Rose. I need to—" He squeezed his eyes shut and forced them open again. "You have Jake Colson's number handy?" He opened the phone directory on his computer. "Never mind."

He hit the button for an open line, and dialed Colson's office.

"Hi, Linda. This is Dave Bell. I need to speak to Jake."

"He's already left for the alumni lunch, Doctor Bell. Won't be in the office 'til one, and his calendar's full for the rest of the day. I could fit you in . . . does Thursday of next week work for you?"

"Never mind. I'll see if I can buttonhole him at the lunch."

"Helen had me RSVP in the negative for you before she . . . got sick. I didn't save you a place."

"I'll manage. Thanks."

He pulled on his jacket on the way out. Rose was on the phone. She went silent as he swept past her.

He jogged the block and a half to Thurston Hall. It housed not only banquet rooms suitable for entertaining alumni but also the college admin offices. He hoped he wouldn't run into Mary. Breathing heavily and moist at the forehead and armpits, he took the broad cement steps two at a time, showed his ID to the guard, and took the elevator to the second floor. The doors to the banquet room were closed. He glanced at his watch. The lunch was half over. He grasped the fist-size knob and pulled.

As the door groaned open, he caught the familiar wood polish and mothball scent beneath the aroma of cooked meat. An amplified voice from the lectern on the dais at the front of the room was telling the assembly, something like fifty people at cloth-covered round tables for six arranged around the wine-colored *faux* Persian carpet, that "more women than men have been enrolled in college since 1980, and women graduates have outnumbered men since 1985."

Dave peered through the darkened room at the highlighted speaker. Robin McAndrew. As Dave let the door whoosh closed behind him, several heads turned. He leaned against the chair rail at the rear of the room. He spotted Jake Colson on the dais, between Jerry and Robin's empty place at the head table.

"We are already spending well in excess of two hundred billion dollars annually on higher education in the U.S.," Robin's voice went on. Caught in the beam of spotlight focused on the lectern from the ceiling, Robin was tall and suave, his longish, faintly unkempt sandy hair edging toward gray at the temples. Jake, small, wizened, and tough, glowered at Robin through his thick glasses. His wisp of a beard, the same gray as his failing hair, was frozen in place along with his attention. Jerry, twice Jake's size, was doodling on his plate with his fork, his eyes downcast, his face in a permanent sneer.

Dave edged along the wall. If he could make his way around the room, he could intercept Jake when the lunch broke up.

"And," Robin intoned, "as Ruby Manikan observed, 'If you educate a man, you educate a person, but if you educate a woman, you educate a family.'" Polite titters. Jake grinned ruefully. Jerry continued to scowl at his plate as if he hadn't heard. "A remark, though made by a woman—and a Native

American woman at that—might be taken today as something short of politically correct." More laughter.

Dave reached the corner of the room and jostled between the seated guests and the wall. "'Scuse me," he whispered. In return, disturbed faces glared at him.

As Dave came even with the dais at the front of the room, a boy he remembered from the gym, now in a dark suit and a name tag that identified him as "Student Staff," rose from the table closest to Dave. His girth blocked Dave's view of the dais.

"Can I help you find your seat?" he whispered.

Half a dozen faces turned.

"I need to see Doctor Colson when the lunch is finished," Dave said. "I'll wait here."

The boy studied Dave's face. "Are you Doctor David Bell?"

"One and the same."

The boy's frown deepened. "I'll have to ask you to wait outside. Doctor Colson will be leaving by the far door accompanying a select group of alumni to his office."

"I'll grab him for a second."

"He's got a full schedule." The boy flexed his shoulder muscles. "You'll have to wait outside."

"Look, I—"

Robin McAndrew paused in mid-sentence and looked toward Dave. Members of the audience turned. Jake and Jerry both looked in his direction.

"It's urgent that I see him, only for a moment," Dave whispered.

"No can do, Doctor Bell." The boy unbuttoned his suit coat.

"It'll only take a minute—"

The boy put the flat of his hand against Dave's chest and pushed. With a flash of rage, Dave knocked the hand away, darted up the steps to the dais, and scurried behind the chairs at the head table until he was in back of Colson. All eyes in the room followed him. Robin stopped again and turned.

"Jake," Dave said in a shaky whisper, "Linda couldn't fit me in—"

Colson turned in his chair. "Are you fucking crazy?"

"This is no time or place—" Jerry said in a hoarse whisper.

Dave waved toward the glowering young man now mounting the steps to the dais. "The staff person wouldn't let me talk to you. I want to arrange a time—"

"Is that Doctor David Bell?" said a voice from the floor. Cameras clicked and bulbs flashed. The boy grasped Dave from behind by both shoulders and yanked. Dave staggered backwards.

"Clear out," Colson said, "or I'll have you thrown out."

The boy dragged Dave toward the edge of the dais. Dave swung. The boy dodged and caught Dave with a swift uppercut. A cry from the crowd was punctuated by the clacking of cameras. Flash bulbs flared like intermittent lightning. The boy seized Dave's arm, twisted it behind him, and forced him down the stairs and out the door.

As the banquet room door closed behind him, he came face to face with Mary. She stopped short in front of him. Papers rippled across the floor.

Two security guards ran up.

On the steps outside Thurston Hall, where the security guards left him, Dave weaved in the glaring gray light. His tongue was parched. His throat was raw. He caught the metallic taste of blood. He'd bitten his lip when the kid's uppercut caught his chin. Little by little, he let his shoulders droop and started toward Scully Hall. He went to his office and read the resignation, signed it, and dropped it on Rose's desk on the way out.

In a fog, he drove to Takoma Park and left the Z on Carroll Avenue in front of Für ein Fremdes Land. Before he went into the shop, he checked the display window. The "help wanted" sign was still there.

The bell on the door jangled. Horst emerged from the rear of the shop, glasses on forehead.

"*Herr Professor Bell*," he said. His face darkened. "Come."

Seated at the table, Dave told Horst everything. "I've come to you because I have no place to live, no money." He swallowed. "Have you found someone to help you run the shop?"

Horst's face turned sad. "The job is far below you. The room is small."

"I would be grateful for both."

Horst nodded. "The room is ready." He smiled. "And I will welcome such expert help."

From the book shop, Dave walked to the library and checked the blue-book value of his 1993 Nissan 300ZX. Over $20,000. He drove to Route 1 and studied the used car lots. He finally chose the most prosperous looking of the bunch and pulled in. Half an hour later, he drove out in a 1990 Chevy Cavalier with a check for $11,000 and two hundred in cash in his pocket. He'd gotten nowhere near the value of his car, but at least he had money again. He stopped at a bank and opened a checking account. Back at the motel, he stretched out on the bed and surveyed the ceiling.

At four-thirty—early enough that Chip and Jeannie would be home but too early for Mary—he telephoned. Chip answered.

"I want to see you," Dave said.

Long silence, then, "When?"

"How about tonight? About nine."

"Where?"

"Parking lot of the middle school?"

"Okay."

Before nine, Dave parked the Cavalier in the empty school lot and got out. The wind was rising, and the air was heavy with moisture. No sign of Chip.

In the woolly light from the single street lamp, a figure trudged up Grant Street. Dave recognized the hooded white sweat jacket. Chip looked like a wind-whipped angel.

Dave put out his hand.

Chip pushed his hood from his head, put his hands in his pockets, and kicked the tarmac. "Where's the Z?"

"I sold it. Want to walk?"

They headed past the tennis courts, under the basketball hoops, down the stairway to the playing field. Dave pulled his coat closer against the gusts.

"I first brought you here before you were ten, " Dave said in a low voice, "to see the fireworks on the Fourth of July. Remember? Then we played touch here. One year the whole family—"

"Dad," Chip said, "what do you want?"

Dave's voice failed. "I wanted to tell you that the story in the *Log* isn't true. I had no idea things would get out of hand."

They reached the bottom of the stairs and headed across the field. Chip kept his eyes on the ground. Dave felt the first splash of rain.

"It's going to get worse, Chip. Chances are my picture will be in tomorrow's *Post*. I don't want to be separated from you and Jeannie."

Almost in the middle of the field. To Dave's left, the haze of light from street lamps on Piney Branch Road dissipated in the mist. An occasional car hummed up the hill.

Chip stopped.

"After this is all over," Dave said, "I'll move somewhere else, away from D.C. and Takoma Park. I want you and Jeannie to come with me."

Chip stood with his back to Dave. The rain whispered in the silence between them.

"Chip, forgive me."

Chip turned. The rain uncurled his hair over his forehead. "I always thought you were . . . I looked up to you."

His eyes settled on Dave's face. Dave blinked.

Chip drew the hood over his head and started across the field.

"Chip."

Chip walked on, his hands in his pockets.

"Chip," Dave said again.

The rain grew louder.

• • •

Monday, Dave took the Metro to the offices of Cutlett & Vickers in Rockville. He recalled that the offices of Scarff & Leibowitz were somewhere in the building. After a short wait and coffee, he followed the secretary into a private office. Inside, a blond man in his forties, in a vest and shirt sleeves, talked on the phone. He motioned to Dave to be seated and hung up.

"Tom Vickers. What's the story?"

When Dave got to the closed accounts, Tom said, "Wait a minute. She's closed all your accounts? Who's representing her?"

"Bob Scarff."

"Was your picture in the *Post* over the weekend?"

Dave nodded.

"You're unemployed?"

"Got a job in a bookstore. Ten dollars an hour."

"And my guess is that with a record of sexual harassment, you're not hireable at any college or university?"

Dave nodded.

"Are you looking for other work," Tom said, "something more lucrative?"

"Haven't had time."

"What can you do, other than teach German?"

"Teach in high school, I guess," Dave said.

"After dismissal for sexual harassment?"

"Translation."

"Sounds like you'll be starting a new career—at the bottom financial rung."

"Never thought of it that way," Dave said.

"Have you considered how you'll pay for the divorce? Our fee? Court costs?"

"Ask Mary."

"From what you tell me, she has a very strong case. If you come down on the losing side, the court costs and maybe even her lawyer's fees will be yours."

"How much?"

"This firm charges two twenty an hour. Scarff and Leibowitz are about the same. We're talking at least 20K." Tom dropped his pencil. "With your financial problems, I can't risk the investment this firm would have to make to take your case. I suspect we need to postpone any further work until you're in a professional position. Have you fought the harassment charges?"

"I've tried to speak to the college president."

"Talk to him. Then come and see me."

That afternoon Dave called the other two lawyers on Bob's list. When they heard Dave's story, they told him they wouldn't be able to take the case. Dave called Bob Scarff.

"No one will take my case, Bob. They don't think I'll be able to pay them. How about representing myself?"

"Bad idea."

Dave hung up. He opened his collar and undid his tie. It didn't help. He was suffocating.

• • •

Dave arrived at the office at nine on Tuesday morning. Rose watched him but said nothing. He inserted the key in his office door. It didn't turn. He forced it. The key bent. He walked to Rose. "Is Doctor Devereaux in?"

She picked up the telephone and pressed the button opposite Jerry's name. "Doctor Bell to see you." She hung up and smiled. "Go on in."

Inside the door, Dave flung his overcoat and briefcase in a chair. "I can't get in my office."

Jerry nodded. "New locks. Routine procedure. I'll tell Rose to let you in."

"What about Colson?"

"He considers the case closed."

"He won't give me a chance?"

"You didn't help your case any with that performance at the luncheon."

"I was frantic."

"One more thing," Jerry said. "The *Trion* papers. Turn them over to me before you leave. The test papers, too, and your translation and article."

"My work belongs to me."

"Not under your employment contract. Research you conducted while representing Lincoln belongs to Lincoln until it's published. Besides, *Trion* was entrusted to the college, not to you personally."

"Who's going to take over *Trion?*"

"We haven't discussed it yet. Where are you staying?"

"At a foreign language bookshop in Takoma Park. I'm working there now."

"I'll call you."

Dave went to his office. Rose let him in. Not much to show he'd ever been here. No knickknacks, photos, mementos. The room was spare and clean, the way he liked his working space. In an hour, no one would know he'd ever been here.

Near the bottom of the stack from his lowest desk drawer, he came across a brochure with a familiar crest, a heraldic shield with an oak tree, a sword, and a torch. University of Nürnberg. He'd been so young. He'd lived in a room barely big enough for his bed, survived on noodles and tea, wore ragged chinos and an old overcoat he found at a flea market. But he'd had Inge Lehmann.

Short, thin, pale, and bouncy as a hyperactive kitten, Inge had ice-blue eyes and frizzy hair the color of leached straw. Her passion was American jazz, American cigarettes, and Jack Kerouac. Nothing about her made sense. While Dave verified the sources of the *Gesta Romanorum* as the last step in his dissertation documentation, Inge read Ginsberg, Baldwin, and Ezra Pound for her dissertation in Modern American literature. She reveled in ancient Greek plays and French post-impressionist painting. She rebelled against her conservative father, Dave's mentor, but she secretly went to church. She loved American culture but hated American food. When she shared his room, she wouldn't sleep if he wasn't there and napped while he studied. In bed she was athletic, playful, and passionate. When he said he was leaving to marry the girl waiting for him in the states, she told him she was pregnant. The abortion left her pale and sickly. *"Ungeheuer,"* she had screamed at him. Monster.

He picked up the brochure. She'd be in her fifties by now. Probably teaching American literature in Nürnberg or somewhere. His heart contracted. He'd left her for Mary. Maybe, if he'd been older and wiser . . . No. Even then, even when he was in Germany, he loved Mary. He'd believed he couldn't do without sex. Mary had never been great in bed, even then. Inge was much better. But he didn't want Inge. He wanted Mary. He dropped the brochure in the waste basket. He still wanted Mary.

• • •

When Dave finished his noodles at Mark's Kitchen, up the street from the bookshop, he stopped at the pay phone outside the restaurant and dialed. After two rings, Mary answered.

"I want to talk to Jeannie," he said.

"She won't talk to you."

"Mary, go tell her I'm on the phone."

He heard words in the background he couldn't understand.

"She doesn't want to talk to you," Mary said.

"What have you been telling her?"

"Nothing. It's all in the papers. Are you staying with Helen?"

"No."

"I don't believe you."

"Believe anything you like."

"You'd do well to be cooperative, Dave," she said, her voice tight. "The way things look, the divorce is going my way."

"Was it really necessary to close all the accounts?"

"Bob advised me to do it, before you did."

"You think I'd do something like that?"

"You've done a good many things in the past few months I didn't think you were capable of."

"So you struck first."

"I did it to protect myself. And the children."

"Bob advised you badly."

"Bob is a good lawyer."

"I'm not talking the law, Mary. I'm talking right and wrong. I've promised myself that when all this is over, I'll be glad that I did nothing as part of the divorce to hurt you and the children."

"*Now* you worry about hurting me and the children."

"I didn't call," he said, clearing the bitter taste from his mouth, "to fight with you. I called to talk to Jeannie." He licked his lips. "Despite how you feel, will you tell Jeannie I love her? Tell her I'll call again."

The bookshop was dark. He walked past it and turned into the alley. At the rear of the building, he opened the gate in the high fence. Inside the postage-stamp-sized yard, he went through the waist-high weeds and garbage cans, up the shaky wooden stairs to the back porch, and up the flight that led to the upper porch. He looked toward the hills but couldn't see his home. Too many trees. But he knew where it was. He could feel it on the hill opposite him.

He found his keys and let himself in. He felt his way down the long hall to the front of the building. The uneven floor groaned under his weight. Probably built years before he was born. The kitchen was dark. So were Horst's living room and the store room at the top of the inside stairs. The door to Horst's bedroom was closed. No sounds. Horst must be out.

At the end of the hall, he felt for the knob to his room and opened the door. The street light on Carroll Avenue shone through the paint-flecked window into his eyes. He switched on the table lamp inside the door and shed his overcoat, jacket, and tie.

He sat on the bed. The tiny room's wobbly furniture left him no room to walk. Only a twin bed short enough that his feet hung over the end, a wooden table painted green, a kitchen chair, and a sagging chest of drawers. Pipes along the ceiling. Miniature bathroom down the hall. Horst had cleaned the room the day Dave moved in, but it needed painting. The linoleum on the warped floor needed replacing. The place smelled of cooked cabbage and mildew. The room reminded him of the dollhouse chamber he'd rented on Lindenstrasse in Nürnberg. That room, the building, even the neighborhood, had an ancient charm. This was merely shabby.

He leaned across the bed and opened one window. Cool air diluted the smell. He took off his clothes and hung them from the pipes. Dust fell in his eyes. He should get a rag and clean the pipes. Not tonight.

He lay on the bed and opened the oversize volume of Rumi poetry Horst had given him. The book seemed to have an aroma, sweet and pungent. He pressed his nose to the pages. Nothing. The impression of sweetness lingered. "My eye is God's eye, and God's eye is mine." A few pages later, "Why fear oblivion in death? I shall die again and bear the wings and feathers of angels. I shall be what you cannot imagine."

Dave put the book aside and stretched out on the bed. Starting over—poor, alone, with nothing but his brains and guts to see him through. Thirty years ago, he'd been young, bright, determined. Now he was a middle-aged failure. The radio from a passing car was playing a rap song Chip played at home . . .

At home. Not his home any more. He'd never live in that house again. The only home he'd ever had. And he couldn't go home.

He closed his eyes. His one catastrophic error, the biggest mistake he had ever made, was to love Mary. That made him vulnerable. Now he had to stop loving her. Otherwise, he'd remain weak, a pawn.

Ungeminnt. Mann's word. Unloved and unlovable. Damned. "Evil has no understanding of love."

He'd dozed off when he heard Horst come in. Dave held his watch in the light from the street lamp. Past nine. Horst's television droned softly. Dave slid beneath the covers.

The phone rang in Horst's living room. The sound was muffled and strangely comforting. Life was going on. Some things were still normal.

A tap at the door. "David, for you."

Dave pulled on his sweats. Who knew he was here? He plodded barefoot down the hall and picked up the receiver.

"Dave, this is Jerry. Got a call from the Prince George's County Police. They were looking for you. I said I'd try to find you and pass on a message."

Dave waited.

"Helen," Jerry said. "Automobile accident. They called you at home. Mary told them to call me."

Dave couldn't speak.

"Helen drove off a bridge, Dave. On some country road between New Carrollton and Bowie. Went into a lake. Drowned."

Chapter 8

Passionless Aliens

I haven't seen Dave since Friday, when the campus security guards took him into the elevator. Why wouldn't he tell me where he's living? Because he's with Helen. I drove by the assigned faculty parking spaces on the way in. No Z. He must have taken leave. She's been out sick. I imagine them giggling together in bed.

And Jeannie's snotty behavior this morning. Where I go at night is *my* business, not hers. If it weren't for Bob, I don't know how I'd have kept going.

"Mrs. Bell?" Emma at the door. "You might want to call Doctor Brecht. She was insistent."

I blink at her. She's looking at my desk top. Then I see it, the yellow while-you-were-out slip. I mumble my thanks and dial Carla.

"Mary, I hope you are all right."

"Fine," I say with forced good spirits.

A nonplussed silence, then, "I am very glad to hear it." She sniffles uncomfortably. "I still have David's book, the *Leverkühn*. I was working on the translation, you remember? Perhaps I can give it to you for him."

I don't have a clue what she's talking about. "We've separated, Carla. I haven't seen him since last week."

"Ach." She sounds confused. "You do not know he is no longer with the college?"

I grip the telephone.

"The investigative committee found him culpable," she says. "He has resigned. He cleaned out his office yesterday."

My ears ring.

"You may rest assured," she goes on, "that his professional career is finished."

She thinks I'm gloating.

"But Helen . . ." I stop long enough to get the shakes out of my voice. What will he and Helen live on? She's been supporting Harry, and a secretary doesn't make that much.

"Ach, Mary. You have not seen the *Post*? Helen drowned last night."

The room sways.

"She drove off a bridge out in the country," Carla says.

I stammer.

Emma, trembling, is in front of my desk. "Mrs. Bell, excuse me for interrupting, but two policemen are here. They want to talk to you."

I look past her. In the doorway are two uniformed figures.

• • •

After the interview, I'm too rattled to work. I call Bob. He's with a client. I leave a message. Somehow I get into my coat and blunder my way to the car. I drive home without remembering how I got there. It's freezing. I turn up the thermostat and wrap myself in the throw. I told the police everything I knew. They referred to it as "Miss Sereni's accident." I asked if they suspected suicide. "We're in the fact-gathering phase," one of them said.

Carla said it was in the *Post*. I find the paper where Chip left it on the kitchen table. There it is: LINCOLN SCANDAL WOMAN DROWNED. Another driver saw her car swerve to the left in front of him. She crashed through the barrier without slowing down. Illegal drugs were recovered from the wreckage. Whether Helen had used anything wouldn't be clear until after the autopsy.

Brutally, the article rehashes the whole scandal.

The phone rings. I can't face talking to anyone. The answering machine clicks on. "Hi." Bob's voice. "Called your office. Emma said you'd gone for the day." Pause, then in a deeper voice, "Call me." The machine bleeps obscenely and goes quiet.

• • •

Days pass with a leaden sameness. Jeannie barely tolerates my presence. Chip's gone most of the time. I have dinner at Bob's Saturday night. At least *he's* glad to see me. I spend the night and sneak home before dawn. No word from Dave. On Thursday, Carla and I share a chilly lunch at L'Espionage in Chevy Chase. Friday at work I get a call from Bob.

"I've found the bastard. He's hiding out in Takoma Park at a German bookstore, a mile from you."

The bookstore where Dave bought his foreign texts.

"How—"

"Jerry Devereaux tipped me off. I got the idea he didn't want the police to think he was withholding information. If someone else tells them where Dave is, Devereaux's off the hook. I called them. They've probably gotten to Dave by now."

"They'll arrest him?"

"Helen's death is being judged an accident. They found cocaine and ecstasy in the trunk, and the autopsy showed that Helen had ingested barbiturates. Odd thing was the right hand door of the car was open. 'Nuff of that for now. Tonight? My place?"

• • •

The days of April are the longest I remember. Why doesn't it get warm? The cherry tree blooms for the first time, but rain and cold wind make short work of the blossoms. Dave's beloved jonquils open, hundreds of them. The roses are putting out new growth. I nag Chip into mowing the lawn. Bob helps me spread bags of mulch. Amazing how he knows how to simulate warmth. Chip and Jeannie watch him in silence. Why did Dave insist on such a high-maintenance yard?

I don't want to see or talk to Dave, but I'm running out of money. I hate to dig into the savings—they're for Chip and Jeannie's college. The mortgage is overdue, and Chip's graduation is a month off. Mid-morning on a Wednesday, I close the office door so Emma won't hear, dial the bookshop, and ask for Dave.

"How are you?" I ask.

"Okay."

He doesn't ask about the children. His voice is distant, unfocused, the way it sounds when he first gets up in the morning.

"I called," I say, "because I don't have enough to pay everything."

Long pause, then, "Send me the bills."

"No," I say, "Bob says you should give me a check."

I hear the German man talking and laughing in the background. A woman's voice.

"Okay," Dave says. "How much?"

"There's the mortgage. I should really pay last month's and this month's at the same time. And the gas and electric and phone. Chip's graduation is coming up. I closed down the cable account. By the way, you should pick up your computer equipment, but if you do, I'd like to buy a computer for Chip and Jeannie to use. And, you know, a printer and modem and all. I had to pay off the MasterCard and American Express when I closed the accounts—"

"Uh-huh." His voice is flat.

"Comes to about $6,100. Not counting the new computer."

"Uh-huh."

The other voices have gone quiet, but I hear the cash register.

"Did you hear what I said?" I ask.

"I'll send you a check."

"Things are overdue."

For one monstrous second, I think the person I'm talking to isn't Dave. "Are you all right, Dave? You sound—"

"I want to see Chip and Jeannie."

"They don't want to see you."

The line goes dead.

• • •

Every time I look at Chip, I see Dave. He doesn't resemble Dave, except for his size, but he holds his chin down and raises his eyes to peer at you, as if he were looking over half-glasses, exactly the way Dave does. He's got that same open laugh, and he bites his lower lip when he's thinking. These days, he's aping his father's aloofness—never home, even when he's here. When he's not fiddling with my car or studying, he's outside pruning or raking or weeding—jobs he used to help Dave with.

I struck the same deal with him Dave did—he maintains the wagon, buys gas, and can use it when I don't need it. Only problem is I have to give him the money for gas since Dave's not here to give him an allowance and occasionally slip him a twenty or two for an evening with Cindy. I had a serious talk with him and Jeannie about money. Both will have to get part-time jobs while they're in college, and we'll have to borrow.

Sunday morning. I awake at five, as I've been doing lately, and make coffee. Now it's Chip who bitches if I turn up the thermostat. I haven't had the heart to ask him to chop firewood.

He comes into the kitchen barefoot, wearing a pair of Dave's cast-off workout shorts, his face dull with sleep, his hair in tangles. He rummages aimlessly, spoons left-over Stroganoff into a bowl. "Didn't think you'd be up."

"Want me to fix you something?"

He shoves his bowl into the microwave.

"Come sit while your food warms." I pat the chair next to me. "Why up so early?"

"Gym gets crowded on weekends."

"Your Dad said it was deserted on holidays. That's why he always went on Saturdays and Sundays."

"That's the campus gym. I can't go there anymore. Have to use the one at Takoma High."

"I still work at the college—"

He shakes his head. He doesn't want any favors from me. The microwave pings. He slouches to it, recovers his bowl, returns.

I take both his hands in mine. "I feel like I've lost you. Talk to me."

He studies me. "We don't have any money, and you're a basket case, and Jeannie's freaked out, and Cindy and me broke up."

"Why?"

He starts eating. "I felt like she deserved something better."

"When did this happen?"

"Back when all the trouble started. I couldn't face anybody."

My skin prickles. "But it wasn't *you!* Why should—"

"Harry Sereni called me before the *Log* broke the story about the harassment thing. You weren't home from work yet. He told me that Dad had forced Helen and she was pregnant. That was right after Dad told me to think before I—"

"Chip, none of that is true. I can't believe Harry would—"

"He said you'd deny it all." He pushes away from the table. "Look, the investigative committee went over the evidence. Dad didn't fight it. He quit and went into hiding. None of us knew where he was for weeks. If it wasn't true, it'd be easy enough to prove it. He didn't even try." He gets up, takes his bowl to the sink.

"Go see your father," I say, my voice shaking.

"I've seen him. Didn't make any difference. He's slime." He starts from the room, stops. "Okay if I drive to the gym? Save me about fifteen minutes."

I nod.

"Oh, and the radio's not working in the wagon."

I nod again.

"Any chance—" he says, then stops. "Since you have to get a new radio anyway, how about getting a CD player with it? You know, a cheap one—"

"I'll see," I say in a wobbly voice.

He clomps up the stairs. Ten minutes later, he's out the door.

Dave and I had always planned to give Chip a car for graduation—nothing fancy, used, safe, cheap, and reliable. That's out of the question now, but maybe I can make the wagon more appealing since it's becoming obvious that he'll be going to Lincoln, taking advantage of my employee tuition discount, not to George Washington, and he'll be living at home. I have to replace the radio anyway. I'll get a snazzy stereo, like the one in the Z. I'll give it to him at graduation and let him install it. I'm not sure how I'll pay for it.

Wednesday I take a long lunch hour and drive to Fairmont Stereo in Bethesda. I leave the wagon in the public parking garage and walk into the bloodless sunshine down Fairmont Street. Twenty feet in front of me, a couple comes out of one of those gaudy little bistros Bethesda aficionados go giddy over. The woman is all breasts and long black hair. The man, in a tight white polo shirt that shows off his build, puts his arm around her. I know that voice. The sun is behind them. I can't make out his face, but as I look at his body, recognition dawns.

"Hi, Bob," I say.

When he sees me, his arm releases her. "Mary—"

The woman doesn't smile.

Bob turns to her. "This is Mary Bell, another of my clients. Mary, Dulcy Stovener."

She takes his hand. He pulls it free and puts it behind him.

"If you'd been a little earlier," he says, "you could have joined us for lunch. Shopping?"

I nod. "On my lunch hour. Don't have much time."

"We're doing a working lunch ourselves," Dulcy says. She has one of those high, nasal, whiny voices that grates.

"Catch you later." Bob gives me one of those lusty looks he gets when he's about to make love to me. Dulcy doesn't see it.

I force myself not to turn and watch them. Instead, I sweep into the store, all business. "Car stereos," I say.

Back in the office, I busy myself with checking the printouts of mid-term grade reports, but I keep seeing Dulcy. She must be twenty years younger than me. Nice body, clear face. She has that same easy confidence Helen had. But she's so young. And that voice? Why is Bob fooling around with someone like her?

For the first time I realize Bob's younger than me, too.

I thought Bob was making love to me because he found me beautiful. He's dehumanized me, made me cock trophy.

Chip's not home when I get in from work. I hide the new stereo and speakers and color-coded wires, still in Fairmont Stereo bags, on the shelf of my bedroom closet. After dinner, Chip says he wants to use Dave's computer. He goes into the study and shuts the door.

Jeannie's in her usual funk. "How come Chip gets to play on the computer and I have to clean up after dinner?"

"We take turns now." I finish clearing the table. "Chip's turn is tomorrow night, mine Friday."

She's about to light into me again when the phone rings. It's Bob.

"How about if we drive over to Saint Michael's Saturday morning and come home Sunday night? Beautiful there this time of year."

"Dulcy busy?"

Jeannie catches the tone in my voice.

"I'm single, remember?" Bob says.

"Did you use that line on Dulcy, too?"

"You know the Dulcy thing is a red herring. I know what's worrying you. I don't know how to say this exactly, but . . . a woman's orgasm is ninety-nine percent in her head. Give it a try this weekend."

Jeannie's watching me as though I'm wielding a chainsaw.

"Let me call you," I say, squirming under Jeannie's gaze.

"Tonight?" He's husky again.

"All right."

I hang up. On impulse I go into the study. Chip's frowning at the monitor. He ignores me.

I haven't been in this room since the day I barged in on Dave and Helen. Dave was staring out the window as she sat in the lounge. He said Harry and Helen had set him up. "Thinking with my gonads." Then they saw me and she ran. He turned pale, and I knew.

"What is it?" Chip asks without looking at me.

"What're you doing?"

"Addressing envelopes for the graduation invitations. Dad taught me how to use these fancy fonts."

"Who're you inviting?" I say.

"Here's the list."

I glance over the names. Emma, the Devereaux's, Chip's friends. "I have your father's address. I'll get it."

He's glowering at the screen again, typing with one finger. "He's not invited."

• • •

Bob works with me to get ready for the divorce sessions. First comes the mediation. Bob advises me to buy subdued, virginal clothes. "You need to look like Joan of Arc." He tells me to ask Dave for the money, "but don't tell him what for. And, by the way, we've about used up the retainer."

Bob coaches me to speak softly and keep my eyes down. Fold my hands in my lap. I practice. He tells me I was born for the stage.

The Parenting Conference is grueling. The master and Bob do most of the talking. Dave doesn't have a lawyer, says little. I'm quiet. We go to counseling sessions handled by an organization called Children of Separation and Divorce. They describe Jeannie and Chip perfectly without ever having seen them. I can hardly bear what we're doing to our children.

I bumble through the end of the semester at Lincoln. Grade reports, matching of requirements against graduation applications, final proofing of class schedules and the catalog for the fall semester. The divorce grinds on—Discovery, *Pendente Lite*, Deposition. Chip graduates. Cindy wasn't invited, but Carla, Jerry and Shirley Devereaux, and Emma are all on hand to applaud Chip, who, as it turns out, is not the biggest kid in the class after all. Dave's absence hurts.

Chip starts his summer job as a busboy at Chez Maigret in Georgetown. They'll let him work part-time when he starts classes at Lincoln in the fall. The pay is poor, but it was the best he could get—he didn't even start looking for a job until the end of April.

Jeannie hangs around school friends and has her first date, with a gawky acne-laden bean pole. After one look at him, I cease worrying about her virginity.

In July, I invite Bob to Chip's birthday dinner. Chip's awkward but friendly enough. Bob courts Jeannie and manages to get a smile out of her. I've never seen anybody who can handle people the way he does. By the end of the meal, he has both kids laughing. Then he gives Chip his birthday gift, a cell phone with the fees paid for a year. The next Saturday, Bob's at our place playing touch football with them on the front lawn.

That night at his place, after we've made love, he brings fluted goblets of champagne to bed. We drink in silence.

"Is it me?" he says finally. "Do I smell bad? Am I doing something to hurt you?"

Shame oozes up from my vitals.

"I'm sorry," I say. "I'm doing the best I can."

"You don't give yourself to me. You hold back. You don't trust me, do you?"

"You scare me."

"Did Dave scare you?"

Did Dave scare me? "I don't know."

Sex with Bob is different, though I'm not going to tell him that. He's less passionate, more calculating. He varies his touch and his speed. He's been slow and sensuous, quick and dominant, romantic and sweet. It all feels the same.

Dave was like a wild stallion, alive with desire, but there was awe in his hands, as though my body were sacred. He reined himself in, his throat growling softly. Then, when he was in me, passion swept over him. Sweat poured from him. His orgasm was thunder in the flesh.

Bob doesn't sweat or cry out or growl. He relishes the moment and makes me feel like the entrée at a gourmet meal. He's the gourmand, never out of control.

With both of them, much earlier with Bob than with Dave, I shut down. But with Dave I at least pretended.

Bob sips his champagne. "The Merit Hearing is scheduled for August 13. You're behind on my fee payment."

"I'll ask Dave for money."

"As soon as you can. I can't afford to do this for charity."

• • •

Sunday night I'm alone, getting myself together for the office Monday morning. I should iron a blouse, but I'm exhausted. Odd. If I disappeared tonight, only a few people would know or care. I'd be easy to replace at Lincoln. Carla would have to find someone else for the weekly lunches. Only Bob would really care—he wouldn't get his fee.

I see the future stretching out ahead of me, gray and barren. I was right. Carla and I are twins. Passionless aliens in a world of people obsessed with love.

Chapter 9

Merit Hearing

Jerry's words, from barely ten minutes ago, echoed and re-echoed through Dave's mind. " . . . off a bridge . . . New Carrollton and Bowie . . . drowned." Dave knew Helen was dead, but he saw her, ripe with life. He heard her voice. He felt her touch. Maybe, as in Vietnam, he had to see the corpse before he believed. Or maybe like Trion, he didn't care.

He got to his feet feeling like he was underwater and pulled on his running shoes. Old Town Takoma Park was closed down. Only the café was lit. Dave turned from the light and walked toward the Sligo Creek Park. Stars shed their cold light. Only two days 'til spring. Once in the park, he stopped on the foot bridge. He could see nothing below him, but he could hear the tension of the running water, feel the moisture rising to his face, sense the panic in his belly. When the car hit the water, the electrical system would have shorted out, leaving everything black. The cold water would have paralyzed her. He knew from his Ranger training that the body is able to avoid breathing for almost a minute and a half, longer if the water is very cold or the victim hyperventilates before submerging. Darkness closing in from lack of oxygen. Then the involuntary sucking of water into the lungs. Still conscious. Did she struggle?

Sweating in the cold, he crossed the bridge and walked along the path he had jogged many times. He knew its curves and bends and hills. He passed wooden tables where he and the children had picnicked, rocks in the stream where he and Mary had dangled their feet, knolls where he had sat while he thought about Thomas Mann. He wanted to laugh. The soul. How little he had understood. You had to touch life to find the soul. You had to feel death.

Did it ever occur to you that I love you? Helen loved him? Mary'd told him that, too, and so had Inge. But he was incapable of being loved. That was his curse. That was why Helen had to die. Loving the unlovable was lethal. It was all there in Mann, and he'd missed it. Unsuspecting, sweet Helen. A gift any man would cherish. And he'd tossed her aside like a broken doll.

The hurt in his abdomen spread into his chest. It moved into his shoulders and arms and neck. He tried to keep it from reaching his head. Too strong. He felt it in his jaws, his cheeks, his forehead, his brain. His eyes blurred. He hurt so much he couldn't stay on his feet.

• • •

"David."

The text before Dave was Italian. Yes, of course. Dante. *La Divina Commedia. "O amanza del primo amante, o diva—"* He'd already read this passage.

"David?" The voice pronounced his name as his mother had, Dahveed.

"David!"

Dave looked up. Horst's glasses were on his forehead. The lenses magnified his wrinkles.

"The lady asked a question," Horst said in German.

On the other side of the counter, a woman scowled through horn-rimmed glasses. "André Malraux."

"French," Dave answered.

The woman's frown deepened. "My question was, where do I find his books?"

"Let me show you." Dave stepped from behind the counter and led her to the third aisle. "His novels are here in French fiction. His non-fiction will be further back. Both sections are arranged alphabetically, and we have some shorter writings in anthologies."

Dave returned to the counter. Horst was waiting.

"David, did you eat breakfast?"

He couldn't remember.

"The phone call last night—" Horst said.

Dave closed his eyes. "Helen drowned."

"Helen?"

"The woman I . . . The department secretary."

"My God!" Horst said. "Accident?"

"I don't know."

"David, I want you to go upstairs and eat. Then lie down. After I finish with this customer, I'll come up and check on you."

Dave was asleep when Horst came to his room, rested his hand on Dave's shoulder.

"I want you to rest today," Horst said. "Tonight, after I close, we will talk." He gave Dave a worried look and left.

Dave slept. The Vietnam dream tried to force its way in. He could feel it almost touching him. In front of it, he saw Mary's face as she told him to move out. Chip disappearing into the rain. Carla saying, "not severe enough." Jerry behind his desk. Helen was there, too, everywhere. So was Trion. But Dave couldn't see them. Nothing but jangled dissonance.

"David." Horst hovered over him with a cup of tea. "How

do you feel?"

"I don't know."

"I left the teapot on your table."

Dave sat up and bent toward the window. Below him, in front of the shop, the jonquils in the flower boxes were opening.

He felt nothing. He repeated the litany over and over. No feeling. It reminded him of his leg wound in Vietnam. Anesthetized, he'd sat chatting with the surgeon while they cut him open and gouged out the shrapnel. He'd commented that he could feel what they were doing. It didn't hurt. "It'll hurt later," the doctor had said.

Horst came through the door with a tray. "We eat, yes?" He gave Dave a plate to balance on his knees. "You like beef stew? The wine is from Australia. Quite good." He sat at the table and lifted his fork. "You should see a doctor."

"I don't have health insurance any more."

"You have the money from the sale of your car. You have your last paycheck."

"Mary and the children can't get by on her salary. I don't know what we'll do when my money's gone."

"I can get you translation work," Horst said. "Translate *Leverkühn* into German. Brenz-Verlag is still interested, yes?"

Dave nodded. "I need money now, not next year or the year after."

"Do some other kind of work."

"What? Sell insurance and work nights at Sears? Mow lawns?"

"You could do worse." Horst shook his head. "David, you must get a lawyer and fight the harassment charges."

"Lawyers cost money."

Horst pushed his plate away and finished his wine. "You do

not sound like my old friend, Herr Doctor Bell. My old friend was—what you say in English—a scrapper."

"I don't know who or what to fight."

"When you get your balance, you will be able to act, but first you must pass through a time of darkness."

"I don't even hurt. I'm numb. Who can I fight? I'm to blame. I'm *Unverzeihlich*."

"Wait until it is dark, then search for the key."

"And until I find it?"

"Let your friends help you."

"I have no friends."

Horst smiled. "What am I, then?"

Dave smiled. "You are my friend."

• • •

As the next week progressed, Dave's waking hours were distorted dreams. Nothing was in focus. He learned to pretend he was normal. No one except Horst noticed that his attention slipped as if he were drugged. Sleep became an addiction. He was in bed every night by nine and napped at noon. The Vietnam dream circled, waited, but never broke through.

On Friday, two Prince George's County police officers came into the shop and asked to speak to him alone. He called to Horst to watch the shop and took them to his room. They asked about Helen. He answered. An hour later they thanked him and left.

He passed up lunch and let Horst take an extra hour for a nap. In the drowsy afternoon, he propped open the front door and hooked the backdoor to let the cool spring air move through the musty shelves. He waited on customers in German and Italian and English. Every face looked like Helen. Every voice was tinged with her speech. Her ginger aroma filled the shop. Finally at eight in the evening, Dave closed up, went to Mark's Kitchen for noodles, returned to his room, and slept.

• • •

The days of April passed in a fog of rains and cherry blossoms. The master named for the divorce called to verify Dave's address and phone number. Mary called again—she needed money. The total was over six thousand. He asked to see the children. When Mary told him neither of them wanted to see him, pain broke through. He cried. As his tears dried, he again emptied himself of feeling.

At the end of the month, Bob Scarff explained to Dave that when children were involved, Montgomery County required two sessions of mediation. Dave paid a hundred and fifty dollars for each.

In the middle of May, along with a fresh demand for money from Mary, was the Parenting Conference. Mary told the master that Chip and Jeannie refused to see Dave. The master recommended therapy for Dave and the children. Dave shook his head. When the sessions were over, Dave paid the requisite three hundred dollars. As he prepared to leave, the master asked to talk to him alone.

"Doctor Bell," he said as Dave sat fidgeting, "we have an old saying in the profession: 'A man who represents himself has a fool for a lawyer.' Not only do you lack legal expertise, but you're not even speaking up on your own behalf."

"I don't have enough money," Dave said.

Chip's high school graduation was coming up. No invitation. Dave found a card in the shop up the street, enclosed a check for fifty dollars, and mailed it. No answer.

The evening of Chip's graduation, as Dave was closing out
the cash register, Horst interrupted him. "For you. I thought you
should have it."

The envelope was addressed to Horst. Inside Dave found
the Prince George's County Coroner's report. Helen's death
was ruled accidental drowning. No signs of physical trauma or
alcohol, but significant traces of barbiturates were found. No
pregnancy.

As June progressed, Dave sent Mary money. He attended
more meetings. He couldn't remember what they were called
half the time. He didn't understand what they were about and
said little. Neither Jeannie nor Chip came with Mary to any of
the meetings. Mary always appeared in demure, quiet clothing
that almost made her look like a widow, clothing he had never
seen before.

By July, the days were muggy, heat in the mid-nineties.
Dave kept the door to the shop open most days. He had no air
conditioning in his room, but he bought a fan for twenty dollars
at the Good Will. Sleeping in his own sweat brought back
Vietnam.

For Chip's eighteenth birthday, Dave shopped for a funny
father-son card. Again, he wrote a check to Chip for fifty dollars
and mailed it, even though the graduation check hadn't been
cashed. He waited. No answer.

More meetings in lawyer's offices. Something called *Pendente
lite* that seemed to be an attempt to settle the divorce without
going to court. Bob Scarff said Mary was unwilling to do that.
Before that was the Discovery. Then came the Deposition. Dave
answered endless questions from Bob. Dave asked Mary almost
none. He didn't know what to ask.

• • •

The date for the Merit Hearing, which Dave understood
to be the final resolution, was set for August 13, 1996, in the
Domestic Relations section of the Montgomery County Judicial
Building in Rockville. He arrived by Metro half an hour early
and entered through the massive doors into the stucco-and-glass
structure—like a hospital with its cheery, open spaces. Inside
the door, he stopped. From where he stood in the sun-splashed
atrium, he could see each of the eight floors of the building
rising above him—a series of receding balconies as in an Escher
drawing, each with its own stucco-and-wood railing. The
architect had created a building of courtrooms in which a suicide
leap would be easy.

Four people joined him on the elevator to the second floor.
One was George Eckland. Dave peered at him but said nothing.

When the elevator's indicator panel showed "2" and the
doors whispered open, Dave followed George onto the marble
floor. George disappeared into the men's room. Dave walked to
the railing. A sheer drop separated the ground floor from this
expansive balcony, open and fresh, quiet and polite, treacherous.

He moved to the nearest bench and mopped his eyes and his
forehead with his handkerchief. Another twenty minutes before
the hearing.

A small group gathered by the entrance to Domestic
Relations. A woman, dressed in black, was tall and willowy with
straight blond hair. Dave wiped the sweat from his eyes. Mary.
The man with his arm around her was Bob Scarff. The large
black man next to Bob was Jerry. Beside him was Harry Sereni.
Apart from the rest were two women and a man. One woman
was Carla acting like a shepherdess in charge of the other two.
The man, the tallest of them all, was studying Harry. The man's
brow was furrowed, and he bit his lower lip. Red hair and—*My*

God! Chip!

Chip was dressed in a suit and tie. His face was serious, even sorrowful. He didn't want to be here. He slouched the way Chip perpetually slouched, with a kind of hang-dog posture that Dave had tried to get him to abandon. "Stand straight and tall," Dave had always told him. "Take joy in your size. You're a man."

The third woman was not a woman at all. It was a girl. Jeannie.

No, she was a woman. Shapely but delicate, like a full-blown chrysanthemum. Dave's heart fluttered. His daughter was beautiful.

The fog lifted. Pain—sharp and violent—struck his chest so hard he nearly toppled. He grasped the plastic seat beneath him.

Jerry broke from the group. Dave stiffened.

"Dave," Jerry said, extending his hand, "you look awful."

"Been having a rough time. What're you doing here?"

Jerry's smile disappeared. "Witness. Called by Mary."

"Carla came to gloat?"

"Mary asked her."

"What the hell are the kids here for?"

"Mary wanted them here." Jerry glanced at his watch. "Better go on in."

Jerry hurried away. Mary and her entourage moved to the entrance of the Domestic Relations suite. Dave waited until the entire group had passed through security. He forced his muscles to relax, dried his face, and dashed to the entrance. The guard behind the counter took his briefcase. Dave could see the group of eight walking toward the hearing rooms. Carla guided Chip and Jeannie into a side room. Dave snatched his briefcase and hurried after the children.

Carla stood brooding out the window. Chip and Jeannie sat

on a sofa. Jeannie was sorting through magazines on the coffee table. She wore the princess ring. Chip read a hard-cover book. They raised their heads at the same moment and saw Dave.

"Daddy!" Jeannie whispered.

Carla stepped between Dave and the children. "They do not wish to see you."

With a single motion of his arm, Dave moved her aside. "Jeannie," he said. "Chip—"

Chip scowled at his book. Jeannie watched Dave warily.

Dave squatted by the coffee table and smiled. "How are you?"

Jeannie frowned at the table. Chip stared at his book.

"I've missed you." He leaned toward Chip. "Getting ready for college? I don't know what's going on with you. Going out for football?"

Chip's eyes stayed glued to his book.

Dave turned to Jeannie and grinned. "My little girl has turned into a beautiful woman."

Jeannie, her mouth open, trembled. She raised her head in pleading to Carla.

"Leave them alone!" Carla said. "They are *ashamed* of you."

Dave's eyes watered. He straightened, took a step backwards, shrugged. "Sorry. I thought—"

Carla's nostrils flared.

He felt a hand on his shoulder.

"Dave." Bob Scarff's voice behind him.

Dave mustered as much control as he could and walked into the hall.

"In here." Bob led Dave to a small conference room. "Mary's willing to settle. Here are her terms."

He handed Dave a legal-length document typed double-space—alimony, child support until Chip and Jeannie entered college, payment for their college education, payment of the mortgage, utilities, court costs, and legal fees; sole custody of the children to Mary with visiting rights twice a month for Dave, as long as the children agreed to see him.

Dave tossed the paper across the table. "You expect me to agree to this?"

"It's negotiable. She'd be willing to lower the alimony in exchange for half your pension—if you get a decent job. She'll pay the court costs if you assume all the utilities—stuff like that. Then there's the question of a new car—"

"You're fucking crazy."

Bob raised his eyebrows. "She's got you by the short hairs, Dave. Infidelity, the sexual harassment, the scandal. I'd settle if I were you. The court might not be lenient with you."

Dave stood. "Forget it."

Bob sighed with a knowing weariness and got to his feet. "Okay, buddy. I warned you." He put the proposal in his briefcase and left.

When Dave entered the hearing room, Mary and Bob were already seated in two of the four chairs at the long, dark table facing the raised judge's bench. Before them were stacks of documents. Empty brief cases lay on the floor next to Bob's chair. In the pew-like spectator bench beneath the windows at the rear wall were Jerry, George Eckland, and Harry Sereni. A young woman sat behind the metal desk at the end of the room with a computer keyboard, two monitors, and an old-fashioned upright reel-to-reel tape recorder. Dave moved across the muted orange rug and sat to the right of Bob at the table. No one spoke.

The chamber reminded him of a hospital waiting room

with recessed fluorescent lights in the high ceiling. Flags at both sides of the judge's desk. The Great Seal of Maryland behind the judge's bench. Potted plants. No dust on the furniture. No lint on the carpet.

The judge entered through a paneled door. He wore black robes—as if to match the sober clothing of all the other players. After he was seated, he led them through the nature of the case, asked for the lawyers' names, and who they represented. He asked all witnesses to leave the chamber. Jerry and Harry shuffled out.

"Doctor Bell," the judge said, "since you are representing yourself, I'll go out of my way to assist you, but I'll expect you to observe the rules of procedure."

Bob called his first witness, Mary. She laid out the case, centering on Dave's forced affair with Helen ending in her apparent suicide. Bob asked about Dave's fitness as a parent. Mary told of Dave's absence when Chip was arrested. "He was with his mistress." She said Dave tried to earn the children's affection by coddling them. As an example, she recounted Dave's refusal to punish Chip for the marijuana incident. She went on to describe Dave's forcible expulsion from the alumni lunch on 15 March. Not exactly role-model behavior. Then, under Bob's questioning, she detailed the family finances, her own career, sacrificed during the early years of the marriage so that Dave could write, and Dave's current employment. "He has deliberately impoverished himself."

Bob returned to his chair as Mary prepared to leave the witness stand.

"Cross examine, Doctor Bell?" the judge said.

"No."

"Doctor Gérard Devereaux," Bob said.

Jerry was brought in and sat in the witness chair.

"Who accused Doctor Bell of forcing Miss Sereni to have sex?" Bob asked Jerry.

"Her brother, Harry Sereni."

"Anyone else?"

Jerry gave Dave a pained look. "Miss Sereni."

"Doctor Devereaux," Bob said, "when Doctor Jacob Colson, the president of Lincoln College, asked for your recommendation as the department chairman—as distinct from your role as member of the investigation committee—how did you advise the president?"

"I did the best I could to defend Doctor Bell."

"But what did you recommend?"

"That Doctor Bell be asked to resign."

"And when the president," Bob said, "asked the investigating committee to reconsider its initial recommendation, how did the committee recommend?"

"For dismissal."

"How was the vote split?"

"Unanimous."

"You, too, believe Doctor Bell guilty of sexual harassment?"

Jerry wiped his forehead with his fingers. His eyes flickered to Dave's, then to the floor.

"No further questions."

As Jerry left the witness stand, Dave's eyes followed him. *The bastard. Did everything he could to get me ousted.*

The next witness was Harry Sereni. When he was seated, his eyes—red-rimmed and unnaturally large as if the pupils were dilated—skirted the room and came to rest on Dave's face. He gave his address as New York City.

Harry ran through his allegations that Dave had given him

the *Trion* papers and forced sex on Helen.

"Where is Miss Sereni now?" Bob said.

"Killed in a car accident on March 19th."

"Do you believe that your sister's death was suicide?"

"Helen didn't kill herself!" Harry shouted. "She was a devout Catholic." He fastened his eyes on Dave. "She died carrying your child!"

"Mr. Sereni," the judge said. "Please confine yourself to answering questions posed by counsel."

"No further questions," Bob said.

The judge looked expectantly at Dave. "Doctor Bell?"

Dave tried to slow his heartbeat and got to his feet. "Mr. Sereni, when did I show you the *Trion* papers?"

"Objection," Bob said, rising. "Immaterial."

"Your honor," Dave said, "Mrs. Bell says she has suffered from my scandalous behavior. I want to show that there's considerable doubt as to the validity of the charges."

The judge raised his eyebrows. "Proceed."

Dave turned to Harry. "When did you see the *Trion* papers?"

"Two or three different times. Eight or nine in the evening. When no one else was around."

"Where?"

"Your office. Scully Hall."

"How did you get in at that hour of the night?

Harry looked at Dave sidelong. "Through the front door."

"And security let you in?"

Harry paused. "I have a student ID."

"Did you ask the campus police to admit you?"

Harry's face didn't change. "I don't remember."

"Where did I keep the *Trion* papers?"

Harry darted a look at Bob, then his face lit up. "In a

strongbox."

Dave waited a beat. "And where did I keep the strongbox?"

Harry's eyes wandered. Then they met Dave's. "I saw it in your safe."

"Which drawer?"

"Bottom."

"How big was the strongbox?" Dave asked.

"I don't know. It was just a strongbox."

"How big was the manuscript?"

Harry shrugged one shoulder. "The size of a book."

"What were the dimensions?"

"I don't remember. Wait. They were . . . Yes. The pages were big, maybe a foot square. I'd forgotten."

"The strongbox in which I stored the manuscript must have been somewhat larger than twelve inches by twelve?"

Harry nodded.

"Let the record show that the witness agreed," Dave said. "What else did I keep in the strongbox?"

Harry shut his eyes as if to remember. "Photocopies, your translation, your article, and the comp exam papers. And maybe some other things."

"How big was the strongbox?

"Maybe fourteen by fourteen."

"How was I able to fit it into the standard twelve-by-ten-inch file drawer of the safe where you say you saw it?"

Harry twitched.

"Let the record show," Dave said, "that the witness did not answer. Mr. Sereni, have you seen the Prince George's County Coroner's report on your sister's death?" Dave leaned toward Harry. "What if I told you that it showed Helen was not pregnant? Would you like me to enter it in evidence, Harry, so that we can compare it to your outburst of a few minutes ago?"

Harry sat perfectly still.

Dave had Harry in his sight's crosshairs. He decided to wing it. "Admission to campus buildings after six at night is only possible if the campus police admit you. What if I told you that campus police records show that you *never* sought admission to Scully Hall after hours?"

Harry's fists tightened.

"Have you ever heard of perjury, Harry?"

"Objection!" Bob shouted.

"No further questions," Dave said.

Dave returned to the table. Harry left the room.

"Is the defense prepared to present its case?" the judge said.

"Yes, your honor," Dave said. "I'd like to call myself."

Dave sat in the witness chair.

"Doctor Bell," the judge said, "since you are representing yourself, you may dispense with the usual question-and-answer format."

"In the interest of showing that my behavior was not irrational," Dave began, "I would like to clarify some things about my marriage. We had not been getting along for some four or five years. Mrs. Bell no longer respected me as a professional or as a man. About two years ago, she lost interest in sex—or so I thought at the time. For the year prior to our separation, we had not engaged in sex at all. My attempts to make love to her were an imposition. Only later did I come to understand that she had never loved me, that she had been pretending."

Mary whispered to Bob.

"Last fall," Dave went on, "Miss Sereni was hired as the department secretary. As our work brought us together, I saw that she was interested. We grew closer. I was lonely and rejected. I was a foolish middle-aged man taking advantage of a young woman. I ended up hurting everyone involved. Even—" Dave's voice went raw. "Even my children."

He mopped his forehead.

"Mr. Sereni has testified that I forced his sister to sleep with me. That's not true. He also says that I coached him in my office around eight or nine, when no one else was there. He says the security guard let him in. Scully closes at six. Anyone who wants in has to go to the campus police and ask an officer to let him in. The police keep records. Mr. Sereni's statements can easily be shown to be false. Mr. Sereni has also testified that I kept the *Trion* papers in a strongbox in the bottom drawer of my safe. The strongbox is too large to fit into the safe. Incidentally, the safe in my office doesn't have a bottom drawer. It sits on a table."

Dave clasped his hands to hide the shaking. "I am guilty of adultery, but not of all the evil I am accused of. For twenty years, I was a good and loving father, despite my failings during the last year." Dave looked at the judge. "I have nothing further to say."

Bob rose.

"Doctor Bell, between October of last year and March of this year, how often did you make love to Miss Sereni?"

"We met usually once or twice a week."

"Fifty times or more?"

"I didn't keep count."

"Doctor Bell, how did you conceal your assignations with Miss Sereni from Mrs. Bell?"

"I didn't tell Mrs. Bell where I had been."

"And when she asked?"

"I lied."

"Over the weekend of February 17th of this year, when

your son, David, Jr.—Chip—was arrested for possession of marijuana, where were you?"

"At a friend's house in Charlottesville, Virginia."

"Who was with you?"

"Miss Sereni."

"How long were you and Miss Sereni alone in your friend's house?"

"Two and a half days."

"Where did you tell Mrs. Bell you were during those two and a half days?"

"At a conference in New York City."

"How often did you lie to Mrs. Bell about your whereabouts?"

"I don't know."

"Fifty times? A hundred times?"

"I don't know."

"Did you lie to your children, too?"

Dave's stomach twisted. "Yes."

"How many times?"

"I don't know."

"Fifty times? A hundred times?" Bob studied the notes in front of him. "No further questions."

"Redirect?" the judge asked.

"No," Dave said.

Mary and Bob whispered. Bob nodded and rose. "Your honor, we request a fifteen minute recess."

The judge frowned but agreed.

Dave bolted from the room. He raced to the fountain and gulped water. As he wiped his chin and straightened, he collided with Jerry. When Jerry saw Dave's face, he drew in his breath and pushed past.

Dave caught him by the bicep and spun him around. "You never tried to arrange for me to talk to Jake, did you?"

"It was hopeless."

"He didn't ask to have my resignation in hand before he'd see me, did he?"

"I thought that's what he meant."

"And he asked the committee to reconsider. He even asked for your personal recommendation as department chair. He wanted to give me every chance, didn't he? Why did you lie to me?"

Jerry tried to pull free, but Dave held fast.

"You knew I never forced Helen," Dave said.

"We were dealing with facts, not my opinion."

"Your personal recommendation was to fire me."

Jerry tried to pull Dave's hand away. "What are you accusing me of?"

"Lying, betrayal and cowardice. You didn't want me to talk to Jake, did you?"

"I thought you might make things worse for yourself. As it turned out, I was right."

"And you wouldn't want it to look like you were rooting for the bad guy. Or, worse, that the guy you were intent on doing in wasn't guilty?"

Jerry wrenched free of Dave's grasp and took a deep breath. "Dave, I did the best I could."

"I think you did, Jerry. The very best you're capable of. Like Long Dinh. You froze. You're a coward."

"I couldn't help it. *I* didn't have the knife—"

"Right. I forgot. All you had was an M-16."

"Me?" Jerry said. "You were the one—"

"And twenty-seven years later, you're still cringing."

Dave shoved him aside. Jerry slammed into the wall, bounced, and stood in Dave's path. He bent his legs, leaned forward, and raised his arms like a wrestler ready for the first lunge. "You son of a bitch."

"Go on," Dave said in a hoarse whisper. "Take me on. Show me you got balls."

Jerry, heaving and sweating, licked his lips. He crouched deeper as though about to spring. Dave braced for the impact. Then, gradually, Jerry straightened his body until he was drawn up to his full height. His hands fell to his sides, and he turned on his heel. With studied dignity, he moved evenly away from Dave down the hall.

Dave stumbled to the men's room. He sat in a stall, waiting for the adrenalin to fade. Too much at stake to vent his rage on Jerry. His breathing finally slowed.

Mary was in for a surprise. He was going to call her. She'd be a hostile witness; he could dispense with some of the procedural niceties. He'd ask her about the marriage, about their sexual relations, about the length of time since they'd made love. He'd force her to admit that she faked, that she had never loved him, that she'd used him. Right from the beginning. As the final thrust, he'd ask her if she was faking during the love-making that resulted in the conception of Chip and Jeannie. "And how did that feel, Mrs. Bell?"

He shuddered. What kind of a monster was he? He imagined her face as she tried to answer. Maybe she'd cry. His chest hurt. He'd promised himself that when it was all over, he'd be able to look back knowing he hadn't deliberately hurt his wife and children in the divorce.

But losing custody would hurt the children more than anything else. All right. He'd stick it to Mary. He took off his jacket, unbuttoned his shirt, and wiped his chest and underarms. He was still wet when he retied his tie.

Bob was waiting. "Dave—" He tipped his head toward the small conference room where Mary sat at the table.

"We figured," Bob said, "we'd give you one more chance to settle before the axe falls. Mary has agreed to drop her alimony to a thousand a month and increase the visitations to four a month if you'll replace the station wagon."

"Things aren't going a hundred percent your way, are they?"

"You're about to get whacked."

"The Spartans would have admired you. Bob, the happy executioner. *No.*" Dave left the room.

He was in his place at the table when Carla and George Eckland came in. Bob seated Mary and took the chair next to her. The judge entered and took off his glasses. "Have plaintiff and defendant attempted to reach a settlement?"

Bob stood. "The defendant refused our offer."

The judge put his glasses on and nodded to Dave. "Doctor Bell, do you wish to call any further witnesses?"

"Mary Bell."

Mary paled, stood, and walked to the witness stand. Bob turned halfway in his chair and looked toward the group on the bench under the window.

Dave rose. "Mrs. Bell, did I ever express dissatisfaction with our marriage?"

"You thought our . . . sexual relations were not completely satisfactory."

"What were my complaints?"

A motion at Dave's left. Carla was leaving the room.

Mary threw Bob a look as if for help. "You felt I wasn't responsive."

"In what way?"

Bob was on his feet. "Objection. Immaterial."

The door to the hearing room opened. Carla entered escorting Jeannie and Chip. Dave gasped.

"Overruled," the judge said. "Let us see where Doctor Bell is heading."

Dave pivoted slowly. Chip sat at the end of the spectator bench. Carla was next to him. Jeannie sat on the other side of Carla.

Dave locked his eyes on Mary's. "Have you really sunk so low?"

"Please speak up, Doctor Bell," the judge said.

"You've won," Dave said in a croaking whisper. "I never thought you'd go this far—bringing the children in to watch. A loveless woman in a loveless marriage. And now your reward."

Bob stepped between Dave and Mary. "Objection."

Dave shouldered him aside. "They won't stay with you long, Mary. He'll be leaving for college this month. Jeannie will follow so quickly you won't know the years have passed. They'll know what you did. I won't have to tell them."

"Your honor," Bob cried.

"Objection sustained," the judge said. "Doctor Bell, you are out of order. Please—"

"No need." Dave raised his face to the judge. "Your honor . . . I—" His voice cracked. "Nothing further."

"Let us then proceed to summation. Mr. Scarff?"

Bob rose. "I can make this brief, your honor. Doctor Bell has admitted that he had a continuing adulterous relationship with Miss Sereni. He was with his paramour at the time his son, Chip, needed him. He maintains that he did not force Miss Sereni to have sex. I remind the court that Miss Sereni herself accused Doctor Bell." Bob walked behind Dave's chair. "In addition to the hurt Doctor Bell's betrayal of his marriage vows has inflicted, Mrs. Bell has had to bear the public humiliation of a scandal in her own work place."

Dave could feel Bob's breath. The movement of air from Bob's gestures brushed Dave's hair. He fought to control his own breathing.

"The point here, your honor," Bob said, "is that scandal resulted from Doctor Bell's indiscretions *whether or not* he actually forced Miss Sereni. Had Doctor Bell not had an extended affair with Miss Sereni, the rest of the unfortunate events outlined in this case would never have occurred. Doctor Bell, in sum, has shown himself to be an adulterous husband, a liar, and a negligent father. As for Doctor Bell's list of extenuating circumstances . . . It seems that Doctor Bell would have us equate sexuality with love. One might well conclude that Doctor Bell has no understanding of love."

Bob's hand swiped the back of Dave's chair. Dave shuddered.

"We ask," Bob said, "the court to find in favor of Mrs. Bell and grant her custody of the children and the financial support she has requested."

"Doctor Bell?" the judge said.

Dave trembled as he struggled to his feet.

The judge scowled at him. "Doctor Bell, are you all right?"

Dave leaned on the table. His damp palms stuck to the polished wood. "May we have a short break?"

Bob smiled at Dave, pulled the agreement from his briefcase. "Now?"

Breathing hard, Dave made his way to the conference room and sat at the table. Bob came in, closed the door, and dropped the agreement on the table in front of Dave. "Sign all three copies."

Dave did.

"Thanks, buddy." Bob picked up the papers. "You understand that you can't meet these obligations working in a bookstore. You'll have to get a job that pays."

"And if I don't?"

"We have a name for that. Voluntary impoverishment. We'll have you arrested."

Bob gave him a friendly smile as he headed out.

Dave sat with his face in his hands. At last, he pulled himself to his feet and walked to the hearing room. Mary and Bob were seated at the table. She was smiling, her eyes bright.

The judge reappeared.

"Your honor," Bob said, rising. "During the recess, plaintiff and defendant have reached a settlement." He put one copy of the signed agreement on the judge's desk.

The judge read it, scowled at Dave. "Do you understand what you have agreed to here?"

Dave nodded without rising.

The judge thanked the parties for shortening the time the court had to spend and expressed hope that the agreement would prove satisfactory in the long run. He declared the session over and left the room.

Beaming, Mary hugged Bob and rose.

Dave heard shuffling and footsteps. He sprang to his feet. "Chip, Jeannie—"

The children, already at the door, stopped. Mary stepped in front of them.

"No," she said. "Keep away from them."

"For God's sake, Mary—"

"They want nothing to do with you. They're *ashamed* of

you."

She turned, put one arm around each child, and walked from the room

Chapter 10

Touchdown

Everything was going our way, until Dave cross-examined Harry. Everyone in the court could see that Harry was lying. Then Dave turned down our offer. Now I'm scared. What else is Dave going to pull?

Harry's testimony compels me to see that Dave didn't force Helen. He didn't help Harry cheat. Dave's biggest flaw is his sex drive. I laugh silently to myself. My biggest flaw is the lack of a sex drive. I'm the sinner amongst us. I hear his broken voice. *Evil . . . Frozen in ice from the waist down. Tell me what it feels like.*

"Doctor Bell," the judge says, "do you wish to call any further witnesses?"

"Mary Bell."

My God. What's he up to?

I can't keep up the fluttering vulnerability I've been faking. His face is determined. This is not the empty husk who sat through our endless meetings up to now. This is the old Dave, the man I married, aggressive, passionate, eyes flashing. He looks enormous standing there, close enough to lay hands on me. I remember what I thought the first time I saw him—he's strong enough to kill me with his bare hands. But he didn't. Instead, he protected me and took care of me. Not any more.

Dave moves closer, asks about sex during the marriage. Carla comes in. I didn't see her leave. I gasp. Jeannie and Chip are with her. Dave wheels to gawk at the children. Bob gives Dave a nasty smile. What's going on? The judge shouldn't allow our children to view this abomination. Jesus. He doesn't *know* these people are our children. I stand. I've got to stop this.

Dave pivots toward me. "I never thought you'd go this far. A loveless woman in a loveless marriage. And now your reward."

Bob leaps to his feet. "Objection."

Dave moves toward me, knocks Bob out of the way. He's going to kill me. Bob shouts, the judge tells Dave he's out of order. Dave stares at me, as if trying to make sense of what he sees. He turns toward the judge. "Nothing further."

We go to our chairs, and Bob begins his summation. His voice rises and falls, his elegant diction and prosody underlining point after point. He pauses for dramatic effect several times. I think he's finished, but he resumes, his voice low, the speech slowed.

I'm hearing with Chip's ears. I can feel his repulsion. I can sense Jeannie's anguish. Why did Carla bring them into the room to witness this horror?

"May we have a short break?" Dave says.

He reels from the room. Bob takes papers and starts out.

I catch his arm. "Why are the children here?"

He gives me an indulgent smile and hurries out.

I dash to the children. "You shouldn't be here. How—"

Carla's smile is suppressed ecstasy. Chip and Jeannie shy away from me. I return to the table. I can't get the picture of Dave out of my mind. My skin shrivels as I see his face, twisted, unhinged. I'm profoundly grateful that Bob advised me to get new locks for the house, complete with dead bolts on every door. I resolve then and there to have a security system installed.

Bob reappears. "He signed our original offer."

"He didn't want the changes we offered to make?"

"He didn't even read it to see which version it was. We got it all. We have a lot to thank Carla for."

"But—"

"We won, Mary. Nothing else matters."

I see George Eckland's face. *It's my obligation as a journalist to report the truth as I see it. Nothing else matters.*

The judge reads the agreement, questions Dave, and thanks us all for saving time. It's over.

I collapse into Bob's arms. Over his shoulder I see Carla herding the children toward the door. Dave starts after them. His face is twisted. I can't let him hurt them. I dash ahead of him. Carla and I drag the kids from the courtroom. Carla hurries them into a side room.

Bob's arms go around me. "Congratulations."

I pull away. "Stop it."

Dave careens past us. People are running after him, calling to him.

I'm getting wobbly. Bob takes my elbow and leads me into the side room. Jeannie's crying while Carla comforts her. Chip, arms folded, is glaring out the window. Bob eases me into a chair.

"Did you see his face?" I say.

"I'll be on my way," Carla says, still beaming. "Call me later, Mary?"

I nod.

Bob takes us home, dripping in the August heat. While the kids and I shower, he spreads a celebration feast on the dining room table, then showers and changes into shorts and a tank top. We eat in silence except for his running comic monologue. He insists that I drink a martini he's made.

"Tell you what," he says with gusto. "Let's play touch." He

starts for the doors.

The kids and I drag out to the lawn. As soon as it's polite, I'll ask him to leave. The kids and I need some time to heal. Bob appears with a bottle of champagne, pours us both a glass, bounds to the middle of the lawn, and snatches the football from Jeannie. He throws a whirling pass to Chip who tosses the ball to Jeannie. It rolls into the ivy.

Chip aims a nasty laugh at her. "Girls."

She runs to the ivy and holds up the ball.

Chip throws up his arms in ironic glee. "Touchdown."

Jeannie starts to cry. Bob puts his arms around her. She pushes him away.

I yell at Bob. He gives me a hurt look.

"Come on," Bob says to Chip and Jeannie.

They head toward me. I refill Bob's glass.

"Hey, you guys." Bob raises his glass. "To victory." He looks at my face and wilts. "Sorry." He puts his arms around me.

After Bob leaves, Chip goes out. I don't even ask where. Jeannie hides in her room. I'm freezing. Chip's set the air conditioning to sixty-five. I raise the thermostat and change into sweats and lie on our bed. I watch it grow darker. I should get up and make dinner. Instead, I go over what's happened. I can't bear the silence, the aloneness. I dial Bob's number. He's laughing as he answers.

"Can I come over?" I ask.

"I'm working with a client."

Tears start down my cheek.

"Hey, kid," he says, "you should be rejoicing."

"The children—"

"They'll be fine."

"Why did Carla—"

"I told her ahead of time," he says, "that if things started to go bad, I'd give her a signal and she'd bring the children in."

"Without asking me?"

"It worked, didn't it? Now it's time to get the sexual harassment charges withdrawn so he can get his job back and pay my fee. What?"

He's talking to someone else. A woman's voice in the background. "Just be a minute," he says away from the phone.

"Should I press for his arrest for voluntary impoverishment?" I say.

"Last thing you want. He can't earn a penny in jail."

"But you said—"

"Trying to scare him. That worked, too."

The woman's voice again.

"I gotta go," he says. "Call my secretary and set up a time we can talk."

Off the phone, I fall back on the bed. What works is right, no matter who gets hurt. *Nothing else matters.* I won't be seeing Bob again. I can't face the sorting out of what's happened. I can at least call Dave and tell him I want to help get his name cleared.

I dial the number for Für Ein Fremdes Land. The German answers. He sounds upset.

"May I speak to Dave Bell please?" I say.

"He moved out this afternoon."

"He must have left a forwarding address, a phone number, something—"

"Nothing. I do not know where David is."

Chapter 11

Ungeminnt

Dave ran through the knots of bystanders. Someone called, "Your briefcase—" A hand swiped at him. Past security, down the stairs, to the street. He dashed to the Metro station, tripped as he jostled his way up the escalator. On the platform, no trains. Shaking, he sat on the cement bench.

"Doctor Bell." George Eckland smiled down at him.

"Jesus. Don't you know when to quit?"

"You think the hearing was fair?"

"Go fuck yourself."

George grinned. "May I quote you?"

Lights flashed at the edge of the platform. A train. Dave got to his feet. It wouldn't take much to push George onto the tracks.

George chuckled. "Your ex-wife is more cooperative."

Dave moved toward the edge of the platform. "Then go talk to her."

"Didn't have to. She came to me."

The train entered the station.

"I shouldn't reveal my sources," George said, "but it's worth it to watch that smug face of yours crumple. Remember the anonymous tip? Mary."

The train stopped, and the doors opened. Chimes. The doors were about to close. Dave lurched onto the train. It pulled out and left George behind, laughing.

At the Takoma station, Dave sprinted down the escalator. His shaking hand took two tries to get his fare card into the slot. He sped across the plaza, through the intersection against the signal, down Carroll to the bookstore. He rushed past Horst at the front counter.

"David."

"I lost. Everything."

"The children?"

"They're ashamed of me. She has custody."

"Ach, Gott!"

"But I'm going to see them."

Dave reached the top of the steps. Horst stumbled after him. In his room, Dave pulled his suitcase from under the bed. "I'm going to see them, then I'm going away. They want to force me to get a professional job. No one will hire me. They'll put me in jail."

"David, don't run away. Sue the college. Clear your name. Ask for another hearing with Mary—"

"I have less than five hundred dollars left."

"Have tea with me," Horst said.

He didn't have time for tea, for Christ's sake. He looked at Horst's face. "All right. I'll pack and dress."

Horst nodded and plodded out.

Dave dropped jeans, a tee-shirt, and his running shoes on the bed and packed everything else. Off with the shirt and tie. He tossed his damp clothes into the suitcase. By the bed were the Dante and the Rumi poetry. He crammed them in next to his shoes, dressed, and carried the suitcase downstairs.

A steaming pot under a tea caddy sat on the little table at the end of the shop. Next to it were *beignets*, napkins, sugar, lemon juice, and a pitcher of milk.

Horst handed him a cup. "A soothing Indian mix I found in Adams-Morgan. You must leave? Do not throw away what you have."

"I've already thrown it away."

"You are what you choose to be. The only unforgivable sin is despair." Horst sagged. "What happened?"

"Chip and Jeannie came into the court room. I couldn't speak. Mary wanted me to cave. I did." He slurped the tea without waiting for it to cool. "Harry said Helen was pregnant, and Jerry, that son-of-a-bitch—"

"David, forgive the weak."

"During the recess, he admitted he hadn't tried to get an appointment for me with Jake Colson. Fucking coward! He hasn't changed in twenty-seven years. He was paralyzed at Long Dinh, and today he whined, said he couldn't help it. Said it wasn't *he* who had the knife—"

Dave stopped. The knife. He saw Jerry's contorted face. "You were the one with the knife." *The hootch. The rattle at the door. The shadow low in the doorway. Jerry frozen, his M-16 aimed. Dave's lunge. The scream. Knife to the gut of the crouching body, the quick twist and upward rip. The expected gush of viscera. The unmistakable stench of ruptured intestines. Then the sick premonition. The body was too small. Tiny guts splattered across his boots. Dave looked down.*

"A child," Dave whispered.

He put his hands to his mouth, bit on his index finger, tasted blood. "It was a child. *A child.*"

Horst reached across the table. "You are bleeding. I will bind your wound."

Dave pulled his hand away. "No."

"Take the time to heal."

Dave snatched his suitcase.

"Leave in peace, not in torment," Horst called after him.

"No."

Horst caught his arm and pressed a paper into his bleeding hand. "The address of my friend in Maine."

Dave ran through the door into the yard. Out the gate to the alley. He forced the key into the lock of the car door and twisted it hard, jumped in, and jammed the key into the ignition. The gears ground into reverse. The car shot down the alley backwards, sideswiping the brick wall. Dave roared across the sidewalk past startled pedestrians and swung the rear of the car out onto the street into the oncoming traffic. He drove to the lot behind the library, swung into the first parking place he saw. Blood on the steering wheel. Blinking the sweat from his eyes, he sprang from the car and bolted up the hill toward the house. He'd force his way in if he had to.

As he passed the intersection at the crest of the hill, he heard laughter. Through the ripe oaks and maples, laden with heavy leaves wilting in the heat, he saw three people with a football on his front lawn. Chip bounded across the grass. Mary, dressed in slacks, lounged on the porch steps. The champagne glass in her hand had been a wedding present. A bottle on the step beside her had the characteristic orange label—Veuve Cliquot, from Dave's wine cabinet. Jeannie ran the length of the yard and lifted the ball in triumph. Chip cried, "Touchdown!" Dave could see the third player now, a tall, muscular man in blue workout shorts. Bob Scarff strutted to Jeannie with a broad grin.

Bob threw his arms around Jeannie. "Hey, cut that out!" Mary yelled. The three of them walked arm in arm to the steps. Bob disengaged from Chip and Jeannie and draped his sweating arm across Mary's shoulder while she poured champagne. They were all talking at once. Mary and Bob raised their glasses. "To victory," Bob shouted. Bob and Mary hugged.

A low cry forced its way from Dave's throat.

He lumbered down the hill to the parking lot, started the Cavalier, and drove without thinking. August sun streamed through the windows. The car was an inferno. His face, chest, and underarms dripped. The scene in the yard blazed before him. He could still see Bob, all muscle and hair, his handsome, crooked grin as he embraced Jeannie. He could hear the happy shouts and clink of the glasses. "Victory." Bob and Mary in a clinch.

He was on Route 95. The signs said he was headed for Baltimore. He opened both windows, felt the wind in his face, and switched on the fan full blast. The blood on the steering wheel stuck to his fingers. The child's blood. Tiny Asian face, dead eyes bulging in terror, blood and human slime soaking through Dave's boots.

Baltimore rose before him in the late afternoon sunshine. Only the tallest buildings escaped the gray-brown smog that filled the streets. He wanted an open place blessed with cold and darkness. A place to search. A place to heal.

He checked his pocket. The scrap of paper Horst had given him. Bloody fingerprints around the crabbed writing in black ink. He hadn't been to Maine since he taught there in the early eighties, but he could see it in his mind.

Baltimore faded behind him in a dinge of smog. "Points north" a sign said. He slammed his foot down on the accelerator.

PART TWO

December, 1996:
Winter Bay

Chapter 12

Trion Incognito

Too much of a coward to die. Next time use weights.

But the shock of nearly drowning had blockaded the unbearables in his memory. If he was going to function at all, he needed to keep them that way. He knew how to do it. Deaden his senses. Routine.

The temperature in the shed was above freezing thanks to the fire in the pot-bellied stove. Dave pulled the blanket tighter around him. The ice in his marrow had yet to thaw. The sky showed blue-black. Nate liked to get moving at sun up. Still quivering, Dave hoisted himself to his feet, refilled his cup, and edged into the utility closet. He had learned how to sit on the jerry-rigged toilet without bruising his knees on the pipes beneath the utility sink. After he flushed and tucked the blanket into the neck of his sweat shirt, he adjusted the shaving mirror and caught himself wondering if he, like Trion, had lost his reflection. What he saw jolted him. His left cheek was scarlet, as if burned. He'd left flesh and a tuft of beard on the frozen Mackinaugh River. His father's eyes were still there, but they were lined and weary. The beard had grown out nearly white. No one from Washington would recognize him. Arianna, in her typical candor, had told him the beard aged him but made him more handsome. Youth was not a commodity she admired. Boys had no staying power.

The scrape of the razor across the angry red slash made him

suck air through his clenched teeth. He washed the shaving cream and blood from his cheeks and neck and tried to trim his beard, but his hand was shaking. He tensed his body to make it stop. If he could be out and splitting logs before Nate came from his place up the hill, maybe he could avoid Nate's invitation for coffee. Nate's wife had been dead for years, and he only saw his children and teenaged grandchildren during the summer. During their coffee times, Dave was wary, silent. He didn't volunteer any information, and Nate was too polite to ask. Dave didn't follow sports, and Nate knew nothing about literature. As a result, Dave had learned a great deal about Maine weather, and Nate had learned nothing at all.

Routine. Numbness. Wednesday. His day off. Wait a minute. It was Christmas. Arianna would turn their weekly dinner into a celebration. Okay, some work on the property before that. Nate wouldn't want him to paint the sitting room or fix the steps on the largest cabin on Christmas. Not enough snow to plow, but they were short on wood. Dave would split logs. His body needed work. Pumping gas all week left him flabby. He forced his brain to focus on the work at hand. Routine.

He let the blanket slip from his shoulders and poured coffee. Arianna. There'd be the unspoken invitation. She thought Dave's celibacy unnatural.

The coffee burned his tongue. He forced it down. He owed Arianna a lot. She'd introduced him to Bill Tracy who'd hired him to pump gas at Tracy's Texaco, popular with the locals because it still offered full service. At the station Dave had met Nate and talked him into renting the shed for the winter. During the summer the hired help—kids from Mackinaugh College—stored their tools in the shed and used it to change and clean up. Nate had lent Dave a cot, a table, and three chairs. Dave even got to pay part of his rent by eight or nine hours of work each week, usually hard physical labor Nate was too old to handle himself.

Thanks to Nate, Dave was accepted in Winter Bay and North Point and Cold Harbor. People said hello, but they didn't pry. He'd found a buddy of sorts—Joe Fallon, one of Winter Bay's three middle-aged police officers. Joe did his paperwork in the mornings, then worked the streets in the cruiser from noon to eight, the same as Dave's shift. Most afternoons between four and five, Joe stopped by the gas station with coffee, something he'd been doing for more than twenty years with all of Dave's predecessors in the job. He and Dave flipped quarters for who would pay. Then Joe sat and smoked and drank coffee for fifteen minutes. If Joe showed up with donuts, he had a favor to ask—usually that Dave tow somebody out of a ditch or snow bank after closing. The city paid Tracy for towing, but Dave got nothing extra, even when he had to work overtime. He didn't mind. The work occupied his attention. It held his memories at bay.

He moved the percolator to the coolest corner of the stove, sat on the floor, and added a log. When he'd asked Arianna why she went out of her way to help him, she tossed her head, jangled her bracelets, and said, "Horst demanded it." Dave had smiled. She didn't mean "demanded." She meant "asked." Like she said, "rest at table" when she meant "sit down," and "you lack repose" when she meant he looked tired.

She was surely older than he. The Marlene Dietrich of Winter Bay, the Mae West of North Point. Not that she wasn't a respected citizen. Her Costa d'Oro coffee house and bookshop thrived. It was an attraction for painters and writers who congregated in Winter Bay, an artist colony too far north to get much tourist trade in the winter. "You're going to be open on Christmas?" he'd said. "Who wants espresso on Christmas?" She'd laughed her opera singer's laugh. "My dearest David, an artist you are not."

Everyone knew Arianna. She got caught up in every civic action, from bake sales for the marching band in Cold Harbor to the special one-time town tax to buy street ornaments for the holidays. Dave had learned early to be wary lest she lure him into collecting old clothing for Saint Christian's or painting the new railing down at the dock.

• • •

"Rest at table and drink coffee as I finish off the last customer." Arianna swept behind the coffee bar, her full-length green-and-purple skirt billowing behind her. Dave caught the scent of lime. She leaned next to the counter-top Christmas tree, her chin on her folded hands, and smiled at the young man with long hair and an earring. Dave couldn't hear their conversation over the Stravinsky on the stereo, but soon Arianna prepared another espresso.

While the man drank, Arianna made a subtle show of turning off and venting the espresso machines and putting the perishables in the refrigerator beneath the counter. The Stravinsky ended, and the man paid. As he went out, the brass temple bells on the front door clanged. They clanged again when Arianna slammed the door tight and locked it.

"I didn't tell you yet." She swabbed the counter. "Monday, I sold three copies of your *Leverkühn Tragedy*. Mackinaugh College put it on the list of recommended readings for a graduate course."

"Maybe my next quarterly royalty check from Smithson will break a hundred dollars." He grunted. "My picture's on the dust jacket."

"Not to fear. That picture has no beard. Makes you look like a twenty-year old homp."

"Homp?"

"What is your word for . . . *un uom ben fatto*—"

"Hunk?"

"Ya. Honk."

"Not honk. Hunk. Honk is the sound a goose makes. My name is on the book."

"No one will think Dave Bell, the sad gas station man, is the same as Doctor David Schliemann Bell." She switched off the lights over the counter and came to the table. "Your beautiful watch—?"

Dave shrugged. "Needs repairs. I took it off."

"And the inflamed cheek?" She took his face in her hands and forced him to look into her eyes. "What did you do?"

He pushed her hands away. "Forget it, okay?"

"I will not have the water rob me again."

"Water?"

She threw on her cape, adjusted the hood, and slipped on gloves. "Come-come. We go." She led him into the alley and locked the rear door behind them. "Tonight I ride home." He unlocked the Cavalier and closed her door after she was seated.

"Do I tell you before about my name?" she said as he drove down Main Street toward the dock.

"Yes."

"Good. I tell you again. Only more this time. My Christmas present to you. 'Arianna' is Italian for 'Ariadne,' a fine lady with many lovers. An enchantress. A seer. Maybe even a witch."

"And d'Amori?"

She laughed like a soprano singing a roulade. "My family, many centuries ago, lived in a little town called Mori, not far from Naples. The town is famous because of the saying in Italian, *'Vedi Napoli, poi Mori.'*"

At the bottom of Main Street, he turned right and drove south along the bay. "'See Naples, then die'?"

"Yes. Or, 'See Naples, then Mori.'"

Dave smiled.

"But in the fifteenth century," Arianna said, "my family move to Veneto, where Venice is, you know? The people there call us 'Da Mori'—'from Mori.' I did not like being called 'Ariadne from Mori.' When I come to the U.S., I change my name a little, to d'Amori. Now I am 'Ariadne of the Loves.'"

She gazed out her window at the snow-covered shore. "Ariadne of the Loves is an outrageous woman. Her fare is not a full feast. She lives her life à la carte." She turned toward him. "I am outrageous to make you smile, you understand?" She patted his leg. "You are too sad."

Dave said nothing.

"You want to tell me," she said, "why you are sad?"

"No."

"Good, because I do not want to be sorrowful. Christmas. We eat penne Carbonara."

Dave allowed himself a small grin. "Charcoal feathers?"

She laughed. "It mean penne—a kind of pasta—in the style of the Carbonari."

They passed the Winter Bay city limits where the long, rocky shoreline arced toward the harbor's mouth and the sea beyond. Dave turned the Cavalier left into a frozen, rutted dirt track on a spit of land barely big enough to hold Arianna's rough-hewn and sea-battered cottage. Frozen snow crunched under the wheels as he pulled up the rise before the front porch.

"You worry me living out here," he said as he opened her car door.

"The sea and I are old enemies, but it does not want me. Only the people I love." The wind whipped her cape. "It is trying to take you. Not so, my love?"

He slammed the car door behind her, and they minced up the incline to the porch added to the clapboard cottage so long ago that the supports were sagging. On either side of the door, frozen geraniums darkened the window boxes. Dave stepped carefully to avoid kicking rows of flower pots with dead plants he remembered as begonias and impatiens.

She led him in, flipped a switch to turn on the Christmas tree lights, and rubbed her hands. "You light the fire. I go change."

By the time she returned in a blue kaftan, he had the fire roaring.

"This is lovely," she said with a smile. "My end parts—hands, feet, ass—"

"Extremities?"

"—turn cold with the first frost and do not warm until the jonquils bloom."

Dave's smile disappeared.

"I have offended you?"

He shook his head.

"Very well. Lacrima Christi. In the refrigerator."

When he returned to the living room, she had turned off all but the Christmas tree lights. Tapers burned on the dining room table. She spread large plush cushions on the floor. He set their glasses on the stone hearth, settled his weight on a cushion, and offered her his hand. She lowered herself with athletic grace.

"You exercise?" he said.

"A lady must be allowed her secrets."

"We've been getting together for almost five months, but I still feel like I don't really know you."

Her fingers stroked the narrow glass. "Shall I ever know you? You tell me little."

He turned his eyes to the fire.

"Horst sent you a letter," she said, "addressed to me, of course. I must not forget to give it to you. I will mail the answer when you have written it." She raised her eyebrows. "You are too careful. Let Horst mail to you care of Nate."

"Don't want to take chances."

"Horst will tell no one."

"Someone might see the address."

"They will find you someday anyway."

"Someday."

She breathed deeply. "Horst worries about you."

"You've been telling him bad things."

"Only the truth. I, too, worry about you."

"I can take care of myself."

"So you say. But you let me amuse you. You do not sign up to take courses at Mackinaugh College for teacher certification?"

"I filled out the registration papers, three pages worth, fine print. They wanted to know my employment history, what college I'd had before." He chuckled bitterly. "The student advisor is a kid. She's a regular customer at the gas station. She called me 'Dave.' I had to call her Miss Finley. I could tell by the look on her face she couldn't believe that Dave, the grease monkey, had ever gone to college, let alone taught at one. She wants transcripts. I won't be taking classes in the spring semester."

"Ah, David."

"Don't have the money for tuition right now anyway."

"I tell you I will pay."

"No, you are too kind."

"You *will* take care of yourself. Foolish man."

"I've gotten as far as I have by depending only on myself."

"And where have you got to?"

He was startled. Her eyes were grave.

She rose. "You can help with pasta and pancetta. Come-come."

• • •

Back at the shed, Dave hung up his shirt and jeans on one of the three dowels spanning the corner next to the cot and pulled on his sweats. One dowel would have been enough. All he had was a shirt, chinos, two Texaco uniforms, and his dress clothes—three shirts and suits in dust-coated plastic. Worth keeping? Maybe. Every once in a while Horst sent him a royalty check, only a few dollars, but maybe things would change. He might be able to come up with the money to go to Mackinaugh for a teaching certificate. If he got a job, he'd need the suits. On the other hand, he'd lost so much weight that the suits would be too big. He ought to try them on. Not tonight.

He turned off the overhead and switched on the camp light by the cot. Of course, now that he'd applied to Mackinaugh, he'd have to write for his transcripts from Berkeley and Nürnberg. Risky. Someone could trace him. Once he had given his address to the universities—Horst's letter. He'd forgotten. He fished it from the breast pocket of his shirt.

My Dearest David,

Arianna writes me that you are morose. I would love to come and see you in the Spring, but I doubt this old body could make the trip. Besides, I would not risk betraying your hiding place.

Are you working? I do not mean selling gasoline and repairing cabins. Are you working with your mind? *Leverkühn* is your masterpiece. Once again, I urge you to translate it into German.

Finally, you have been searching long enough. I beseech you to find yourself, return to Washington, clear your name, and resume your career. I know that lack of money is a major difficulty, but I would be glad to help. If you were able to find work that uses your real talents and especially if you published *Leverkühn* in German, I am persuaded you could find enough money to cover the legal fees.

But it is not for me to pester you, my friend. I will remain faithful to you, no matter how you decide.

Ever,
Horst

Dave pulled *Leverkühn* from its spot on the shelf next to the Rumi and the Dante. He flipped open the cover. There, in purple ink, Arianna had written in her flowing script: "17 September. Happy Birthday to my dear David. Love, Arianna d'Amori." At the bottom of the page, she had added, "Translation soon, *mio caro?*"

These two old coots were conspiring. He hadn't made the connection. Why wouldn't people leave him alone? He turned to the first chapter.

"Adrian Leverkühn," he read, "is, before all else, like Thomas Mann who created him, a man with a soul."

How he'd labored over those words. Ungainly sentence. He'd learned since then, but he had lost passion, the passion that made *Leverkühn* so successful. His soul had soared with excitement as he wrote. His body had been strong, able to bear the strain of writing at night and teaching during the day. Chip and Jeannie had been little. He and Mary . . . lovers. Enchanted with the children, in love with each other.

He put the book aside, lay on the cot, and switched off the light. Illusion. She was pretending.

The translation? Not yet. He'd have to do it longhand. No computer. Shit, he couldn't even afford a telephone.

Sadness pushed in from all sides. He resorted to reciting Dante in his mind, passages he'd had to memorize as an undergraduate. Their soft undulations would carry him off to sleep. The dream and Helen and Inge and the child awaited him. *Nel mezzo del cammin di nostra vita . . . Tanto è amara, che poco è più morte . . .* "In the middle of our life's journey . . . The going is almost as bitter as death . . ."

• • •

In the days after Christmas, Dave's face healed, and the mercury dropped below zero. Several times a night, the cold woke him. Shivering, he cranked up the fire. He invested in a Casio watch and heavier gloves, bought at the Thrifty Mart's "Blizzard Special." On work days, he wore his parka over his Texaco uniform. Under it were his sweat clothes. Under that, long underwear. Nate told Dave it was too cold to work outside, but Dave, wanting to stay busy, worked alone. Routine.

New Year's Day dawned dull and dark. Snow was forecast. Dave delayed his outdoor work until ten, hoping the temperature would rise. It didn't. He poured the coffee into a thermos and checked the stove. Bundled in his parka, gloves, ear muffs, and baseball cap, he headed up the hill to the woodpile. After fifteen minutes of log splitting, he stopped, pulled his bandana from his hip pocket, and wiped his forehead.

As he picked up the wedges and sledge hammer, a figure came through the trees at the crest of the hill and edged down the snow-covered gravel road. Someone for Nate. Odd that he was on foot. Dave held the wedge on the end of a log and poised the hammer.

"Excuse me, sir."

Dave looked up.

"I am seeking Doctor David Bell," the man said in soft German-accented English. "You can tell which is his place, yes?"

The man wore an overcoat and a stocking cap. His face looked very young. He reminded Dave of Chip in his first suit.

Dave scratched his head. "I'm Dave Bell, sonny," he said in his best Maine accent, "but I sure as hell ain't no doctor."

The young man's gaze moved from Dave's forehead to his eyes, nose, mouth, beard. "We can talk, yes?"

"Who are you?"

"My name is Hans Lehmann." He lowered his eyes, as if shamed.

Dave studied him. Unlined face. Looked like it had never felt the pull of a razor. Blond arched eyebrows. Eyes brilliant blue in the gray light. Troubling eyes. A kid, a youngster. An academic groupie?

Dave waved the hammer. "Got work to do."

The young man raised his head. His eyes were moist. "Please, sir. It is very cold." He blushed and looked away. "We could talk inside, yes?"

Dave threw aside the hammer. "Okay. Come on."

Side by side they plodded down the gravel road to the shed. "Go on in." Dave followed him. "Coffee?"

"Thank you."

Dave added a log to the fire and poured two cups from the thermos. Hans took off his coat and hat. The kid was wearing a suit and tie. He was an inch or two shorter than Dave but over six feet. Blond. Wiry. His eyes—something startling about his eyes.

"Sit down." Dave pointed to the table with his elbow and pushed a cup toward him. "All right. You found me. How?"

"When I called your office, they told me you had resigned. Your wife didn't know where you were. My fellowship at Christ House ended, and I returned to Stuttgart. I wrote to everyone who knew you." He folded his hands on the table. "I recalled that Brenz-Verlag in Wiesbaden published your first book. The only address they had for you was a bookstore in Takoma Park, but they had two canceled royalty checks cashed at the Fleet Bank in Winter Bay, Maine."

"Why did Brenz-Verlag tell you where the checks were cashed?"

Hans gazed at Dave's face. "You have a beard."

"Who are you?" Dave said. "Why would Brenz-Verlag—"

"I am Hans Lehmann, named for my grandfather, Johann Lehmann."

"Doctor Johann Lehmann at the University of Nürnberg? He was my teacher many years ago."

"You remember his daughter, Inge?"

Dave waited, wary.

"She was my mother." Hans put his hands flat on the table. "And you are my father."

Dave's heart bolted.

Hans nodded slowly without taking his eyes from Dave's face. "You and my mother lived together. You took her to an abortionist. She did not submit to his surgery. She stayed in his office some hours. You were waiting. Then you left for the U.S. in December, 1975. I am born in August 1976." Hans handed him a photo from his breast pocket. "My mother and me at Christmas, 1976."

Dave put on his glasses. The woman was Inge. No question. She held a blond infant on her lap and smiled at the camera. Dave turned the photo over. The back bore the imprint, "Krüger, Photohändler, 27-12-76."

"This doesn't prove anything," Dave said in a shaking voice.

Hans gave him a folded paper. He opened it. A birth certificate for Johann David Lehmann, child of Inge Lehmann and David S. Bell, dated 3 August 1976.

Hans held out his right hand, palm down.

On the fourth finger was a gold ring set with a square blue stone. Around the stone were the words, "University of California." On one side of the ring were the letters, "BS." On the other, "1968."

Hans slipped off the ring. "Inside is etched 'David S. Bell.'"

Dave held the ring to the light. "Where did you get this?"

"You told my mother you would be getting another when you were awarded your PhD. The one you now wear?"

Dave sat on the cot. The river was white, the bay beyond it charcoal, the sea almost black, the sky colorless. It would snow again.

"I have read everything you have written," Hans said. "In German and English. Your books, your articles. My mother told me about you, showed me pictures. She had a grocery list you wrote. A pair of socks. A notebook."

Silence.

"You are angry," Hans said.

Dave turned to the window. A dull white boat skimmed

across the bay, leaving behind a gray wake. Flakes were falling, scattered and tormented. "Why didn't Inge write?"

"She was sure you never wanted to see her again. She resumed her studies. Then, she worried about me growing up without a father and telephoned you in San Francisco, where you were teaching. Your wife, Mary, answered. Before my mother died—"

Dave caught his breath.

"Lung cancer," Hans said. "She told me to search for you, sir. I decided I would find you before I finish my studies." Hans looked at the floor. "She said you were impetuous and quick to anger."

"I'm not angry, Hans."

Hans raised his head. His lips parted in a timid smile. "I am very glad."

Dave stood. "Where are you staying?"

"I book a room at the Comfort Inn. I come by taxi."

Dave nodded. "We'd better get your stuff. It might snow. We may have trouble driving into town if we wait too long."

Hans smiled again. His eyes were sparkling. "I like you with a beard," he said.

• • •

"Arianna—"

"Ah, my David, you are early."

"Arianna, I've brought someone with me."

Her eyes moved to Hans by the shop door.

"His name's Hans Lehmann," Dave said. "Showed up this morning."

Arianna's face registered alarm. "Who is he?'

Dave hesitated. "My son."

Her eyes swung to his face. "This is Chip?"

"No. Hans."

"I did not know—"

"Neither did I."

A smile spread across her face. She sailed from behind the counter to the door, pressed both of Hans' hands, and kissed his cheek. "You are Hans?"

Hans grinned and blushed.

She took Dave's arm. "You both rest at table. I bring you *caffè latte*. You like Chinese food, yes? Then we go to the Golden Pavilion for dim sum. It is New Year's."

She swirled away.

"She is a friend?" Hans said.

"My only friend other than Horst—I'll tell you about him— and a policeman named Joe Fallon. You'll meet him. Remember to ask Arianna about her name."

Arianna was back with a tray. She served Dave and Hans and placed a chocolate tort before Hans. "Too thin. Like your father. Eat." She was off again, to the front of the shop.

Dave grinned at Hans and shrugged.

Hans laughed. First time Dave had seen him laugh.

"Nearly nine o'clock," Arianna called. "I close a little early." She snatched their cups and plate and carried them behind the counter. She turned off the machines and opened their steam valves, flipped off the lights, and tossed her cape about her shoulders. "Come-come." She led them to the front of the shop. "We walk. Not far."

Up the hill away from the bay through the piercing cold to the corner, two blocks to Elm. At the neoned entrance to the Golden Pavilion, she took them by the hand and marched through the double glass doors. As she burst into the dining room, the small Christmas tree on the cashier's desk swayed from the impact. The half a dozen diners halted their conversations. "Mr. Sung," she said to the startled maitre d', "happy New Year." She embraced him and swept one arm toward Dave and Hans. "My friends. You give us a good table, yes?" The flustered Mr. Sung motioned toward a round table in the middle of the room. "Three glasses of white wine," Arianna said to Mr. Sung as they seated themselves, "hot and sour soup, three orders of my usual dim sum, mu shih pork and kung pao chicken." Mr. Sung scooted away. "The wine—" Arianna wrinkled her nose and waved her hand from side to side, palm down. "But it is a Chinese restaurant." She turned to Hans. "How handsome you are! You are German, no? Are you long in the states?"

"I only arrive in New York yesterday," Hans said, "then I mount a bus."

Dave repressed a grin. "He got here this morning."

"Where you are staying?" Arianna asked Hans.

Hans pointed at Dave. "With him."

Arianna laughed her musical laugh. "You are . . . cute."

Hans blushed and looked at Dave.

Arianna took Hans' hand in hers. "I am sorry. I am embarrassing you. You ride all night to get here after a flight from Germany?" Hans nodded blankly. "David, I hope you allowed him repose in the afternoon."

"We talked all day," Dave said. "I never thought—"

"I am not tired," Hans said. "I sleep on the bus."

Their wine arrived. Arianna lifted her glass. "I drink to Hans and David!"

"And to Arianna," Dave said.

They touched glasses and sipped.

Hans pushed back his chair. "You would allow me to excuse

. . . I mean . . . you would excuse to allow me—"

"Of course," Arianna said. She nodded toward the rest rooms. Hans moved away.

Arianna turned to Dave, her face grave. "He is from your student time in Nürnberg?"

Dave nodded.

"You have never before seen him?" she said. "You are happy?"

Dave hadn't considered the question before. "Yes."

"He is a beautiful child. His eyes! They are exactly your eyes. You must be proud."

Proud? Dave cocked his head. "Yes."

"You talk in German or English?"

Dave smiled. "We started in English and gradually drifted into German."

"You call him 'son'?"

"I call him 'Hans.'"

"He calls you 'father'?"

"He calls me 'sir.'"

"You want him to call you 'father'?"

Dave cleared his throat. "Yes."

Arianna took his hand. "David, when one needs a teacher, a teacher appears."

"He is to teach me?"

Hans returned to the table as the soup arrived.

"You are a student?" Arianna said to him as soon as he was seated.

"Theology. At the Lutheran Seminary in Stuttgart."

"How long will you stay in the U.S.?"

"I don't know. My visa is valid through three months."

"Then," Arianna said with a smile, "I shall be able to know

you."

Over dim sum, Hans asked Arianna about her name. She soon had him giggling. Dave smiled to himself. Hans *was* cute. Especially when he laughed. By the time the pork and chicken arrived, Hans' weariness was obvious. Arianna asked Mr. Sung to pack the left-over food.

"We haven't paid," Dave said.

"It is done. Hans is very tired."

They walked to the bookshop, and Dave drove Arianna home. Then he turned the car north en route to the shed. Before they passed the outskirts of Winter Bay, Hans was asleep. Dave pulled over long enough to take the bag of Chinese food from Hans' lap and put it on the floor. He retrieved a tattered blanket from the back seat and spread it over the boy. At last, he put the car in gear and eased away from the shoulder. He drove more gently than usual.

Chapter 13

The Gator

Awake at five again. I shamble to the hall closet and put my overcoat on over my sweats, crank open the living room window, and look down six stories to the leafless trees in the park across the street from our apartment. Sligo Creek is frozen. Bare roots press through muddy snow along the bank. I thought the house was cold. This place is Siberia. I close the window and start coffee. No need to get Chip up—it's New Year's Day—but I'll have to waken him in time for him to get to work at eleven. He says he can carry more than twelve credit hours next semester and still work twenty hours a week. I don't tell him I'm doing more than twenty hours as a teacher of remedial English at Montgomery College, in addition to my regular job at Lincoln. We're making it. Barely.

Maybe Jeannie will sleep in. I need some respite from the sniping one minute and stony silence the next. I won't answer the telephone in case it's Bob badgering me for the rest of his fee. I explained to him that I cashed in the life insurance policy and have nothing left in savings. The bastard won't even help me look for Dave—unless I pay him. He told me to ask the DMV to trace Dave's car license and report his absence to the police. I agreed to an arrest warrant for non-payment of alimony and child support. Not because I want him in jail—I want to know where he is. I talked to the German man, Horst. He knows nothing, he says. I don't believe him.

I pour myself coffee and flop down at the kitchen table. That beautiful maple piece we had in the dining room had to go—no room in the apartment. That reminds me. I haven't gotten a rent check from the Daltons. They're using the same late excuse I am, the holiday. At least they're responsible and honest and take good care of the house. I probably should consider their offer to buy. Not until I know what happened to Dave.

As far as I know, the last person to see him alive was George Eckland. George called me for a statement, said he'd seen Dave after the hearing. A week after that, I called George, hoping I could get some clue as to where Dave had disappeared to. The kids at the *Log* office said George had dropped out of school. They didn't know where I could reach him. I didn't believe them, but within a few weeks all his grades were being reported as incomplete. At the end of the semester, I entered E's in all his academic records.

The Cavalier has disappeared, too. If Dave chose Helen's way out, they might never find him or his car. Maybe that's what he did. He'd lost everything, his career, his family, his good name.

If I keep this up, I'm going to get sick again. The horror I can't get past is that I did this to us.

I get to my feet and tiptoe to the bedroom. I take clothes from the closet. I don't want to waken Jeannie. In her most recent crying fit, she told me she hated sharing a bedroom with me. She keeps saying I did something to make it happen. She's completely on his side now. She beatifies him, keeps his picture on her side of the dresser, accuses me of knowing where he is, says she wants to go live with him.

As furious as I am, I miss him. I yearn to be held. As long as we were close, his desire fulfilled me, even if I felt nothing myself. For twenty years . . .

"Mom?" Jeannie's sleepy voice. "What's wrong? Are you crying?"

"Nothing. Sorry. I was trying not to waken you."

"Why're you standing there?"

I clasp my clothes to my breast and hurry to the bathroom.

• • •

When I got the call from the D.C. police, it was instant recall of Helen's death. When the knock on the door comes, I jump. Two of them, both black, both in suits. They decline coffee and sit side by side on the sofa.

"Mrs. Bell," the taller one begins, "do you know this man?"

He slides a glossy black-and-white photograph from a manila envelope . A smiling young man in a plain polo shirt with an Izod alligator logo.

"Harry Sereni," I say.

The policeman lays the photo on the coffee table between us where it can watch me while we talk. "Do you know if he ever went by the name of Aroldo?"

"That's his given name, according to the school records."

"Did you know his sister, Elena?"

I shudder. "She went by Helen. Died in a freak auto accident. Might have been suicide." I sit back. "Is that why you're here? Do you think *he*—"

"When did you last see him?"

"At my divorce last August. The only time I ever saw him. My lawyer called him as a witness."

"Why was that, Mrs. Bell?"

I go through the grisly tale once again.

The shorter one says. "How can we contact Doctor Bell?"

"I don't know where he is."

"Who else knows Mr. Sereni?"

I pause and think. "The German faculty at Lincoln College. All the professors know him."

"Anyone else?"

I search my memory. "Yes. At least I think so. George Eckland, a student reporter for the *Lincoln Log*."

"Do you know how Mr. Eckland and Mr. Sereni knew each other?"

"I don't know for a fact, but I suspect that Harry was a primary source for the reporting George did on the scandal involving my husband. Why are you investigating Harry Sereni? His sister's death?"

"Do you know Mr. Sereni's current address?" the taller one says.

"He was living in New York at the time of the divorce."

The front door bangs open and Chip bumbles in. He puts down his knapsack and looks at the two black men.

"My son, Chip," I say. "These gentlemen are from the D.C. police, Chip. Would you mind waiting in the kitchen until we're through?"

He's fixed his eyes on the photo of Harry. "You guys looking for Harry Sereni?"

"Chip, please," I say. "You're interrupting."

"You know Mr. Sereni?" the short one says.

"I only met him once, at the divorce. Is he in trouble with the law?"

I'm astonished that Chip is being so rude.

"Chip, *please*," I say.

"Sorry." He picks up his bag and lumbers off. The tall policeman puts the photo in his briefcase. "Mrs. Bell, how much money did Mr. Sereni receive from his sister's insurance policy?"

"I didn't know she was insured."

"By Lincoln College. I understand all employees have the option of life insurance. As the college Director of Administration, you control access to the insurance records, right?"

I'd never thought of that. "Let me check the files. I'll call you."

He gives me his card. With polite nods and thanks, they're gone.

Chip's at the kitchen table, frowning at the sandwich he's made himself.

"That was really rude of you," I say.

"Sorry. As soon as I saw that picture, everything kind of clicked into place."

I sit across from him and wait.

"It was that Izod symbol on his shirt," he says. "When I saw him at the divorce, I knew I'd seen him somewhere, but not in a suit and tie. One time I took Mark and Phil to the gym on campus. He passed us walking the other way. They knew him. They told me he's a candyman, sells pot and ecstasy and cocaine and stuff. They called him 'The Gator' because he always wears shirts like that. They told me the other day they haven't seen him since last summer."

"He moved to New York," I say. "Probably living it up on Helen's insurance money."

"You won't hear me crying over him," Chip says. "The guys say that some student at Lincoln OD'ed on stuff The Gator gave him. Nearly died."

"Who?"

Chip shrugs. "A journalism major, they said. George something. Dropped out of school, went into rehab. Understand he was permanently damaged. Can't talk or anything. He was a reporter for the *Log*."

I lean forward, short of breath. "George Eckland?"

"Isn't that the guy that wrote those stories about Dad?"

I nod.

"Jesus." Chip shakes his head. "I never made the connection."

I look at my hand. It still holds the card the policemen gave me. It has a cell number on it.

"Chip," I say with lead in my voice, "I'm going to call those policemen. I want you to tell them everything you told me."

He twitches. "Okay."

Harry. Sometimes vengeance is so easy. Medea was an amateur.

Chapter 14

Der Bastard von Nürnberg

At the shed door beneath the naked bulb, Dave knocked the snow from his boots. Nate had promised a warm February. Warm*er*, all right, but still in the teens as soon as the sun went down. When Dave opened the door, warm air caressed his face. Brahms Fourth on the radio, novels and dictionaries spread on one side of the table, silverware and tumblers and the gallon bottle of red wine on the other. The aroma of cooking meat, the scent of burning wood and hot cast iron.

"You are late," Hans said from the stove.

"Had to tow a guy out of a ditch." Dave dropped a white-and-pink paper bag on the table. "I brought donuts." He hung up his parka. "Your hair's getting long."

Hans wiped his hand on his jeans. His tee-shirt was speckled with grease. "I let it grow, you know, like you. It is okay?"

"Sure."

"Tonight, we have a Bavarian meal. Sausage and potatoes." Hans pushed the books to the far end of the table and poured wine. "Come eat." He took two plates from the utility closet and spooned food from the stove, switched off the radio, and sat next to Dave. "When we finish, I want to ask you about my reading."

"What has Arianna got you on now?"

"*Catcher in the Rye.* And *Clockwork Orange.*"

Dave laughed. "Just like her."

"*Vater*, if she can read books like these, why isn't her English better?"

"Old world charm."

"She smells like lime. She is very sexy."

Dave eyed him. "Has she ever—"

"She says that I am a boy. She has other men."

"She told you that?"

"No. I notice things."

Dave nodded. "Does that upset you?"

"It is not my place to judge her."

"She's a good woman."

"She is very fond of you, *Vater*. She says when you leave, it will break her heart."

Dave put down his fork. "One day soon, they'll find me, Hans. There are too many clues—my royalty checks, my Maine driver's licence, the car registration. Month after next, I'll have to file income tax." He picked up his fork and cut a bite of sausage. "When they find me, they'll put me in jail."

Hans tasted his wine. "Arianna says you should face your past and overcome it."

"Arianna and Horst are well-meaning meddlers."

"She says you should teach and translate your book."

"You're spending too much time with Arianna."

"I have learned much from her."

"Too much," Dave said, squelching his irritation.

"You think she is wrong?"

"She should mind her own business. The hole I dug myself into is very deep."

"Mr. Sung says a journey of a thousand miles begins with the first step."

Dave flared. "You guys ganging up on me or what?"

Hans looked at his plate. "I want you to have a better life."

"I don't like it when people fuck with me."

Hans blanched. "I'm sorry."

Dave growled. "Let's make some coffee and see if I can answer your reading questions."

After coffee, while Hans read at the table, Dave washed dishes in the utility sink and left them to dry on the floor close to the stove.

Hans looked up from his book. "I don't have much time left on my visa."

"Almost two months."

"No one in the states knows where I am. Maybe I could—"

"No," Dave said. "One fugitive in the family is enough."

"I will come again."

"Maybe I'll come and see you."

"No, *Vater*, you must stay here and work to clear your name."

"Stop messing with me. I told you."

Hans averted his eyes.

"Look," Dave said more softly, "I've had to depend on myself since I was six. Depending on someone else would be hell for me."

"My mother was right. You are impetuous and quick to anger."

Dave allowed himself a frustrated huff. He looked at the grime permanently under his nails. "I am not the father you deserve, Hans. A bum living in a shack."

"A good man doing the best he can."

Dave put on his parka. "Need to get more wood in."

When the wood box was full, Dave looked over Hans' shoulder. "What are you reading?"

"'He is despiséd and rejected of men,'" Hans read. "'A man

of sorrows and acquainted with grief.'"

"The Bible?"

"King James Version. Arianna says it is the most beautiful of all English writing."

Dave grunted. "'Acquainted with grief.' Sounds like us. 'Despiséd and rejected.'"

"All people have not despised and rejected us."

"Most have. Starting with my father. I always promised myself I'd never let my kids down. Look at me. I'm just like him, a real bastard."

"I am a bastard," Hans said. "I do not despise and reject you." Hans lowered his eyes. "When I was little, I hated everyone. I was a pariah and determined to exact vengeance on the world. Then my mother got sick. It was the beginning of the cancer that finally killed her. She told me she had done it to herself by smoking. 'In the end,' she said, 'our fate is what we do to ourselves.' Lying in bed, she read to me Goethe, Shakespeare, the plays of Aristophanes. Everything referred to the Greeks. As soon as I could, I read them myself—Homer, Aeschylus, Sophocles, Euripides. The stories were wonderful, but the Greeks thought we must bear the consequences of our actions, even if we don't understand what we do. Oedipus had to pay for his crimes, even though he didn't know he had murdered his father and married his mother. Trion was punished, even though he didn't know that he had disemboweled his own son."

"Profoundly unfair."

Hans smiled. "The Bible does not say that life is fair. The Greeks did not say so. What is fair about my being born a bastard? What is fair about my growing up an outcast? I, too, was despiséd and rejected. I decided to choose my own fate and be the best man I could be with what God gave me to work with."

"At least you fought back."

"I chose loving, not fighting," Hans said. "Whom should we fight? People we have sinned against? Do we blame them for our sins? People who have sinned against us? They, too, must live with what they have done. God, who gave us what we have? Ourselves? Hating and hurting oneself does not even the score."

Dave huffed. "You've been in the seminary too long. Sounds like you believe you should surrender to fate."

"Is that what you have done?"

Dave caught his breath.

"One must not surrender," Hans said, "but perhaps one needs to decide where and how to fight evil."

Dave glared at him. "Are you counseling me?"

"No, my father. I dare not counsel you."

"And why do you insist on calling me 'my father'? You want to remind me of my sins?"

"No. I wait and I hope."

"For what?"

Hans bit his lip. "For you to call me 'my son.'"

Dave's mouth opened. Hans reddened.

Dave stood. "My son."

Hans lifted his head. His eyes watered.

Dave took him in his arms. "My son."

• • •

The next day, Hans dropped Dave at the Texaco and took the car. By four-thirty, light had vanished from the sky. Dave lit the oil heater in the car bay, drained the oil from the '87 Sentra, and lowered the hydraulic lift. He had finished replacing the oil filter when the customer bell rang and headlights swept through the bay. A police cruiser labeled "WHPD" parked in back. Joe Fallon let himself into the bay through the inset entrance in the large glass garage door.

"Hey, mate. Looks like you're workin' hard. Or are you hardly workin'?"

Dave checked the dipstick and walked to the sink to wash his hands. "Go on in and get warm." He followed Joe into the office, still drying his hands.

"Clean enough to flip?" Joe pulled out a quarter.

"Be prepared to pay, officer," Dave said.

They used their thumbs to catapult coins in the air at the same moment, caught them, and slapped them on their wrists.

"Call it," Joe said.

"Heads."

Joe frowned. "Tails." He pulled up a chair next to the stove and lit a cigarette. "That kid I saw here the other afternoon. I seen him here before. Friend of yours?"

"My son."

Joe reared and tilted his head. "Didn't know you had kids. He had a foreign accent, sounded like."

"Grew up in Germany."

"Sorry," Joe said. "Wasn't being nosy."

Dave slurped his coffee.

"You know," Joe said, "you belong in Maine. You're tight-lipped as us natives."

"I wouldn't call you tight-lipped, Joe."

"Naw. Too ornery. Your kid, huh? How about that?" He lifted the crinkled cardboard cup to his lips and fixed his gaze on the shopping center across the street. "Carrie and me always wanted kids." He puffed on his cigarette. "We tried. Even went to the doctor. Too late now, of course." He held his cigarette before his face and gazed into space. "Carrie would of been a good mother, you know? And I'd have given anything—" His voice faded. Then his face brightened. "Say, is he working? If he's looking for a job—"

"He's just visiting."

Joe nodded, then put out his cigarette. "Guess I'd better get back to making the world safe for democracy. Let me know if the kid needs anything. What'd you say his name was?"

"Hans."

"Like in Hans Brinker, the Silver Skates guy?"

"Yep."

Joe got to his feet. "Well, listen, Dave, don't do nothin' I wouldn't do. Maybe I'll see you tomorrow."

He clapped Dave on the back and left the office by the front door.

At eight o'clock, while Dave was moving the tow truck into the darkened bay for the night, Hans drove up in the Cavalier.

"You want help?" Hans called.

Dave shook his head, jammed the folding glass door into its socket, and checked it. "Only be a minute." In the darkened bay, he washed up and changed. After he locked the front door, he slid into the Cavalier. He craned his neck to the rear seat. "Jesus. What all did you buy?"

"Only what you listed," Hans said, "and sausage, potatoes, salt pork, and black beans."

"You like salt pork?"

"My mother used to cook it with black beans. She said you taught her. An Irish dish from your father. Cheap and nourishing. You forget. I am one quarter Irish. Not tonight. The beans must cook a long time."

Dave grinned. "You are a good *Hausfrau, mein Sohn.* You'll

make some woman very happy."

Hans shrugged. "Maybe I never marry. I don't know what to do around girls. I always act very stupid. Went to private boys' schools. And no girls at the seminary."

Dave turned toward the windshield. "I'm not one to advise you."

"Women like you. Arianna says so."

"Lot of good it does me."

"But you could tell me how to act around girls."

"That's only the first step."

A mischievous grin lit Hans' face. "Mr. Sung says a journey of a thousand miles begins with the first step."

When they arrived at the shed, Dave started dinner while Hans put away the groceries and carried in firewood. After the dishes were done, they settled on the floor next to the stove.

"Arianna sent you the new *German Literature Review*." Hans handed Dave his glasses and the magazine. "She thought you would want to see it right away,"

The magazine was unusually bulky. The front cover listed the authors and the titles of the articles. Gérard Devereaux's "Thomas Mann's *Trion*: A Study in Lovelessness" led the list. Next came "Thomas Mann: *Trion* (German text)" and "Thomas Mann: *Trion* (translation by Gérard Devereaux)."

Dave looked at Hans. "Have you read this?"

"You read. I pour coffee."

First Dave scanned Jerry's translation. *Verstehen* was rendered as "knowing." He turned to the article. There, in language far more pompous than Dave ever would have allowed himself, was the speculation about the dating of the story, the references to Mann's later work, the link to the theme of *Doktor Faustus*. Dave let the pages fall closed.

"*Trion* was the novella you found?" Hans said. "You have copies of your work?"

Dave shrugged. "It's all in the past. A battle lost."

"And no one to help you or defend you."

"Defend me? Come on."

"Do not laugh at me, *Vater*. When I was a boy, I defended you. My schoolmates said you were a drunkard and a thief and that I'd never see you. They called me *der Bastard von Nürnberg*. I told them, watch out, one day you would be back. You were strong and big, a famous scholar and writer. My mother forbade me to tell who you were, so I gave no name, but my schoolmates and I fought. I never let them say bad things about my father."

Dave flinched. "Maybe you should be ashamed of me."

"Do not be sad," Hans said. "After you have translated *Leverkühn—*"

Dave bared his teeth.

Hans nodded. "The night is late. We must rest."

• • •

Dave, Jerry, and the woman hurry along a trail under the jungle canopy. The woman whispers, "Killer!" Dave looks at her. Inge. "Killer." Now he's leaving the airport. Crowds on both sides, jeering. "Baby killer!" someone calls at him. Inge is in the crowd screaming at him. "Ungeheuer!" She spits on him. He covers his face with his hands. When he takes them away, the crowd is gone, but he can still hear them screaming. He's with Jerry in the hootch with the dirt floor. Someone is jiggling the latch trying to get in. He tries to yell at Jerry to fire, but he can't. He grasps his knife. The door swings open. He lunges. Knife up into the gut, the twist and upward rip. The scream. He looks down. The little head, eyes wide in terror, mouth forced open, blood, intestines.

Dave leapt to his feet, then crouched, panting. Sweat dripped from his face. He looked at his hands. In the dark he couldn't see the blood. The knife was gone. Something came at him in the dark. He edged sideways, crablike, ready to spring.

"*Vater,*" a voice said. The light went on. Hans hurried toward him in pajamas. Eyes Dave knew from somewhere stared down at him in horror.

"You're alive," Dave whispered.

"*Vater!*" Hans knelt beside him.

"Don't touch me."

Hans put a blanket around Dave's shoulders. "You dreamed again?"

Dave pulled away, but Hans held fast. He got Dave to his feet and sat him on his cot. Dave folded his arms on his knees and rested his forehead on his wrists.

"Here," Hans said. "Drink."

Dave took the glass and drank. Water. Hans sat beside him on the cot. Dave turned away his face, ashamed.

Hans put his arm around Dave. "Tell me. Vietnam?"

Dave nodded.

"Tell me."

"No."

"When I come to the U.S. to find you," Hans said, "I do not know what kind of man you are. I am not disappointed. My father is a fine man."

Dave put his face in his hands.

"And I learn," Hans said, "that even a fine man suffers sometimes. And I think, 'I know how suffering is.' I can understand my father. And maybe God will allow me to help him. Then I learn a fine man will not allow a boy to help him."

"Drop it."

"The day I come here, I tell you about my childhood in Nürnberg, growing up alone, a bastard. And you tell me about your work, your trouble, your divorce, but not Vietnam."

"I can't."

Hans' face was sad. "You think I am ashamed if I know."

"Leave me alone."

Hans touched Dave's arm. "I know what you are suffering. In German it is *posttraumatische Belastungsstörung.* Post-traumatic stress disorder. Combat trauma. Tell me what happened. You hurt someone. You hurt yourself."

Dave squeezed his eyes shut and shuddered. "I killed someone. I didn't mean to. We were near Long Dinh. Someone was trying to get in. I attacked. Then I looked." Dave's eyes blurred. "I killed a child." He saw the face, the frozen eyes, the blood, the innards at his feet. He wiped his face on his sleeve and felt Hans' hand on his shoulder. Hans pressed a wad of tissue into his hands. He mopped his face. "I tried to have you aborted. I tried to kill you."

"I am alive," Hans said.

"That doesn't matter, don't you see? I *did* it." His voice broke. "I didn't even know you survived. Shit. Go away, Hans. Go home to Germany."

"The sin can be forgiven," Hans said.

"Why don't you pack?"

"A man has to repair the damage if he can. Then he can live with what he has done."

Dave stepped to Hans' cot and dragged out the suitcase. "You can't repair the murder of a child."

"You can find forgiveness."

Dave snatched clothes from the shelf, opened the suitcase, and threw them in.

"Only despair of forgiveness is unforgivable," Hans said.

"I can't find forgiveness for what I am."

"*Vater*, go to Long Dinh. Ask the people to forgive you."

"I can't."

Hans got to his feet, emptied the suitcase, put it away, and sat next to Dave. "I will go to Long Dinh with you."

"*No.* This is crazy. I don't have enough money to go to Cold Harbor."

"You will, after *Leverkühn* is published in Europe, after you clear your name."

Dave straightened. His brain wouldn't function.

"Dawn comes soon," he heard Hans say. "You fix breakfast while I dress?"

Dave wiped his face with his hands. "Yes."

• • •

When they arrived at Costa d'Oro at 8:30 Wednesday night, Arianna rushed forward and kissed them. "You are come, you are come. I need two strong men." She pulled them to her office at the rear of the shop. "My old equipment—" She wrinkled her nose. "I buy a new computer and printer. I am up-to-date once again."

Dave tried to hide his grin.

"But I cannot *lift* the machines!" she cried. "And I do not know to start them, you understand?"

Beside the desk were six cardboard boxes, four of them open. Packing material, cables, wires, and plugs littered the floor.

"I know nothing of this," she said, false despair ringing in her voice. "You take out the old ones, install the new ones, and help me copy from the old to the new, yes?"

"Poor, helpless thing," Dave said. "How about if you make

us some sandwiches and coffee? Hans and I will see what we can do with the computers."

"We eat first, then work," Arianna said. "*Ecco.*" She whisked a red cloth cover from the desktop. "Better than sandwiches." On the desk were three plates with chicken and salad, three pieces of chocolate cake, and three glasses of red wine. "Come-come. We eat."

Dave sat in the desk chair, Hans in the chair beside the desk, and Arianna on the step-stool from behind the coffee bar.

"New letters from Horst," Arianna said between bites. "He tell me some man has been to his shop to ask about you."

The front door opened with the resounding clatter of brass bells against plate glass. Arianna dabbed at her mouth with her napkin. "Customer." She hurried off.

"How long would it take you to translate *Leverkühn*?" Hans said.

"A month, maybe, if I could work full-time. I wrote the first draft in German."

"I told Arianna so. You would perhaps let me help?"

Dave sagged. "Leave me alone, okay? Look, *mein Sohn*, the whole idea is impractical. I'd need a computer, dictionaries, copies of Mann's *Doktor Faustus* in English and German."

Arianna turned off most of the lights in the shop. "Finish quickly. Much work to do."

By ten o'clock they had the new computer up and running. By ten-thirty they had transferred all of Arianna's files from the old computer to the new hard disk. Arianna sat at the desk like a frightened child. "It is the same like my old one?"

"Just the same," Dave said. "You should get more up-to-date software."

She moved the mouse and clicked. The accounting

program appeared. "Yes, I see. Good." She closed the program and switched off the machine. "Now we must move the old computer and printer to your car. You parked on the street?"

Hans stooped and lifted a carton. Dave looked from Hans to Arianna.

"My car?"

"I have no room to store my old machines. I lend them to you. You can perhaps find a way to use them, yes?"

Hans carried the carton toward the door. "Bring the printer, please, *Vater*."

"I have more bundles," Arianna said. "Some surplus things, you know?"

"Arianna—"

"Quick-quick. It is late, and I am tired."

Dave swallowed. "Arianna, I don't like interference."

"Yes, yes," Arianna said, her voice edged with irritation, "you have got as far as you have by depending only on yourself. *Dio m'aiuta!*" She looked heavenward and wrung her hands. "God protect me from male pride. Very well, then. *Store* the computer. Give the printer to Nate or Tracy or Mrs. Reed. Can you find within that macho heart the humility to do me one small favor and take them?"

With a grunt intended to sound disgusted, Dave carried the printer to the car.

They drove Arianna home, and Dave headed north along the bay.

After they had passed through Winter Bay, Dave broke the silence. "What's in the third box?"

Hans gave him a quick look. "Printer toner cartridges. Books. Floppies—"

"What books?"

"Mann's *Faustus*."

"German and English, right?"

"And the Cambridge Unabridged German-English dictionary."

"And the fourth box?"

"Paper."

"Goddamit. You and Arianna and Horst."

"There is something I have not told you. I have written to Brenz-Verlag. They are eager to publish a German translation of *Leverkühn*."

"That does it." Dave pulled the car off the pavement, killed the engine, turned his body toward Hans. "Stop mucking around in my life."

Hans turned to face Dave. "You will not do for yourself."

"That's my business. Not yours. Clear?"

"I act because I love you."

Dave drew in breath to speak but stopped as Hans' meaning sank in. He drummed the steering wheel with his fists and peered through the windshield.

"I need my father," Hans said. "We came to know one another. I was very happy. But then you pulled away. You are afraid. You don't trust Arianna. You don't trust me."

Dave's throat closed. "You don't know me."

"I know you. You have done things that horrify me, but you are good man. I am a lesser man than you, my father. I am good because I am afraid to be bad. You are good because you have tried to be the man God made you."

Dave sucked his lips against his teeth. Without looking at Hans, he started the engine and drove onto the pavement.

• • •

*Dave raises his body carefully, lifting his weight with his
arms. Jerry lies flat in the tall undergrowth, not moving. As Dave's
eyes near the ragged top of the curling vines, he sees a sun-soaked
meadow broken here and there with clumps of trees. Coming toward
him up the slight rise from the river is a woman with frizzy blond
hair. Inge. She has seen him. She comes straight for him. She is
weeping. "Ungeheuer." He stands. She walks toward him holding a
tiny body and drops it at his feet. Intestines splatter across his boots.
"No," he says. "I am forgiven." "No, Trion, never," she cries. "You
can never be forgiven, because of what you are."*

Dave woke with tears in his eyes. Even before he opened
them, he caught the aroma of Costa d'Oro Special Blend and the
sound of a comforting hum. He sat up. Hans' cot was already
cleared of blankets. Flames showed through the stove vent. The
computer and the printer were on the table. A goose-neck lamp
on an extension cord had been twisted to shine on the keyboard.

Dave pulled on his mukluks and made his way to the table.
Leverkühn was propped open in a copy holder. The first edition
lay next to it. Beside the keyboard were a notebook, a yellow
legal pad, and three sharpened pencils. A partly emptied ream
of paper was behind the printer. The printer's paper feeder was
already filled.

Hans came from the utility closet in his bathrobe toweling
his hair.

"What the hell is all this?" Dave said.

Hans went past him. "I get up early and arrange." He took
off his robe, slipped into boxer shorts, jeans, and one of Dave's
sweat shirts. "We have special coffee. Gift from Arianna. It was
in the box of supplies."

"Along with the lamp, copy holder, notebooks, floppies—"

Hans put on his tennis shoes. "We have everything."

"How did Arianna know I like to use steno notebooks?"

"I tell her."

"How did you know?"

Hans pushed up the sleeves on the sweat shirt. "My mother told me you like this kind. She had one you left behind."

Dave trudged to the stove and poured himself coffee. Hans sat at the table across from the computer. Dave sat beside him.

"Please not to be angry," Hans said.

"Your English goes to hell when you're stressed out."

"I apologize."

"I know you meant well. I know Arianna means well. It's just that . . . I don't think I'm ready, that's all."

"I wanted to help you get started," Hans said.

"I'm not used to having people help me."

Hans brightened. "I could help a great deal. I cannot type English, but I can type German. I have already capped the keys with German script and reset the keyboard software to German. Or if you would teach me about cars, I could fill in for you at Tracy's Texaco and you could translate full-time. Mr. Tracy said it would be like getting two good men for the price of one. We could work together while I learn."

Dave carried his coffee to his cot. "I need more time."

"You have no time."

"You don't understand. Nothing will change what I am."

"You are Dave Bell. A good man."

Dave looked at his grease-stained hands. "I am damned by what I am."

"My father—"

"I am a child killer. I had Mann's *Trion* before my eyes. I was looking in the mirror. I have no shadow, no reflection. I am Trion."

Hans was on his feet, his face flushed. "You are *not* Trion. Unless you choose to be. You are *not* damned. Unless you surrender. *Ungeminnt?* Have not Arianna and Horst and Helen and I loved you? Have you not loved me? Have you not loved Chip and Jeannie?"

"Don't you talk about Chip and Jeannie."

"I am not allowed to speak of your legitimate children?"

Dave cringed.

"I dare," Hans said, coming from behind the table. "I risk your fury to tell you the truth. You cannot escape your fate? You told my mother once you could not live without sex. Now you are celibate. Did you not change? You are *not* Trion. You are Herr Doktor David Bell, a wise man, a strong man, a loving man. A fine father. But now, you choose despair."

Dave leaped to his feet. "*That's enough!*"

"Not enough," Hans yelled. "Don't you see? You blame us, the people who love you. You say you're damned or *Ungeminnt* or despiséd. And now, when time is running out, you say it's too sudden, that you are not ready." Hans paused, trembling, his face close to Dave's. "Coward."

"You bastard—"

"Yes. I am your bastard. God in heaven, you make me *ashamed!*"

Rage like lightening. Dave swung. His fist slammed into Hans' belly.

Hans staggered backwards, clutching his stomach, and fell against the table. His feet lost traction, and he turned halfway, then toppled. His face struck the corner of the table before he hit the floor. He lay with his face to the floor rasping for breath.

Dave stood panting over him, his legs spread, his fists still doubled. His muscles loosened. He brought his feet together and straightened.

Hans was breathing again. He folded his arms on the floor and rested his forehead on his wrists.

Dave fought off an impulse to run. He wanted to be gone, out of this. Instead, he slumped onto his cot. His pulse thudded in his ears and temples. Burned into his memory was Hans' face, the bulging eyes fixed on Dave's in a mix of fear and pleading, as if to say, *please don't kill me,* like those other eyes in a hootch near Long Dinh, but these were eyes he knew, eyes he had known before he ever saw them.

Coward. You make me ashamed. Dave had run away from the dead child in Long Dinh. He'd tried to kill his own child to escape what he'd done and fled Inge's anguish. He'd hid in his study rather than face Mary. Finally, when Helen died, when his job was gone, when his wife and children turned on him, he hadn't stood his ground and fought. He'd turned tail. *Coward.*

And he'd committed the unforgivable and most selfish of all sins, despair. Now Dave had lost everything, maybe even Hans. The Eucharides still waited on the banks of the Mackinaugh.

What could he do to make that shame go away from Hans' face?

Slowly, Hans' breathing became quiet. He wiped his nose with the back of his hand and reached under his cot and dragged out his suitcase. He stumbled to the shelves and took his jeans, underwear, socks, and tee-shirts to the suitcase and threw them in.

"What are you doing?" Dave said.

Hans went to the corner and lifted his two suits and three white dress shirts from the dowel and carried them to the suitcase.

"Hans?"

"I must return to Germany, resume my studies." Hans went into the utility closet. He came out carrying his toiletries. Blood trickled from a cut above the arch in his eyebrow.

"Wait," Dave said. "You're bleeding."

Hans put his hand to his forehead and looked at his fingers.

"Sit down," Dave said. Hans turned away, but Dave took him by the arm and guided him into the chair. Dave took gauze, peroxide and band-aids from the shelf over the sink in the closet, cleaned the wound.

"Hold still," Dave said.

"Stings."

Dave covered the cut with a band-aid. "Won't hurt very long. Stay put for a minute."

Hans' lips trembled, but he stayed seated.

Dave put his elbows on his knees. "I'm sorry."

Hans wiped his nose. "I apologize."

"I'm the one who needs forgiveness."

Hans smiled. "You have my forgiveness. You had it long ago. But—" The smile disappeared. "But will you promise me not to say bad things about my father?" He got to his feet, picked up his shaving gear from the table, and tossed it in.

"You don't have to leave," Dave said.

Hans scooped up the books Arianna had given him and laid them in. The suitcase clicked closed.

Dave wanted to yank the suitcase out of Hans' hands. He wanted to tackle Hans like a quarterback. Knock him out. Anything. Maybe he should plead with him. He couldn't stand to lose Hans, too.

Hans went into the utility closet and washed his hands and face. Next he'd go up to Nate's to phone for a cab. After half an hour, he'd put on his coat and walk out the door. Dave would watch him climb the hill. He'd become smaller and smaller in the distance until he disappeared into the trees at the ridge line. What could Dave do?

He turned to the table to rest his face in his hands. The computer cursor blinked. He wanted to shatter the screen. The word processing software was already booted. What did Hans want him to do? With a groan he hoped Hans didn't hear, he put on his glasses and read the first line of English text in chapter one of *Leverkühn*. "Adrian Leverkühn is, before all else, like Thomas Mann who created him, a man with a soul." He typed, *"Kapitel 1,"* double-spaced, indented, and typed, *"Adrian Leverkühn ist vor allem ein Seelenmensch wie sein Schöpfer Thomas Mann."*

Hans walked behind Dave. Dave could feel his breath as he read what Dave had typed. He straightened, kissed the top of Dave's head. Then he walked to the suitcase, knelt, opened it, and hung his suits on the dowel in the corner.

Chapter 15

The Leverkühn Conspiracy

"Use a rag to turn the crankcase cap," Dave said. "That way, you won't burn yourself if it's hot, and you won't have to wash every time you wait on a customer."

Hans leaned further over the engine. "Where is the dipstick?"

"On a '93 Honda Civic, it's over here."

"Now all we need to do is put the oil in and it's done?"

"Except to double check with the dipstick. The last thing you want is a customer driving out with no oil in the crankcase."

The customer bell sounded. Hans banged his head on the raised hood.

Dave chuckled. "You'll get so you don't do that." He wiped his hands with a red rag from the tool bench, gave it to Hans. "Always carry a rag in your hip pocket."

They started toward the pump island. Dave spotted the police cruiser parked out back. Joe let himself into the bay. When he saw Hans, he stopped. "You got your kid workin' with you?" He swept Hans with his eyes. "Wherever you got that uniform, you ought to return it. 'Bout three sizes too big."

Dave rested his arm on Hans' shoulder. "Joe Fallon, this is my son, Hans."

Joe smiled. "If I'd known you were going to be here, I'd have brought you coffee."

"We'll share," Dave said.

The three of them moved into the office. Dave and Joe flipped.

"Damn." Dave gave Joe two dollars.

Joe pulled the chair close to the stove and lit a cigarette. "So you're workin' with your pa?"

"He's already got the customer routine down," Dave said. "By the weekend, he'll be ready to fly solo."

Joe faked a sneer. "How's his flipping?"

"Flipping?" Hans said.

"You know, heads or tails," Joe said.

"I'll add that to the stuff he'll have to know by tomorrow afternoon," Dave said.

"No fair teaching him to cheat."

"With you, he won't need to."

The customer bell rang. A '97 turquoise Towncar waited at the pump.

"That'll be Mrs. Reed," Dave said to Hans. "Can you handle it?"

"Wait a sec." Joe pulled the red oil rag from Dave's hip pocket and beckoned to Hans. "Oil." Hans paused before him and closed his eyes. Joe dabbed. "Okay, kid, hop to it."

Hans hurried to the island.

Joe gazed after him. "How come a bum like you's got a good kid like that?"

"Unlucky in money, lucky in kids."

Joe watched Hans set the automatic nozzle in the Towncar gas tank and raise the hood. "Hope you don't mind my mentioning it, but you ought to tell him to shave before he comes to work."

Hans came in as the Towncar pulled away. "Mrs. Reed say I

remind her of her grandson."

"Mrs. Reed *says*," Dave corrected.

Joe pulled himself to his feet. "Time to get back at it. Tomorrow I'll bring three coffees, and Hans can flip, okay? You take care of that old man of yours. He ain't as bad as what he looks like." He gave them a wave and headed out. Dave and Hans went into the bay. Dave opened plastic bottles of motor oil while Hans filled the Honda's crankcase.

"You should shave before you come to work, *mein Sohn*."

"I haven't shaved for three days. I want to see if I can grow a beard."

Dave studied Hans' face. "I don't know. It might look scraggly—at your age—"

"Let me try, *Vater*."

"All right, but be sure to tell Tracy what you're doing so he won't think you're being a bum."

Hans grinned. "I tell him this afternoon. He say 'Okay.'" He finished filling the crankcase and checked the oil level with the dipstick. "Mrs. Reed ask if I am your son. She say I look like you. My beard grows out light color, like yours, see?"

"You never grew a beard before?"

Hans shook his head.

"It'll make you look older," Dave said, "more mature. Maybe even handsomer."

"Arianna said so, too."

Dave clapped him on the shoulder. "Put the Honda out back and bring the keys in."

• • •

Saturday, Dave's first full day of translating, was all stops and starts. He'd no sooner type a sentence than he'd delete it and try again. He hadn't written in German in almost a year. Besides, *Leverkühn* was peppered with word plays and alliterations that made no sense in German. After fifteen minutes of struggling with "lowlier than Thou," he left it and went on.

That day was Hans' first day working alone at Tracy's Texaco. It went fine. So did Sunday—after his sojourn to Smallville to attend Lutheran services—and Monday. On Tuesday, Dave left him at the station at a quarter to twelve and drove to Acme Hardware in North Point to buy replacement tiles for the cabin bathrooms. Late in the afternoon, he washed up and returned to the computer. He was pleased that the words were flowing faster now. Then he came to the sentence describing the concerto that Leverkühn had written for Rudi: "Was it a precociously passionate parody or a passionate pronouncement buried in parody?" He wouldn't even try to reproduce that banality in German. His eyes flicked to the bottom of the screen, and he swore aloud. After seven. Too late to start dinner.

At seven-thirty, Dave stopped by the Golden Pavilion to buy take-out. Mr. Sung, all smiles and bows, offered him a glass of white wine and sat with him while the food was prepared.

"My little friend, he is well?" Mr. Sung said.

Dave squelched a smile. Hans towered over Mr. Sung.

"I buy gas from him." Mr. Sung looked at the table and covered his mouth with his fingertips. "Many young lady also buy."

Dave raised his eyebrows.

"Your son," Mr. Sung said, "is very hand-some, very hand-some."

"Thank you."

Dave pictured Hans, the prickly blond hair, scraggly beard, spare frame. It was the eyes, he decided, those intriguing eyes, blue and deep, looking familiar even though you'd never seen them before.

"And your journey?" Mr. Sung said.

Dave grinned. "Heck, all I can afford is an occasional trip to Smallville to shop at the Walmart."

"Your work. You are near your destination?"

"How did you know about that?"

"Missus Arianna tell me. And Hans. I can help?"

"No, no. Thanks."

So Mr. Sung had joined the conspiracy with Horst, Arianna, and Hans.

Dave paid and drove to the station. He parked out back next to a red '97 Mustang with a "Mackinaugh College" sticker in the back window. As he opened the door from the bay to the office, Hans, holding a Styrofoam cup stiffly in both hands, sat erect on the high stool next to the service desk. Beside him on the sill was a buxom young woman with dark brown hair pulled back from her face. She wore gold hoop earrings, lip gloss, and a brown jersey tucked into tight-fitting jeans.

When she saw Dave, she smiled. "Hi."

"Trish," Hans said, "my father."

"I know Dave." She rose and put out her hand. "He's waited on me a zillion times."

"Miss . . . McCormack," Dave said.

She looked at her watch. "You know what time it is? You're supposed to be closing."

Hans shrugged and smiled, then gave Dave a pleading look.

"I'm out of here." She slipped on her too-large leather jacket and pulled her hair from under the collar.

"Thank you for the hot chocolate," Hans said.

"Anytime. Night, Dave."

She left by the front door and bounced to the rear of the station. The Mustang zipped away.

"Wow," Dave said. "I've never seen her except in her car. Very attractive."

"She say I look cold and lonely. She bring me hot chocolate."

"Where did you meet her?"

"I wait on her Saturday night," Hans said with a blush. "And yesterday. How did you know her name?"

"Credit card. Her father's Steve McCormack, owns the paint store on Main, Arianna's landlord. Mrs. Reed's son-in-law."

Hans turned his eyes to the wall clock. "Time to close."

On the way home, the Cavalier reeked of General Tso's Chicken and pork egg foo young. Dave waited a decent interval before he spoke. "What's the deal with Trish?"

Hans looked out the window. "She ask me to go out Saturday night. Can I use the car? I come home and shower after I close up, then pick her up at nine-thirty. I will meet her father and mother."

Dave kept his eyes on the road. "Sure."

"For burgers at Busby's in Cold Harbor and a movie. Two other couples are going. I tell her I not have much money, and she say since she asked, she will pay."

"That girl doesn't let grass grow under her feet."

"She say I am cute," Hans said with a frown. "Like Arianna say."

"Not the same. When a girl says a boy is cute, she means he's attractive."

"*Ach so.* I thought—"

"It's a compliment. How long was she at the station?"

"She come in at seven-fifteen, but we not talk the whole time. I must finish off customers."

Dave chuckled. "Your English is in a state of collapse."

Hans' ears reddened. "She is very sexy."

"Things are sure different. No girl ever asked me for a date."

At the shed, Dave spread the red paper mats next to the computer and took plates from the closet shelf. Hans rebuilt the fire, poured wine from the gallon jug, and put water on to boil for tea. They spooned from the paper cartons and ate with plastic chopsticks.

"You don't seem very happy," Dave said.

"I am pleased, but—"

"You're scared, right?"

Hans' ears reddened again.

"You'll do fine," Dave said.

"I don't know how to act."

Dave poured boiling water into the teapot. "Pretend that you've done this a thousand times, but in Germany it's different. Pretend that women find you attractive. Pretend that you're relaxed. If you act confident, everyone will think you are."

"I do not like to fool people."

"You're not fooling anyone but yourself. After you've pretended for a little while, you'll believe it, and it will be true. If you weren't so unsure, I'd tell you to relax and be yourself."

Hans dallied with a piece of breaded chicken.

• • •

Wednesday. Hans' day off. When the sun was well above the horizon, Dave knelt in the frozen mud and held the wedge point against the uprighted log. "You hold the wedge in your left hand and the sledgehammer in your right hand, like this. Then you tap the wedge until it's firmly lodged in the log. See?"

Hans scratched the back of his neck.

"Then stand up and swing the sledgehammer, arms bent a little, and hit the top of the wedge hard—like so—" Dave hit the wedge full force. With a metallic thud, the wedge drove into the log. The log split, and the wedge fell to the ground. "Keep splitting until you get pieces no more than four or five inches thick."

Hans' mouth turned down at one corner.

"Ready to give it a whirl?"

Hans knelt in the mud. After several tries, he got the wedge to stay upright in the log. He got to his feet, swung the sledgehammer, and hit the log. The wedge rang and fell on a nearby log with a dull *plink*. Hans blew the air from his lungs.

Dave muffled his grin. "Try again."

On the fourth try, Hans gave the wedge a glancing blow and drove it halfway into the log.

"Okay. Now drive it all the way in."

Hans struck the embedded wedge again. It went into the log. The log groaned and opened but didn't split. Hans tried to pull the wedge from the log. It didn't budge.

"That's why we have extra wedges," Dave said. He showed Hans how to drive in the second wedge to split the log far enough that the first wedge fell out. "Keep doing that until the log comes apart."

Hans looked at the log as if it had insulted him.

"You work on this pile, and I'll work on the next one."

Hans gave him a sour look.

"Sorry," Dave said, "but it's got to be done. We'll need firewood to keep warm at night 'til June. Nate will start getting renters soon."

Hans went to work while Dave moved down the hill to the next pile. Dave drove and split and piled. His body came to life.

His pulse thumped along at a happy clip. After fifteen minutes, he took off his parka.

He tried not to watch Hans, but he could hear the *whomp* and *ping* that told him Hans was hitting the log and knocking the wedge into the air. He wished Hans would enjoy the work. Chip used to love working with Dave.

Finally, Dave pulled his bandana from his hip pocket and wiped his forehead. The sun was as high as it would get in a Maine winter sky. Hans was kneeling on one knee and trying to tap his wedge into a log. The hammer hit the top of the log, and the wedge flew. Hans gnashed his teeth, walked to the wedge, and picked it up.

"Finish that one," Dave said, "and we'll break for lunch."

"We must do more this afternoon?"

"'Fraid so."

After three tries, Hans got the wedge to stay in the log. It took him four swings to drive the wedge in. When he did, the log split clean.

"Nice going," Dave said. "You're getting the hang of it."

Hans wiped his face but said nothing. They trudged down the hill to the shed. Inside, they took off their shirts and toweled their bodies. The tang of male sweat made the room smell like a gym minus the undertone of bleach and deodorant.

Dave smiled. "Hard work, isn't it?"

Hans nodded. His chest was thin and white. What little body hair he had was blond. His arms were long and spindly.

"You should get more exercise," Dave said. "And some sun. You look downright puny."

"I spend my time studying."

"Your brain works better when your body's fit."

"My grandfather say the only purpose of the body is to carry around the brain. The only purpose of the brain is to do the work of the mind."

"A man's body is built for work, Hans. It's not healthy to let it go."

"My grandfather say that is male foolishness."

"'My grandfather *says*,'" Dave corrected.

"Says."

Dave wiped under his arms. "You think I'm a fool?"

Hans put down his towel and sat at the table. "You are my father. I admire you and respect you. Your body is stronger than mine. You are a man of the earth. I am an ascetic."

Dave hooded his eyes. "You don't consider me an intellectual?"

"*Ach, ja.*"

"You remind me of your mother. She took terrible care of herself." Dave wiped the moisture from Hans' neck. "Tell you what. Let's work out at the gym in North Point."

Hans said nothing.

"All right, but we do have to split wood."

Hans grimaced.

By mid-afternoon, the piles of split wood were of respectable size. Dave put down his sledgehammer. "That's enough for today." Hans dropped his tools. "At least finish the one you're on," Dave said. Hans picked up the hammer and swung.

• • •

Saturday night, after Hans left, the shed smelled like an after-shave factory. Dave smiled and went on working. The sluggishness he'd suffered through in the early chapters, when his academic German came out in spurts and clots, was gone. The German text raced across the screen as if on its own. He had matured as a writer since the *Leverkühn* days. And for the first time in years he felt a glimmer of the passion that gave the book life.

The first draft of the book, in German, had been simple and direct, but successive revisions in English were increasingly flavorsome. His own arch prose, so often sardonic and parodistic, and the challenge of finding the right words to capture the shadowy distinctions implicit in Mann's work forced Dave to the limits of his ability. He found himself distilling the underlying meaning of his own American English, putting aside the words themselves, roaming through German and asking himself, "How do we say that?" The dictionaries were already getting ragged, and *Roget's Thesaurus* was coming apart. When he went back to the original Mann in German, he was brought up short by the similarities between *Doktor Faustus* and *Trion*. How could he have missed the parallels, sometimes inverse, between the characters of Leverkühn and Trion? Granted one was an artist and intellectual and the other a bully. One sold his soul to achieve artistic perfection; the other lost his soul in the pursuit of power. And how could he have overlooked the characteristics he himself shared with Trion? The same addiction to dominance, the dependence on brute force, the willingness to intimidate, the impulsiveness, infanticide, *cowardice*. His throat went dry. "Great literature," he translated, "offers the willing reader a mirror in which to see himself."

As he typed he forced himself to check the time at the bottom of the screen. He didn't expect Hans home much before one, but when two came and went, his stomach muscles knotted. He knew all the worrying in the world wouldn't make a whit of difference, but his son was out in a car on icy roads.

At two-twenty-five, the Cavalier pulled in. Dave turned

as Hans came through the door and stripped off his coat.
Dave pulled a chair close to the stove. "Come get warm. Want
something hot to drink?"

Hans shook his head.

Dave waited. "Well? "

Hans shrugged.

"Did Trish enjoy it?

Hans wiped his mouth with his handkerchief. Dave caught a
glimpse of lipstick.

"I go to Trish's house and meet Mr. and Mrs. McCormack.
They are very nice. Then we drive to Cold Harbor and meet her
friends at Busby's Burgers. Her friends, they are loud and funny.
I am quiet. They think I am odd."

Dave waited.

"Then," Hans said, "I remember what you tell me. I pretend
I am in Germany and Trish is nervous because she is afraid I
won't like her. I start laughing at her friends. In the movie, she
leans against me. I put my arm around her and she kiss me.
After the movie, we drive to Lookout Point and talk."

"Talk?"

"She tell me about her studies. I tell her about the gas station
and the seminary. We kiss some more. I take her home."

Dave put out his hand. "Congratulations on your first
American date."

Hans shook his hand.

"You unwound enough to sleep?" Dave said. "I'm bushed."

"I am very tired."

Dave saved his work and turned off the computer. In bed,
he listened to the occasional spit and rustle from the stove. Peace
settled over him like the dusk of a summer day. He was doing
good work, work he loved. The shed was warm and his child

was safe by his side. With a start, he recognized in himself a contentedness he had forgotten even existed. He was learning all over again to be happy.

"She tell me she is on the pill," Hans' voice said through the darkness.

Dave raised himself on his elbows. "Sounds like a setup."

"I think the same."

"Women expect a long term relationship when sex is involved."

"Not to fear, *Vater*. I will not have sex with her. I cannot violate the rules I preach."

Dave let his weight fall on the cot. "We sure see life differently."

"*Vater*, you must make your way with your God even as I make mine. No two men are the same in God's eyes."

Dave nodded. "I wish you could be pleased that a gorgeous young woman is attracted to you."

"She ask me to see her next weekend. I tell her I don't know. She say her parents will be away. She fix me dinner at her house."

"Uh-oh."

"Maybe I must be busy next weekend."

Dave chortled. "I need you to help me split logs."

Odd that his son doing well with women made him feel proud. He tried to see Hans as a woman would see him. When he thought of Trish, he thought of a sexy woman, but Hans still looked like a boy. What *did* women find attractive in a man?

Hans spoke again. "No, I explain. If she really like me, not just want sex, she will understand."

Dave let his head fall on his pillow. Chip had almost slobbered every time a girl walked by. Dave had actually been relieved when Chip started going steady with Cindy, even though he guessed they were sleeping together. Here was Hans, also his son, running away from women. Afraid to sin? Probably, but it would take courage to tell Trish the truth. Dave still didn't get it. He'd always been the hunter rather than the quarry. He didn't know how to advise Hans.

"*Ach, mein Gott! Wieviel Uhr ist es?*"

The voice sliced through Dave's dream. He sprang from the cot. Sun streamed through the window.

Hans was upright on his cot staring at the clock. "We forget to set the alarm. I will be late for work, and I have missed church."

Dave sank onto his cot and scratched his armpit. Hans was on his feet en route to the utility closet stripping off his pajamas as he went. Dave found his mukluks and checked the fire. While he was adding wood, Hans dashed past him, grabbed his clean uniform, and ran to the utility closet. The shower started. Dave shuffled to the sink and filled the coffee pot. While he measured coffee into the percolator basket, he glimpsed the clock. After eleven. Hans wouldn't have time for breakfast.

Dave fished in the pockets of the jeans draped over one chair. "I'll put a couple of dollars on the table. Stop by Larkin's and pick up donuts or something. I'll give you coffee."

"Trish is coming by the station with hot chocolate and pastry," Hans muffled voice said from the shower.

A touch of envy tweaked Dave's heart. His kid had it made, and he was about to blow it—all for the sake of his goddam virginity. If Dave had been in Hans' shoes, he wouldn't have even come home last night.

Dave checked the percolator. "Coffee's ready." He carried a cup to the closet.

Hans was shaving his neck. "Put it on the toilet tank."

Dave leaned against the door jamb. "Your beard's looking good. Thickened out. Needs trimming."

"Don't have time. Maybe tonight."

Dave ambled to the stove, poured himself a mug, and sat in front of the computer. He flipped it on and put on his glasses.

"I'm outta here," Hans said as he headed for the door.

"Sounds like Trish is teaching you American slang."

"She says her father says that. She thinks it's, like, quaint and really funny." Hans threw on his coat and pulled on gloves. "Later."

Dave turned to the computer. As he worked, English streaming through his brain and spinning into German, his mind turned again to *Trion*. He wished he could point out the family resemblance between *Trion* and *Doktor Faustus*, but this was, after all, a translation, not a new book. Besides, he wouldn't stoop to citing Jerry's work, especially the stuffy translation and patronizing article. Maybe he'd add some footnotes drawn from his own work.

Odd that his fascination with *Trion* was as strong as ever, even though he now understood why—the striking similarity between Trion and himself. He saw now why Horst had asked him if *Trion* and his Vietnam dream were alike. What Trion had been trying to do, to use Hans' phrase, was to be the man the gods made him to be. He was not condemned to commit the crimes he did, any more than Dave's male genes determined him. Both Trion and Dave had a choice, though neither had known it. Both had chosen badly, but Dave was lucky enough to catch on before it was too late. "When one needs a teacher, a teacher appears." Arianna's words—though it sounded for all the world like Rumi. Hans had appeared. Dave had learned from him, and Hans had learned from Dave.

He stretched and sipped coffee. He and Trion. Trying to be
the man God made him to be. The y chromosome, testosterone,
the male genetic makeup. Smart men, like Hans, knew that love
was more important than sex. Dumb men, like Dave, had to
discover love. Men like Trion didn't even know that love existed.
Dave had used Inge. And Helen. All without seeing what he was
doing. And Mary? He *had* loved Mary, without understanding
what was driving him. He shook his head. Real love was wanting
the other *to be*, rejoicing in her existence. The focus of love
has to be on the object, not on the source. He'd been so self-
absorbed, so inwardly centered he hadn't given Mary the rapt
attention she deserved and needed. If he had, he'd have seen that
she was faking and tried to find out why.

The stab of remorse was like the icy waters of the
Mackinaugh. He wished he could go back, undo what he had
done. Helen and Inge dead. Mary would never forgive him. And
he'd love her as long as he lived.

He put down his coffee. A man *can* love a woman without
erotic desire, if he is mature enough and wise enough. Could
Dave ever love Mary that way? He recognized with a shock that
he already did. Why did he always come to understanding too
late?

And yet . . . the old rage kindled in his chest. She used his
manhood against him, tried to destroy him, and she'd do it
again. He must never, never fall into her hands again.

Maybe that was the life-long punishment he'd have
to endure, the suffering that would save him from eternal
damnation—to love her knowing she'd kill him if she could.
Bereft of peace until they were both dead.

When Hans drove in that night, the Cavalier seemed to
move slower than usual. The engine idled before it died and

the brake was set. Dave went on working at the stove. The door opened. He took one look at Hans. "What's the matter?"

"Trish is angry with me. She not wants to see me again."

Dave started to correct the English, then stopped. "You told her you didn't want to, uh . . ."

Hans nodded.

"There are lots more women around. Wait and see."

Hans took off his coat.

"Dinner's ready," Dave said.

Hans sat. "I like her a lot."

Dave rubbed Hans' shoulder. "You'll like the others, too."

"But Trish, she is not any other."

"You'll say that about the others, too."

Hans gave him a look so sad that Dave's heart twinged.

"It'll be okay, I promise," Dave said. "Look, someday, you'll meet the woman you'll love more than anybody you've ever known. And—" Dave's own hurt rose in his chest. "—if you're lucky, she'll love you, too."

Hans looked unconvinced.

• • •

Dave stopped typing.

Hans looked up. "You have finished the chapter?"

"Yes. And it's *good*, Hans."

"It is good, yes. But you are ahead of me."

Dave turned toward him. "Where are you?"

"Not quite finished with chapter eight."

"I'll print out nine for you. Then I'll start ten. As soon as you finish chapter eight, I'll go over your suggestions."

Hans folded his arms. "You do not accept my suggestions."

"I accept all the typos, but your changes—excuse me, *mein*

Sohn—sound too formal sometimes."

"Sometimes *you* change the text. I like the original best."

"Author's prerogative. Wish I had time to revise. I've learned a lot since I wrote *Leverkühn*."

"I find words I don't know. What is this word, 'scapulate'?"

"A made-up word. It means to cover only partially, as with a scapular."

Hans rolled his eyes. "I thought it was a printing error. I checked both editions of *Leverkühn*. What other made-up words do you use?"

"You'll find them."

"And waste time trying to find their meaning." Hans looked at his watch. "It is after midnight. We sleep now?"

"Go ahead. I want to work a little longer."

"We are a very good team. We finish nine chapters."

"Not finished yet. They're drafts, but I never imagined we could get so much done so quickly. You have been a great help."

Hans held up his hands, palms inward. "And now I am grease monkey, too."

"You look silly in my uniform."

"Arianna say I look cute."

"'Arianna *says* I look cute,'" Dave corrected.

"No, she say you are a honk."

Dave chuckled. "You know what she means?"

"I know." Hans paused, embarrassed. "Why do you not stay with Arianna sometime? I would not object."

"It isn't you, Hans. The time's not right." He looked sidelong at Hans. "Have you ever . . ."

"I wait, you understand? A man of the church needs to restrain himself."

"Guess I'd have been better off if I'd been a man of the

church."

"But," Hans said, "I have a date Saturday night."

Dave raised his eyebrows.

"Sally Mercer," Hans said.

"Drives a Mazda? She's Joe's niece."

"She is in classes with Trish. Trish told her all about me. She stops in at the station sometimes. I asked her to have hamburgers and go to a movie."

"If Trish told her all about you—"

Hans grinned. "Sally is, what you call, safe."

"Don't bet on it."

• • •

By the middle of March, Dave and Hans had finished the first draft. They celebrated at Costa d'Oro with chianti and scampi.

"Now comes the hard work," Dave said. "The revision."

"We read aloud each to the other," Hans said to Arianna. "Then my father stops me, and we mark changes, and I type in the changes and he reads proof."

"Proof reads," Dave corrected. "We'll have the manuscript in the mail before Hans has to leave for Germany."

Arianna turned to Hans. "When must you go?"

"We decide 29 March."

Arianna looked away. "Then, sometime after that, your father will go." She pulled a handkerchief from her bodice and wiped her eyes. "Arianna is sentimental tonight." She emptied the bottle into their glasses. "To *Leverkühn*." She raised her glass.

• • •

On the morning of Saturday, the 29th of March, they were

up at five. Dave fixed breakfast while Hans trimmed his beard. They sat at the table.

"I fixed eggs, sausage, potatoes," Dave said. "I'll fix a lunch."

While they ate, Dave watched Hans, wanting to cement the image in his memory. "Be careful who you talk to on the bus and in the airport. Keep an eye on your suitcase and your wallet and your carry-on luggage."

"*Vater*, please."

Dave picked up their plates. "Get dressed and finish packing. I'll clean up here a little and—" He shrugged and carried their plates to the utility sink. He rinsed them. He'd wash them later. He made two sausage sandwiches, put them in a bag, and added two apples and two chocolate bars. "Did I already give you aspirin?"

"*Ja.*"

As Dave fastened his belt, he looked up. Hans wore his dark suit and tie with his gray overcoat over one arm. Hans was a man, not a boy. Damned good looking, too. Those startling eyes. The long lashes, the arched brow . . . All at once, Dave knew what it was. They were Dave's father's eyes. No. They were Dave's own eyes in somebody else's face. Like Dave's reflection, living, breathing. Hans caught him watching.

Dave smiled a sheepish smile. "You look like me, you know that?"

They drove into town and headed into the city hall lot where the bus would pull in. Almost seven. They hadn't left any extra time. Dave scanned the sky. Dark. The wind was rising.

At the curb, in front of the banks of plowed snow, four people waited. Dave was surprised. The bus didn't even stop in Winter Bay unless someone was getting on or off. Then he recognized Sally Mercer. She had been crying. Nearby, Joe Fallon was pacing and smoking. Next to him was Mr. Sung, arms folded, face down. The fourth, a woman in a midnight blue cape, stood apart.

As Dave and Hans got out of the car, Sally came flying across the lot. She flung her arms around Hans. Dave busied himself with opening the trunk and getting out the luggage. After simultaneous jabbering and blubbering, Sally sprinted to a blue Mazda and sped away. Hans turned to pick up his suitcase.

Dave wiped Hans' cheek. "Lipstick."

"All set, kid?" Joe said with a smile as Dave and Hans came up.

"Yes, sir," Hans said.

"I'll look after your father. He ain't as much of a bum as what he looks like."

"Yes, sir."

Joe stuck out his hand. Hans shook it.

Mr. Sung grinned up at Hans and bowed. "May heaven smile upon my little friend for ten thousand years."

Arianna hadn't moved. The wind jostled her hood, but her face stayed hidden. Hans stepped toward her. She embraced him.

"Thank you," he said, "for all you did for me. I will come back."

Arianna kissed his cheek. "No, love. Go your way. Your time here is past."

The bus pulled in. The driver got out and opened the cargo hold. Dave helped Hans stow his suitcase. He folded his arms while Hans took off his overcoat and loosened his tie. They stood looking at each other.

"Write to me," Dave said in German.

Hans nodded.

"You'd better get on. They need to get going."

Hans bit his lip.

Dave grabbed him and held him. "*Mein Sohn.* I love you."

Dave stepped away. He couldn't speak. Hans wiped his eyes and got on the bus. The engine rumbled to life, and the bus pulled to the exit of the parking lot. Dave watched the amber turn signal. He waved. The bus veered right and, with an audible shift of gears, revved its engine, filled the air behind it with gray exhaust, and groaned up the hill.

Dave watched the smoke melt to nothing. He listened until the last shadow of the engine whine faded into the undulating noise of the town. Even then, he strained for some sound, some sight that would tell him the bus had turned around and was bringing his son back to him. Finally, he turned away from the others and walked alone to the Cavalier.

Chapter 16

Decent People

Bob's threatening to attach my salary. I offered to pay him a hundred dollars a month. He laughed.

Carla's been a faithful friend, the only person who doesn't avoid me. Even Shirley and Jerry Devereaux never call any more. And Carla agrees to bring a bag lunch because I really can't afford to eat out once a week. We alternate offices.

The last Thursday in March, we settle in her office. She tells me George Eckland won't be returning to the college. He's dropped out permanently, suffering from some kind of brain injury. We've heard rumors about Harry—that he's been arrested in connection with Helen's death. I change the subject and fill her in on Jeannie and Chip.

Jerry's in the door with a smile too broad to be sincere. "Look who's decided to honor us with her presence. We never see you anymore, Mary." He grins his way into the room.

I put down my sandwich. "How've you been?"

"Jerry is being considered for a prize," Carla says.

His eyes warn her not to continue.

"The 1997 Marsdale Award," she says, "for the outstanding contribution to German Literature scholarship. For his work on Thomas Mann's *Trion*."

"No big deal," Jerry says. "How're the children?"

"Doing well considering," I say.

"Glad I caught you," he says. "How about stopping by on

your way out?"

I've learned a lot about Jerry since the trouble started. When Jerry gets chummy, something's in the wind.

"Sure," I say.

After he leaves, Carla returns to her chatter. It occurs to me that she spends time with me not only because I'm her twin. She feeds on misfortune. She gets off on my troubles.

On my way down the hall, I wonder if any decent people are left in the world. Jerry's door is open. When I come in, he takes off his glasses.

"Sit down." He walks to the door and closes it, returns to the desk. "I got a phone call that might interest you." He's playing with a pencil, holding it with both hands and looking down its length. "From Mackinaugh College."

"Never heard of it."

"It's in Maine. Seems Dave applied to take courses there to be certified as a teacher. A Miss Finley, his faculty advisor, called me to verify his previous employment. She was surprised when I confirmed what Dave had stated in his application."

"Maine?"

"Near Winter Bay. This Miss Finley says he works in a gas station. I asked what he looked like—to be sure. The man she described doesn't sound much like our Dave. He's probably disguised himself. I'm surprised he didn't use a false name."

He's alive. "Did you ask for his address?"

"He's living out in the country somewhere. His mail address is care of Nathaniel Gains at a post office box." He writes it for me on a piece of his monographed note paper.

I fold the address carefully and put it in my purse. "Jerry, thank you."

"Glad to help. I know how hard it's been."

"Frankly, I'm rather surprised you told me. I thought your sympathies would lie with Dave."

"Dave and I were as close as two men can be, but after what he did . . ." He shakes his head sadly. "I know you need money . . ."

Something phony going on. Jerry was instrumental in getting Dave fired.

"I didn't want to go to the police," Jerry says. "I thought I'd leave that up to you."

So *that's* it. He'd be happier if Dave were in jail.

I spend the rest of the day deciding what to do. If I tell Bob where Dave is, he'll probably have him arrested. Besides, the police want to talk to him about Harry. I'll go to Maine, find him. I'll offer to withdraw charges if he'll come back for the children's sake and get a decent job. Before I leave the office, I put in for time off. I'll have to borrow money for the trip. Jeannie can stay with Carla. No. I don't want Jeannie under Carla's twisted influence again. She can stay with Chip. Chip can take care of her. And he can take care of himself.

Dave's absence has scarred them. He must come back. Jeannie would be so happy. Maybe when Chip understands what really happened, he'll forgive us both.

What if Dave says no? Maybe there's nothing I can do, but I have to try.

Chapter 17

The Bloated Thing on the Beach

Dave left the city hall parking lot and drove to the shed. He forced himself not to think about Hans. Speculate about *Leverkühn*. Because of Dave's German mother and his stature as a native speaker, the Germans had always accepted him as one of their own, despite his U.S. citizenship. He wouldn't have to battle the xenophobia that beleaguered foreigners in German literary circles, especially if they wrote about things German. Maybe Brenz-Verlag would underwrite a book tour in German-speaking countries. He could visit Hans. That would mean meeting Doctor Lehmann again after all these years. Never mind. If the book sold well, he might be able to clear his name and settle with Mary and still have enough to live on.

Too many ifs. He'd have Mary and Bob Scarff to fight off while he was struggling to get on his feet. If he were in Germany, they couldn't get to him. No. Too far from Chip and Jeannie. Maybe that would be the price. It'd be him and Hans. He saw Hans in his suit and tie, his blue eyes—Dave's eyes—moist as he boarded the bus.

Concentrate on the here and now—his luck in flipping with Joe, Horst's latest letter, the need to fix the steps to the large cabin with the weather finally warming up. The snow was melting. That meant slush and mud slides and car towing and donuts from Joe. The one thing he'd never let Hans do at Tracy's Texaco was tow. Too dangerous. *Damn.* He was thinking about

Hans again.

The next morning, in the diffuse light of the dawn, he saw his wallet, keys, and change still on the table. The wood by the stove hadn't been touched. No coffee was brewing. No cot on the floor next to the wall. He felt for his mukluks, slipped them on, and lumbered to the window. The Mackinaugh was as black as the bay now, the snow on the hill as worn as fraying fabric. The sea was a stripe of gray against the dull glare of the sky.

Wednesday night, Dave picked up Arianna at Costa d'Oro. In the harsh light of the street lamp, he saw for the first time that her eyes were sunken, her neck flabby, her hands bony. They drove to her cottage in silence.

Once there, he lit the fire. She changed, then placed breaded veal cutlets in the microwave to thaw and put frozen spinach on to boil. Dave opened the Beaujolais Bâtard. They sat before the fire on cushions.

She drew a yellow paper from her bodice. Hans' telegram, now scented lime. Dave wished he could keep it, but Arianna hadn't offered it to him.

"We'll see him again," Dave said.

The microwave pinged.

"Bring our wine to the kitchen," she said, rising. "I will sauté the cutlets."

They ate at her glass-top table, then extinguished the candles, and moved to the fire.

"Nice dinner," he said. "Thank you."

She nodded.

They watched the fire.

In the quiet, he could hear her breathing. She bowed her head and ran her index finger along her eyelid.

"Arianna, Hans will be back—"

"*Non dir niente.*"

"Holding it in won't help."

She watched the fire.

"Okay," he said with a smile. "Then tell me the story of your à la carte life. Were you ever married?"

"I loved a man once."

"A lover?" Dave asked.

"My son."

"Son—"

"We were on a holiday at Cinque Terre. He was nineteen."

Dave closed his eyes.

"The bloated thing they dragged up on the little beach," she said, "was not Pietro. He was not that color, not shaped that way. I knew it was the thing the water had made of him, but it was not him. Pietro was tall and brown like the earth. He smelled salty and musty, like a man. The girls loved him, like they love you. I watched him swim out from the little cove at the foot of the mountain until I couldn't see him any more. What they heaved ashore with hooks and ropes the next day was not my Pietro."

Dave took her hand.

The tears on her cheek caught the fire light. "He laughed at my fear of the water," she said. "I don't fear it now."

He put his arms around her. "Arianna." Her arms circled his neck. Her forehead rested on his shoulder.

"Shush now," he said. "It's going to be all right." He stroked her hair. She clung to him.

The fire dwindled to embers. Cold seeped through the windows and rolled under the doors.

She moved closer to him. "Don't leave me tonight."

"I won't."

She took his hands and led him away from the fire.

They undressed in the dark, and she guided him to the bed. Lying next to her, his cheek against hers, he felt the remnants of her tears on his face. He kissed her, surprised at how quickly his passion rose.

"Not yet." She held him close.

He stroked her neck, back, buttocks. His hand found her breast.

"Not yet," she said.

"I thought—"

"Go slowly. Be with me. Don't force me to be with you."

• • •

He awoke to the distant sound of a piano. Mozart, the middle movement of the sonata in F. He smelled coffee, something frying, a tinge of lime. The sheets, smooth as rose petals, were damp still. He sat up. The door to the hall was open. She was singing in the kitchen, her contralto doubling the gentle melody of the sonata. He pulled a long honey-colored hair from his mouth.

"You are awake." She stood in the doorway in a dressing gown. "Coffee." She handed him a demitasse. From the closet she brought him a silk robe and a pair of men's slippers. "Shower. Then come to the kitchen for breakfast. Chorizo hash and omelettes. You will drink mango juice?"

In the tiny bathroom at the end of the hall, he found a new razor, a toothbrush still in cellophane, toothpaste, and towels.

Bathed and wrapped in the robe, he entered the kitchen. They settled at a wooden table barely big enough for two.

"Eat," she said. "You must restore yourself after last night. Thank you for staying, David. I apologize. I was too sad."

"I'm sorry I rushed things. It's been a long time."

She reached across the table and patted his hand. "David, when a man makes love, he must use all his senses to understand where his woman is and go there to be with her. Sometimes leading is following."

"It was new to me."

"You were delicious." She took his hand. "You were kind."

"You're disappointed."

"David, some men love only once."

"I wanted to be with you. To have lost a child—"

"No, *mio bello*. I loved my Pietro, more than I have ever loved anyone. Sometimes I am weak and fall into grieving. But I did not live for my son when he was alive. I must not live for him now that he is dead. Some sins are unforgivable. That is one."

• • •

Back at Nate's, Dave surveyed the steps on the large cabin and made a list of supplies. He left for town early so that he could stop in Longenecker's Hardware. By noon, he was at the station in his uniform. As he greeted regular customers and pumped gas, he saw Hans laughing at Arianna's story about her name and tears sparkling on Arianna's cheek in the firelight.

"Be with me," she'd said. Had he ever been with Inge or Helen or Mary?

To have lost a child. He shook his head as he checked Mrs. Reed's oil. Arianna had suffered more than he, and she saw his staying with her as a gift of love. Maybe her pain had made her wise. In the lube bay, he filled the '92 Pontiac's crankcase and figured the bill. When you came right down to it, the only thing that mattered was the children.

Late in the afternoon, Trish pulled her Mustang up to the pumps. "Fill it, please." She sat rigid, staring straight ahead, and refused his offer to wash her windshield. She thrust her credit card through the window without looking at him, then signed and drove off without a backward glance.

He closed the station at eight and drove to the shed. Inside the door, he flipped on the light. Yesterday's coffee cup on the table, his towel over the chair, the cot undisturbed since he made it the morning before. Somehow he still suffered a stab of surprise when he came in and found things as he had left them.

He eased onto his cot. He yearned for his children. All three were effectively fatherless now, but what could he do? If he went back, he'd go to jail, and if Mary found him, he'd have to run again.

Better for Chip and Jeannie to be fatherless than ashamed. Yet how could he be a father even to Hans if he had to spend his life running?

Too tired to fix dinner, he got the fire going and changed to sweats.

He hadn't wanted to stay with Arianna, but he didn't want to hurt her. She'd taught him. She'd even thanked him. "Some men love only once." Mary was the only woman he'd ever loved, but he'd never been with her. He hadn't even known being-with existed. Maybe Mary's coldness was his doing. Instead of trying to help her, he'd been unfaithful. Had she responded to Bob Scarff? The thought sickened him.

She hates me now. I must never get within the range of her claws. I did this to myself. No, I did this to her.

• • •

The next afternoon, Joe Fallon parked the police cruiser

at the rear of the station. Dave snatched the ash tray from the office desk, went into the bay, and pulled up a stool. Joe came in through the door to the garage bay.

"Hi." Dave reached in his pocket for a quarter. "Ready to get beaten again?"

Joe took out a cigarette and started to light it, then put it back in the pack. "Sometimes I hate my job."

"What's wrong?" Dave's heart thumped. "Hans?"

"Hans? No. You. Stuff you did in Maryland."

The quarter in Dave's hand was wet against his palm.

"Dave, I've brought somebody to see you."

He tipped his head. The cruiser door opened, and Mary emerged.

Dave froze. "What's she doing here?"

"Calm down, Dave," Joe said. "She says she's your wife."

"Not any more. The bitch divorced me."

Mary walked into the bay.

Chapter 18

Lost and Found

I ask the woman at the Comfort Inn, a Mrs. Reed, if she knows Dave. She says he lives out at Old Nate's place, works at Tracy's Texaco. She doesn't know if he'd be there now or not. I could ask at Costa d'Oro, a coffee shop. The owner, Arianna d'Amori, is a good friend of Dave's. I catch the inference. She suggests I check at City Hall for Officer Fallon. He knows Dave. I find him, explain. He says he's going to the station where Dave works. I ask to ride with him. He parks behind the station.

"I'll tell him you're here," he says.

The glass doors to the repair bay are down. Inside is a man in a Texaco uniform, tall and gaunt with a white beard. I watch the way he moves, like a nimble bear. Fallon talks to him and nods to me. I get out of the car.

Dave's lost weight, gone gray. He's raw-boned and gawky but still big enough to kill me with his bare hands. Or protect me and care for me. I open the door and walk into the bay.

"Get her out of here," Dave says in a hoarse whisper.

"Your call," Fallon says, "but maybe you ought to hear what she has to say."

Dave turns toward the office door.

"Dave," I say, "I'm not here for me. For Chip and Jeannie."

Dave stalls. "What about them?"

"For their sake, I want you to come to Maryland. I can arrange—" I turn to Fallon. "Is it possible for me to talk to my husband alone?"

"Don't go anywhere, Joe," Dave says in the same strangled voice.

"Sorry, ma'am," Fallon says.

I swallow the bile. "If you'll come to Maryland, you won't be arrested."

"I don't trust you," Dave says.

"You want to go on living like a fugitive?"

"I'm getting good at it."

"I can make things rough for you. Or I can give you another chance. If you'll cooperate."

"I won't put my neck in the noose," Dave says through his teeth.

"You bastard." I'm shouting. I rein in my voice. "Haven't you learned anything?"

"I've learned to keep my back against the wall."

Dave's eyes don't leave my face. I try to control my trembling, take a deep breath. "Let me help you."

He doesn't move.

"Then let me help the children." I swallow hard. "I can withdraw charges."

"Bob would let you do that?"

I set my jaw. "I can negotiate with the court to allow you to be on probation if you'll get a decent job."

"I can't get a job. You saw to that. Your tip to George Eckland. The splash in the *Lincoln Log*—"

I'm shaken. "How did you—"

"Eckland told me. You got even, didn't you? Did you ever stop to think how much you were hurting Chip and Jeannie? And yourself?"

I want to scream. I open my mouth to lash at him, then

close it. "I'm here for them."

His stone face cracks. "How are they?"

"Chip's a freshman at Lincoln."

"Not George Washington?"

"Not enough money. He's quieter than he used to be. Getting good grades."

"No drugs?"

I shake my head.

"Jeannie's finished with her braces?" he asks.

"Morgan took off the last band in August. She's rebellious. Some days I don't know." I wipe my forehead. "Come back."

"And put myself at your mercy?"

"I give you my word of honor, I *promise* you—"

"You think I could ever trust you again? After you brought the children into the courtroom?"

"Dave, it wasn't me. Bob—"

He bares his teeth. "Right."

My heart sinks. It's hopeless. Fallon slips a hand under my elbow.

"I'm all right," I say.

"*Brava*," Dave says without emotion. "That was almost as good as the martyred virgin you played during the divorce."

Rage sweeps through me. "One last time. Come back."

"No."

"I'll attach your salary."

"No pittance too small?"

"I'll seize your car."

"God, you *are* grasping."

"All it takes is one call to Ray Parsons, my lawyer."

"What happened to Bob Scarff?"

"I fired him."

"Are you sleeping with Ray now?" Dave says.

"*No!* And by the way, I know about the Arianna d'Amori woman. From what I hear, she's about as subtle as a drag queen rendition of *Aïda*."

No reaction.

I flare. "Don't you realize how much power I have over you?"

"I'm here, aren't I?" He smiles. "And now that I'm here— don't you realize how little power you have over me?" The smile withers. His voice goes gravelly again "You'd do it all over again, wouldn't you?"

Breathing hard, I turn away. Fallon opens the door for me, and I stalk out.

Chapter 19

Nothing Hopeless

Dave closed the station at a quarter to eight. He drove too fast over icy pavement. He skidded down the gravel road and bolted from the car. Where this time? Utah? Montana? Or someday, if he ever had the money, Germany.

He pulled his suitcase from under his cot and looked at the suits hanging on the dowel. What about the food? What about Arianna and Tracy? Would he leave without saying good-bye to Joe? What about cleaning the shed? Nate was too feeble to do it and wouldn't have a cleaning crew in until May—

Arianna's computer, the printer, the goose-neck lamp, the books. He couldn't abandon them. He eased down on the cot. He was beholden to too many people. He couldn't cut and run.

Before settling for the night, he packed the food, his books, most of his clothes. The disconnected computer and printer lay in boxes by the door.

• • •

By ten the following morning, Dave was parked behind Costa d'Oro. As Arianna inserted her key in the door, he left the car.

"I brought the computer and printer," he said.

After the boxes were behind her desk and the coffee machines started, Arianna unlocked the front door, and they sat at a table with coffee.

"Joe told me about Mary," Arianna said. "What will you do?"

Dave hesitated. "Take off."

"And the children?"

Dave wiped his neck.

She nodded slowly. "Why did Mary come here, David?"

"To fuck me over in style."

"Joe says she did not need to come here to do that. He says she can get court order without coming here." Arianna gave him a wry smile. "You're here to say good-bye to me, no?"

He fidgeted with his cup.

She tilted her head. "Listen to me. Don't run away yet. Talk again with Mary."

Dave flinched. Arianna took his face in her hands and kissed his cheek.

The temple bells rang. Mary stood inside the front door, her face white. Her eyes went from Dave to Arianna.

"What do you want?" Dave said.

"To see her."

Arianna rose. "You are Mary. You are welcome in my shop." Arianna took her hand. "David has spoken of you."

"I can imagine."

"Please to rest at table," Arianna said.

Mary gave her a quizzical look.

"Sit down," Dave said.

"You, too, David," Arianna said. "I bring hot chocolate, yes?"

She hurried away.

Mary watched Arianna working behind the counter. "She's sexy. In a decrepit sort of way."

"Stop it."

"I'm trying to understand what she's got that I haven't."

"Warmth and kindness."

Arianna returned with three brown mugs topped with whipped cream. "Perhaps you are hungry?" she said to Mary. "I have pastries—"

"No. Thanks."

Arianna sat. "You're at the Comfort Inn? You would be welcome to share my cottage."

Mary gave Arianna a blank-faced look and picked up her mug. "I wouldn't want to impose on you and Dave."

Dave wanted to slap her.

Arianna's smile gave way to sadness. "I will tell you the truth." She reached across the table and took Mary's hands. "I want him. He does not want me."

The brass bells sang.

"Customer." Arianna left the table.

"She's in love with you," Mary said.

"I came to tell her good-bye."

Mary started. "What does that mean?"

"I'm out of here. Before you take my car."

"I haven't gotten the court order. I wanted to talk to you first." She avoided his eyes. "Jeannie's still wearing the ring you gave her. Won't take it off. Chip might take some time to come around, but we can get a court-mandated series of therapeutic sessions if it comes to that."

Arianna returned to the table. "It is close by eleven, David. Perhaps you should arrive at the station early to talk with Tracy, yes?"

Dave gave Mary a sideward look. He didn't like leaving Mary and Arianna alone together. Arianna was a meddler. At the door he looked back. Mary was alone at the table holding her cup with both hands. Arianna was busy behind the counter.

That morning, before Tracy left for the day, Dave told him that he'd better look for a replacement—Dave could be leaving as early as tomorrow.

• • •

Around six, Dave dashed from the pumps to answer the station phone. Arianna. "I have a letter from Hans!"

Dave was at Costa d'Oro by eight-fifteen. Arianna was busy with a customer at the book counter. At last, she thanked the customer with a smile, the temple bells sounded, and she hurried to her desk. She returned with an envelope.

Hans said he had arrived safely. His grandfather had aged. Hans would be returning to the seminary at the end of the summer. Meanwhile, he would be studying at home. He told Dave he missed him.

> I've met a girl here. I'm sure you would like her. And I found a gym on Kaiserstrasse. I am trying weight lifting just to see.
>
> I hope you are well. You're in my prayers. I'll remember this year as the year I found my father. I'm proud to be able to tell people at last who my father is. I'm the son of David Bell.

"Something bad?" Arianna asked.

Dave blew his nose and read it to her. His voice quavered as he neared the end.

"You will go home to Maryland," she said.

"No."

"You will leave Winter Bay. Tomorrow." She rose and put her hand to her throat. "You depart from me now, yes? I must prepare to close."

"I'll give you a ride home."

"I will walk tonight. It is not cold."

She moved away from him and sat at her desk as if reading, but she wasn't wearing her glasses.

• • •

The fire was dead. In the dark, Dave kindled a new one with newspaper and twigs, added branches, finally a log. Warmth spread from the stove hesitantly, as if checking the shed before deciding to stay. He should eat. The gallon wine jug was still on the table. He tried to remember which boxes he'd packed food in.

He remembered Mary at the table in Costa d'Oro, red-rimmed eyes, forehead lined from too much frowning. No makeup. Her cheekbones were still high, like two triumphant wings, her eyes the green of the afternoon sea, her hair now streaked with gray. She was old, beaten, her strength and beauty stripped bare. Despite the flashes of rage, the venom he knew so well was all but gone from her.

He opened a box. Wrong one. Winter clothes. In their years together, she was always cold, wanted to be close to him, as if she didn't understand that her body next to his would arouse him. She lay on her left side, her left arm under her pillow, her right leg and arm across him. He shook his head. He didn't need this. He opened a second box, found two pots, started water to boil in one. He took a can of beans from the next box and dumped it into the second pot. His hands shuffled through the box looking for instant rice.

The sound of a car approaching slowly. It came down the hill, past Nate's place, past the cabins. It was in front of the shed. The engine stopped. A tap on his door.

Chapter 20

We'll Have Many More Days Like These

Back at the motel, I raise the room thermostat and sit in the plastic chair at the synthetic table. His cheeks have sunk. So have his eyes. His face looks pinched. Boniness on a man that size is menacing. If we shared a bed now, his body would be like nails. I remember how he used to feel when I lay with my arm and leg across him, solid and warm and furry. I wonder if the hair on his chest is gray. He used to be muscular. Now he looks like a cross between a wino and a cult charismatic.

Wind is thrashing the shrubs outside my window. I close the drapes. Sad ending. Dave used to say that you have to play the hand that life deals. I'd quit if it weren't for Chip and Jeannie. Dave doesn't want me. What's the use of an unwanted woman?

I feel defeat settling over me.

Arianna said not to give up, even gave me her card. "If I can help, you must call me." What does she know? A garish spinster who couldn't get him. She's willing to cede him to me. Whoop-de-doo. The gift of a has-been to an incapacitated from an incompetent.

The vitriol isn't helping. The old defenses don't work anymore. Aging and hurt force me to taste the ashes.

From here to the end of the road it's the real thing.

God, can I stand to see him again? I'll have to go through the hurt of holding in my feelings and endure his hatred. He's right. When all is said and done, God will lay the guilt on me, not him. The worst hurt I've endured wasn't being raped. It was Dave's infidelity. "As God is my witness," I say aloud, "I'll never make myself vulnerable to him again." But if I don't try one more time, I have to swallow failure. If it were me alone, I'd do it. Chip and Jeannie deserve better.

All right. One more try. I'll wait until he's through work and go to his place so we can talk alone. When it's past nine, I set out.

It's eight miles to the north, out a winding country road that follows the meandering of an angry, boulder-laden river. I turn the car heater up to high. Naked trees dance like phantoms on steroids. Arianna told me to watch on the right for a large, white boat turned upside down. The headlights pick it out of the darkness. I pull over and find the sign, "Nate's Playground— Camping and Cabins." I turn down the gravel road and go past the cabins to the high bank over the river. The white Cavalier is in front of a shack. I pull up and get out. The wind tries to rip off my coat while I knock.

A dim light goes on inside. Dave opens the door. He's in sweats that hang on him like a shroud over a skeleton, his hair matted. He turns on the outside light, an exposed bulb. His face takes me in, turns stony.

"Can I come in? The wind—"

The door shudders open, and I stumble in. My God, he's living in a storage shed. A cot, boxes and suitcase on the floor. He's already packed, ready to run again.

"Make it fast," he says.

"Can I sit down?"

He takes a deep breath, nods at the table. A half-empty gallon bottle of red wine is the only item on it.

"I'm here to beg," I say. "The kids—"

"They're better off without me. So are you. You're all ashamed of me."

"That's not the issue."

"Then what is?"

"They need you. Come back."

He feeds the fire in a black pot-bellied stove and pours instant rice into a pot of boiling water.

I glance over open boxes on the floor. "You have a lot of food."

"I had someone staying with me."

"I guessed as much. Who was she?"

Dave ignores me and pulls out silverware.

"You have a well-established record," I say, "of lying to me about your mistresses."

He stirs the rice.

"Not a woman, huh?" I say. "Sounds like you've broadened your sexual horizons."

He puts covers on both pots without answering.

"Who was he, then?" I say.

"His name's Hans Lehmann. He's . . . my son."

I open my mouth to speak, then close it.

"You might as well know. When I was studying in Germany, I lived with a German woman named Inge. I thought she'd had an abortion. Hans is studying to be a minister. Deserves better than me." He stops, swallows. "I love him, Mary. He's my son. I deserted him twenty years ago. I tried to have him aborted."

"If I'd known . . ." I say.

"You wouldn't have married me?"

I'd like him to believe that, but it's not true. "I was so in love with you that nothing else mattered."

"The important thing now is the kids. I owe Hans a lifetime

of fathering. I'll never be able to make it up to Chip and Jeannie." He spoons rice onto a plate, adds beans.

"Doesn't it matter at all," I say, "that I loved you so much that even Inge wouldn't have made a difference?"

"If I believed you."

"Why would I lie?"

"I don't know why you lied twenty years ago."

"I didn't lie."

"You pretended."

"I wanted to please you."

"When you didn't care about me?" Dave says.

It's hopeless. I get to my feet and wipe my nose with a paper towel.

Dave sets the plate on the table. "Bob Scarff knew how to push your buttons."

I turn to face him. "I loved *you*."

He puckers. Is he going to cry?

"I never lied to you!" I rip off another paper towel and blot my face.

He ladles beans and rice onto another plate and sets it in front of me. "You'd feel better if you ate something."

He finds paper cups in a box and sits.

I pick up the fork. "You look older."

"The beard. You've aged, too. Your hair—"

"I don't color it any more." I wipe my lips. "How old is Hans?"

"Twenty-one next August."

"Two years older than Chip."

He chews in silence, then, "Chip and Jeannie would never accept him."

"We have to get them to accept us first."

He pours us wine. "I don't know how much difference it makes, but I'm sorry for what I did." He avoids my eyes. "I told Hans, even what happened in Vietnam, and he's still proud. Sometimes we have to live up to how our kids see us. Even if they're wrong."

I sip wine. "Looks like we've both learned a few things. The hard way. Vindictiveness *is* my weakness. I never told you. When I was fourteen . . ."

He waits, watches me. "What?"

I can't say it. I take a long, slow drink. "I guess we'd better get used to being without the children. Before we know it, they'll be grown up. Hans, too. I look at us, and I think, 'God, we're old already!' Why does it take so long to grow up?"

"Maybe you never know what you need to know until it's too late."

"We still have some years left."

He chuckles sadly. "Remember when I used to read *Babar, the Elephant* to Chip? 'We'll have many more days like these, days we can be glad of. We'll be as happy as ever you please—'" His voice breaks.

I put out my hand to touch his arm but catch myself in time. "Come back. Nothing's ever hopeless."

His laugh is bitter. "You sound like Hans. He said the only unforgivable sin was despair."

"I think I like him already. Is he like Chip?"

"Hans isn't ashamed of me."

I press the paper towel to the inner corner of both eyes and pick up the fork. "Wouldn't it be nice to be young enough that you can blame others all the way, free of personal guilt, or love all the way, without reservation? When you get old like us, your mistakes hang on like parasites. They make you feeble. You can't quite fight your way to the surface anymore, even though you know you're going to drown if you quit trying." I take a bite of beans. They're tasteless. "The thing that caused me so much trouble wasn't even a mistake. You've never told me what happened in Vietnam. I've never told you . . ."

He stops eating.

"When I was fourteen . . ." I can't tell him. He mustn't know. But he has to know. "When I was fourteen, the boy next door raped me." I make myself look at him. "Multiple times. I had—" I can't say it. I have to. "—an abortion. Nearly bled to death."

"God," he whispers.

The whole ugly story hemorrhages out of me. My parents, the smell of chewing tobacco, the way I clutch up. I'm confessing to him, laying my sins at his feet, pleading for absolution. "Bob didn't know how to push my buttons. Nobody does. I don't have any buttons."

I put my face in my hands. I've given him one more weapon. I raise my eyes. Tears are starting down his cheek.

"My God, Mary." He bows his head, chokes back a sob. "I had no idea. God forgive me. I thought . . ." He laughs. "We were in the same boat and didn't know it." He puts his hand on my shoulder. Something in his eyes . . . He tightens his grip. "Do you think there'd ever be a chance that you and I—"

I jerk away.

"We'd have to work hard," he says, "and—"

"You're out of your fucking mind."

"Mary, when I saw you today—"

"What about sex?" I say with a nasty smile, wiping the tears from my cheeks.

"Maybe we can help each other. I can't run away from you. I

take you with me wherever I go."

I pull away from him. "Now you listen to me. I have limits. You pushed me past them. Love?" I laugh. "Don't you think I loved you? How much hurt do you think I can take? You want me to go back to that hell of knowing that someday you'll go off with some slut?" I get to my feet. "Have you any idea what it's like to be told over and over that you don't measure up, that you're not good enough, and no matter how hard you try it won't ever be good enough?" Sobbing, I grab my purse and throw on my coat. "Don't hurt me any more."

I'm at the door. I look back long enough to force a smile. "This really is good-bye, Dave. Who'd have ever thought it would be so hard—after all that's happened?"

I hurry to the car. It groans its way up the gravel road. I blink fast to get the tears out of my eyes.

Chapter 21

Trion Redux

Mrs. Reed was behind the desk at the Comfort Inn as Dave came through the office door.

"You're in town early this morning," she said. "Heard from Hans?"

Dave was relieved. He assumed the town was buzzing about him and Mary. "Got the first letter yesterday. He's doing fine."

"Such a sweet boy." She slipped her glasses on her nose. "I suspicion you're looking for Mrs. Bell. She told me she had a 10:00 a.m. flight out of Greenhaven, checked out a few minutes ago, but I didn't see her drive off."

"What room?"

"Third down on the right."

The door stood open. He tapped. "Mary?" He mopped his forehead and stepped inside. The bed was unmade, the closet open and empty. He bolted to the Cavalier. What kind of a car was she driving? Past the city limits sign, onto the bridge over the Mackinaugh, past the muddy fields glaring in spring sunshine. To his right, the ocean sparkled and glittered as if in mockery. To his left, fields gave way to heaving cliffs.

Would he be able to spot her in the crowd waiting to board the plane? If she refused to talk to him, he'd threaten her. He'd say he was going to create scenes on the street, get himself arrested, fake a public suicide attempt on a bridge. He'd plead. Fall to his knees and beg. Anything.

He was leaving the outskirts of Cold Harbor when he saw the cruiser in the rear view mirror, lights flashing. He eased the car onto the shoulder and switched off the ignition.

The cop let him fret while he wrote something in a metal notebook balanced on the cruiser's steering wheel and spoke into a dashboard microphone. Dave squeezed the steering wheel. Finally, the cop opened the door to the cruiser and got out.

"License please."

Not one of the cops Dave knew. Must be a new hire. Dave pulled his license from his wallet and put his hands on his knees so the shaking wouldn't show.

The cop tore off the ticket and handed it through the window. "Take it easy, buddy. No emergency is worth getting yourself killed over."

Wrong.

Dave waited until the cruiser pulled out, then drove onto the road behind. At this rate, he'd never catch her. Several miles down the highway, the cruiser turned left. Dave eased forward. *Keep at twenty-five 'til he's out of sight.* When he went over a hill, he pressed down the accelerator. Then in the rear view mirror, far away, he saw the cruiser. He took his foot off the gas and let the car slow. By the time the cruiser reached him, he was down to the speed limit. No flashing lights, no siren. The wet wool of his shirt chafed his chest and back. As he passed through Smallville, the cruiser turned off, but before Dave could floorboard it, another cruiser appeared behind him, this one labeled "SCP."

By the time he hit Greenhaven, the car clock showed fifteen minutes to ten. He cut into the Shell station. "Where's the airport?" he yelled at an old man in a baseball cap sweeping the concrete.

The man leaned the push broom against the pump and

sauntered over. "Fill it?"

"Need directions to the airport."

The old man took off his hat, scratched the top of his head, and gazed to the north. "Let's see. Greenhaven Airport?"

"Right."

He put his hat on again. "Stay on the main drag. The road curves around some, 'cause the ocean makes a harbor. That's why it's named Greenhaven. Well, that's the 'haven' part, anyways." He chuckled.

Dave clung to the steering wheel.

"Airport's about two miles out."

Thirteen to ten. Dave raced from the station, picking up speed as he went. True to the old man's words, the two-lane road curved along the coast, swung west at the harbor, then east. Dave finally spotted the sign, "Greenhaven Airport."

He swung into the parking lot at eight minutes to ten and dashed into the terminal building.

"Air North Flight 1762 for Washington National boarding at Gate 2," said a voice through the loudspeaker. Five or six people milled among the seats in the waiting area. No Mary. Then he saw her, standing by the gate attendant at the open door. She was in slacks, her hair pulled back. She'd slung her coat over one arm, and her carry-on bag hung from her shoulder.

"Mary."

She spun.

"It's *not* too late," he said.

"Last call," the attendant said. "All passengers for Air North Flight 1762 please board immediately."

He took her arm.

"Let me go." She slipped from his grasp.

Dave's skin burned. "*Mary . . .*"

She flashed her ticket to the attendant and was out of sight. The attendant closed the door to the tarmac. Dave tried the knob.

"You can't go out there," the attendant said.

He went to the window. Engines revving up. The plane wheeled south, hesitated, and roared down the strip and rose into the shining sky.

"Mary."

Chapter 22

A Face at the Window

The plane is one of those rattletrap leftovers, probably from World War II. The single flight attendant checks us for seat belts. The engines roar. Through the porthole window, I see that the quivering wing almost reaches the terminal. At the observation window is a man. Bony, white beard. *Dave!* My God, is he weeping?

The plane lurches, and we howl down the runway and shudder into the air.

I have succeeded in reducing Dave to a mangled wraith. I have triumphed. Medea incarnate, he called me. Like Trion, the destroyer of children.

I haven't destroyed my children. But I've hurt them. No excuse, right? Like Dave told Chip so often, you can blame fate for your problems, but only you can solve them.

Seeing Dave again brought out the old feelings. I've lost him. He was already packed. By the time I land, he'll have hit the road. He won't tell anyone where he's going. Maybe he doesn't even know. This time he'll change his name. Even if I wanted to find him, I couldn't.

So now what? How do you stop hating? By forgiving. Who? Dave, first of all. Could I ever forgive him? I'm stunned to realize that I already have. I no longer hate him or want to crush him. I'd do anything to stop that hurting in his face at the window.

Helen? Inge? I don't hate them. I understand why they loved Dave. *I* love him.

That leaves *me*. It feels like the first step would be to remember the opposite side of me, my love for the kids and even for Dave.

The flight attendant is speaking to me. "What would you like to drink? Coffee, tea, soda?"

"Nothing, thanks."

She moves on.

Dave said one time, "Life doesn't make us unhappy. We make ourselves unhappy by trying to be what other people want, by wanting things we can't have." I'll choose to be happy even if I never see Dave again.

The attendant again. "We'll be landing in about forty-five minutes."

• • •

Chip is inside the gate in his usual slump, frowning at the floor.

"Stand straight," I say. "You're a man."

"Mom?"

"Were you expecting Mata Hari?"

I give him a bear hug. All at once, I'm so proud of him.

His arms go around me. "You all right?"

"Compared to whom?" I step away and take his hands. "I missed you."

He's looking down at me, full of concern. "Did something happen?"

I give him my biggest smile. "How long have you got? We'll talk when we get home."

He smiles, relieved. "It's like old times."

That hurts. Have I really been such a slug?

Not any more. I'll put away my hate and learn how to be happy without having what I want. I'll stop trying to be what Dave wants. I'll be Mary Bergstrom. No, that Mary was crushed by rape. I'll be Mary Bell, the happy mother of Chip and Jeannie.

All the way to Takoma Park, I draw Chip out. He talks about school, says he's dating somebody.

It's going to be okay. It's going to work.

At home, I'm surprised to find the apartment ship-shape. After dinner and dishes, I sit Chip and Jeannie down at the kitchen table and tell them everything. Chip can't unclamp his jaw. Jeannie watches me like someone waiting for the next shoe to fall.

"You found him," she says.

"Not for long," I say. "By now he's on the road." I have to tell them. "He wanted a reconciliation. I couldn't."

I force myself to tell them about Hans.

Chip shies as though from a gunshot. "He was like that even then."

"But he left Inge to come home to me. He'd broken up with Helen a month before the trouble started. He wanted to stay with us. I drove him away." I grind out the three words. "I was wrong."

"Jesus," Chip says, "you're defending him?"

I take his hand. "He's not a monster. Someday, you and Jeannie will have to find him."

Jeannie puts her arms around me.

"I never want to see that son-of-a-bitch again," Chip says under his breath. "If he shows up, I'm out of here."

"And make the same mistake he made?" I say. "Run away?"

"Forget it." He stomps out.

So like his father. When the going gets rough, disappear.

Jeannie's still holding me.

I stroke her hair. "I can't search for him anymore. I'll help you find him when the time comes."

Chapter 23

The Key

Dave rummaged through the garbage cans behind the station until he found another cardboard box relatively free of oil stains. The customer bell sounded. Joe climbed out of the WHPD cruiser carrying a brown bag and came into the bay.

"Whatcha doin' there, big fella?"

"Cleaning out my stuff. New guy started today."

"What about your wife?"

"She flew home this morning."

"What're you going to do, Dave?"

"If you get the court order tomorrow, could you sort of misplace it? Give me a head start?"

Joe bobbed his head without looking at Dave. "Coffee's getting cold. You want to flip or what?"

It took Dave a few seconds to grasp what Joe meant. He smiled. "You old cheat. You think you're getting your coffee free?"

After Joe left, Dave carried the last box to the Cavalier. Nothing of his left here. He went into the office. He was done.

If he slipped out of town early tomorrow, Joe and Arianna wouldn't be able to tell anyone where he was. They wouldn't have to lie when people came looking for him.

He'd miss Joe. The old cuss had a way of worming his way into your thoughts. Thirty-plus years as a policeman had taught him a lot about human beings. Not smart. Wise. The kind of man Dave wanted for a father.

Desolation came with the darkness.

I had a son-of-a-bitch for a father. A weakling, a coward. He ran away, deserted us. Just as I ran away and abandoned my own kids. All three of them. My father all over again.

He slumped on the stool in the office. He should turn on the lights.

I'm not forced to relive my father's life. Hans forgave me my cowardice. Can I forgive my father?

He raised his eyes to the cobalt sky above arc lights of the mall parking lot.

I forgive you. And I love you.

He felt as if gravity had loosened its grasp. Release. Had his forgiveness released his father? Or had Dave released himself?

• • •

By seven-thirty the next morning, Dave had the Cavalier packed. He checked the shed one last time. Nothing to mark the times he spent with Hans or the birth of the German edition of *Leverkühn* or the conversation with Mary. No trace of his tortured dreams or his search in the dark for the key that Horst said he must find. Like many other times in his life, nothing of him was left.

He crossed to the window and looked through the clean glass. The Mackinaugh flowed blue in the slanting morning sunshine. The hill was clear of snow. Grass of the palest green stretched between the shed and the shore. Green spikes pushed up here and there. So many bitter hours he'd spent in the dark watching the silent Mackinaugh, the bay, the patternless sky. One last look before he began the sad journey west. He lifted his parka from the hook on the door and headed down the hill.

Halfway to the shore he knelt and examined the green spears waving in the sea breeze. Jonquils, ready to bloom. All over the place. He gazed out to sea. The jonquils would be in bloom in Takoma Park by now. Barely a year since that Sunday afternoon when he saw them budding from his study window. Only a year? He'd been young then. *A man is a man when he's strong, nurturing, and wise.* The line he'd used on Chip. He himself had been none of those.

He moved down the hill to the river bank. The current pushed toward the bay. The breeze bore the scent of the living earth, wet and ripe. No evidence the Eucharides had ever been here. They'd be waiting for him out west. On the far shore two boys were running and hollering, innocent of the remorse that ages a man.

He squatted at the edge and trailed his fingers in the water. He knew how cold it could be. Helen had found out, too. Drowning. He fought off a shudder. She'd loved him. Three times in his life—maybe four, if he counted Arianna—he'd been given the greatest gift a man can receive, a woman's love. He'd never been with a woman until Arianna taught him how. Each time he'd shielded himself from the gift, believing he was *Ungemmint.* An excuse. Love frightened him, made him feel dependent. He'd even screened himself from his children's love, always trying to give without the vulnerability of receiving.

And Mary . . . He winced. Raped repeatedly. An abortion. She'd never told him. Just as he'd never told her about Long Dinh. *What fools these mortals be.* He could have helped her, been with her as Arianna would say. If only he'd known. Maybe that was his worst sin, worse than despair. His eyes moistened.

Maybe the Eucharides weren't so far away after all. *It's not about me. It's not even about Mary. It's about Chip and Jeannie and*

Hans. He couldn't let the Eucharides take him. He had to live up to what the children needed him to be, no matter what the risk, no matter whether Mary took him back. He'd have to build a respectable life somewhere. The only thing that mattered was the children.

His brain tripped on that thought, as though he had made a grammatical error. Something wasn't right here.

He sat on the bank and pulled his legs to his chest. Live up to what they needed him to be? "Some sins are unforgivable." Arianna's words. Living for one's children? Kind of a mirror image of Trion. Instead of killing his children, as he had tried to do with Hans, as he *had* done with the child at Long Dinh, he'd tried to undo his own damnation by being more than Chip and Jeannie wanted him to be. A super father. A Trion in penitent's clothing. What a crock. And if that wasn't bad enough, living for someone else was too much of a burden to put on that someone. He had to live for himself, be the man God made him to be, make himself into the man he was. He chuckled. A dichotomy worthy of Rumi. The only way he could live up to the way his children saw him was not to do it. This time, get it right.

The boys on the opposite shore whooped and ran up the embankment. People told him this truth when he was their age. It was there in the Bible, in Shakespeare, in Goethe, in the Greeks. Like the oracle's warning to Trion—they told him, and he didn't believe it.

He trudged up the hill toward the shed. He'd come here to escape, to go through the dark time Horst foretold. "Search for the key not in the light but in the dark." The same key would open two secrets, Mary and the Vietnam dream. The key was Trion. Understanding the story for the first time, seeing that Trion, like Dave, had a choice. Despite everything that had happened to Trion, despite everything he'd done, despite his genes and the y chromosome and testosterone, he was not condemned by fate. He could have lived up to the good in him.

Dave stopped dead. That *was* Trion's sin, wasn't it? Not having the balls to be the man the gods made him to be. Settling for too little. Dave looked down. His shadow was there, clearly etched on the new grass, firm, bold, solid. And he had a reflection, too—Hans, his eyes, his mere existence. Dave still had his soul.

He looked over his shoulder. The Eucharides *would* always be standing by in case he backslid, settled for too little. Never mind. He'd found the key. Running away again would mean searching for what he'd already found, turning again toward the Trion side of him. It would be dancing with the Eucharides, and most of all, it would betray Dave Bell.

What if Mary never took him back? She probably wouldn't. What if Chip and Jeannie rejected him? They wouldn't want the tramp he'd become for a father. What if he had to do construction work or teach German in high school or wait tables or pump gas? What if he landed in jail? What if the whole world turned against him, ridiculed him, spat in his face, called him a baby killer? If he wanted not to be Trion, if he wanted to be himself, he had to go home to Maryland no matter what else happened.

He watched the Mackinaugh, the boys, the Eucharides dancing at the shore. He'd grown a couple of notches. How many more notches lay ahead? Would they all hurt so much?

• • •

Dave found Joe at his desk next to the jail on the city hall's top floor. He was reading in the smoky fluorescent light, a cigarette between his lips.

"Officer," Dave said, "don't you know there's no smoking in city hall?"

When Joe saw Dave, his eyes opened wide, and he smiled. "Jeez, we just let anybody in here nowadays." Joe's smile faded. "Heading west?"

"Maryland."

Joe gave Dave a close-lipped smile and nodded. "Figured."

Dave shrugged one shoulder.

"Got time for a last cup of coffee?" Joe said.

"Sure."

"Cost you a dollar."

"Flip you for it."

Twenty minutes later, Dave turned down Main Street toward the dock. As he entered Costa d'Oro, Arianna was swabbing the counter. She dropped her rag and threw her arms around him. "My dear honk! You are still here. I give you hot chocolate. Come-come."

"Brought you something." He handed her the half-empty gallon of red wine.

She wrinkled her nose. "So." She set it on the counter and wiped her hands on the cleaning rag as though the bottle had contaminated her. "When you leave?"

"Car's packed. Gas tank full." He smiled broadly. "Maybe tonight I'll see Chip and Jeannie."

Her face bloomed.

"Will you call Horst for me?" he said. "Tell him I'll be in tonight. Maybe he can find me a place to stay. And—" He handed her an envelope. "Will you mail this for me?"

"The mailbox, it is on the corner." She read the address. "Hans."

"I want him to go to Long Dinh with me when I have money again."

She frowned. "I do not understand."

"I can't do it by myself. I have to ask pardon for my sin." He smiled. "And when I'm strong enough, I'll tell Mary and Chip and Jeannie what I did. It's what you wanted. I won't let the water take me."

"Then thanks be to God."

"What's important is that this letter pass through the hands of an enchantress. Mail it for me."

She blinked and nodded.

"I'll be back."

Arianna let go of his hands. "No, *mio bello*, this is good-bye."

"Good-bye?"

"Our time together is finished. I had you a little while. I had Hans an even shorter while. But there will be others. Arianna lives life à la carte." She put one hand on each side of his face and looked down at him through half-closed eyes. "Go to her, the woman who loves you and wants you."

The front door opened with a clangor of temple bells.

Arianna stood. "Customer." She tilted her head and smiled. "Your dark time is finished. Go now, quick-quick!" She hurried toward the front of the shop. He heard her jewelry tinkle, her kaftan swish. She looked at him over her shoulder. Her eyes sparkled. She blew him a kiss, then wrinkled her nose, waved her hand at him, side to side, palm down, and turned to her customer with a smile.

Author's Note

The Trion Syndrome resulted from my own struggle to come to terms with the unspeakable things I went through and participated in during the years I served as a clandestine signals intelligence operative working under cover with soldiers and Marines in Vietnam. I began to wonder if men who had demonstrated that kind of ferocity were even capable of love. I returned from Vietnam an emotional wreck, after living through the fall of Saigon and escaping under fire after the North Vietnamese were already in the streets of the city. I had all the classic symptoms of Post-Traumatic Stress Injury—panic attacks, flashbacks, nightmares, irrational rage. My marriage crumbled, and I was afraid I was going to lose my children who were my reason for staying alive. I turned to helping others—AIDS patients, the homeless, the dying in the hospice system—and writing. I resumed my study of German and sought the wisdom in Greek mythology to heal me. In the process I rediscovered my most cherished author, Thomas Mann. Then Dave Bell, the protagonist of *Trion*, took me over. To find peace, I had to tell his story. Hence *Trion.*

I am grateful to the many people who helped me with the book. Ellen Kwatnoski, author of *Still Life with Aftershocks*, offered sage advice on the manuscript. Circus performer and writer Greg May, author of *Blood and Sawdust*, gave me the kind of tips only a writer of his flare could offer. And Su Patterson, patient and meticulous, did the final edit. She spotted errors I had read past a dozen times and failed to catch. I am beholden to countless others who, over the years, coached me in facing my own past and reshaping Dave Bell's story with honesty. Writers are the most generous people I've known in my life. God bless them all.

Tom Glenn

About the Author

Tom Glenn has worked as an intelligence operative, a musician, a linguist (seven languages), a cryptologist, a government executive, a care-giver for the dying, a leadership coach, and, always, a writer. Many of his prize-winning short stories (sixteen in print) came from the better part of thirteen years he shuttled between the U.S. and Vietnam as an undercover NSA employee on covert signals intelligence assignments before being rescued under fire when Saigon fell. With a BA in Music, a master's in Government and a doctorate in Public Administration and trained as a musician, actor, and public speaker, he toured the country lecturing on leadership and management, trained federal executives, and was the Dean of the Management Department at the National Cryptologic School.

His writing is haunted by his five years of work with AIDS patients, two years of helping the homeless, seven years of caring for the dying in the hospice system, and his bouts with Post-Traumatic Stress Injury as a result of his Vietnam experiences. These days he is a reviewer for *The Washington Independent Review* of Books where he specializes in books on war and Vietnam. His Vietnam novel-in-stories, *Friendly Casualties*, is now available on Amazon.com. His article describing the fall of Saigon and his role in it was published in the *Baltimore Post-Examiner* as a three-installment article in August and September 2013. Apprentice House of Baltimore brought out his novel, *No-Accounts* in 2014.

Apprentice House is the country's only campus-based, student-staffed book publishing company. Directed by professors and industry professionals, it is a nonprofit activity of the Communication Department at Loyola University Maryland.

Using state-of-the-art technology and an experiential learning model of education, Apprentice House publishes books in untraditional ways. This dual responsibility as publishers and educators creates an unprecedented collaborative environment among faculty and students, while teaching tomorrow's editors, designers, and marketers.

Outside of class, progress on book projects is carried forth by the AH Book Publishing Club, a co-curricular campus organization supported by Loyola University Maryland's Office of Student Activities.

Eclectic and provocative, Apprentice House titles intend to entertain as well as spark dialogue on a variety of topics. Financial contributions to sustain the press's work are welcomed. Contributions are tax deductible to the fullest extent allowed by the IRS.

To learn more about Apprentice House books or to obtain submission guidelines, please visit www.apprenticehouse.com.

Apprentice House
Communication Department
Loyola University Maryland
4501 N. Charles Street
Baltimore, MD 21210
Ph: 410-617-5265 • Fax: 410-617-2198
info@apprenticehouse.com • www.apprenticehouse.com

CPSIA information can be obtained
at www.ICGtesting.com
Printed in the USA
BVOW06s0454120118
505148BV00005B/58/P